A WALTZ IN BATH

Before she could reply to Richmond's comment, the band struck up another waltz. "Would you care to dance, Miss Wyndmoore?" he asked cordially.

Cassie frowned. *Why is he being so nice to me? He couldn't actually be attracted to me. That's out of the question.* Once again, she couldn't think of a reason to say no, so she replied, "Yes, of course," and they headed out to the dance floor.

As they began their set, Cassie noticed something odd. Lord Richmond was holding her a trifle too close for propriety. In fact, he was holding her much too close for propriety. Cassie could feel his hand on the small of her back, gently pressing her closer to him, and if she were of a romantic sentiment, she could have closed her eyes and imagined that the handsome and dashing Lord Richmond really wanted to be with her, the unexceptional Cassandra Wyndmoore.

As he guided her across the floor, she wished she could lose herself in the moment and enjoy the feeling of his strong, muscular form against her . . . .

BOOKS BY SHARON STANCAVAGE

EMILY'S CHRISTMAS WISH

AN ENCHANTING MINX

A BATH INTIGUE

Published by Kensington Publishing Corporation

A Bath
Intrigue

Sharon Stancavage

ZEBRA BOOKS
Kensington Publishing Corp.
www.kensingtonbooks.com

Chapter 1

"What do you mean you won't be able to have the axle fixed until tomorrow morning? The inn is filled and we're expected in Bath," Miss Cassie Wyndmoore exclaimed.

The somewhat grimy and rather shabbily dressed gent from the Pig and Crow Inn who was charged with helping her coachman looked sympathetic. "I'm sorry, miss, that's when it'll be done," he explained with the patience of Job.

Cassie was at the end of her patience. She had endured her sister Daphne's complaints about everything from the roads to the weather to her lack of a proper suitor for hours and hours, and now there was the problem with the carriage. *If I was Lady Somebody, I'm sure they'd make my carriage a priority,* Cassie thought wryly. Then she looked down at her rumpled gray muslin traveling dress and realized that she rather resembled a badly dressed governess—or, worse yet, a poor relation.

Cassie sighed slightly and looked at the rumpled man in front of her. As she was about to explain her situation to the man once again and try to cajole him into fixing her carriage, a deep, male voice behind her interrupted.

"What seems to be the problem?" the man asked.

Every fiber in Cassie's well-turned figure stiffened. *It couldn't be him, not after six years,* she thought, in a slight panic. Cassie slowly turned and stared up into the gray-blue eyes of Derek Leighton, the Earl of Richmond. The only man who had touched her heart and caused her pulse to go aflutter. The man who had filled her dreams ever since his passionate, ill-fated romance with her goddess-like older sister Pandora.

She took in his unruly dark hair, the sparkle in his eyes, and the slight tan that graced his figure. *He looks more like a gypsy than a nobleman,* she thought, her eyes never leaving him. His black hair was longer than she remembered and curled over his collar in the most enchanting way. His tanned skin was most unfashionable, and even though his features were too severe to be called classic, Cassie thought he was incredibly handsome, albeit in a very un-Byron-like way.

After the episode with Pandora, Cassie had been sure she'd never see him again. It would have been easier not seeing him again so she could forget all about him, as she had tried to do for the past six years. But here he was at the Pig and Crow Inn, ever so cordially inquiring about the problem with her carriage.

As she gaped at Richmond in shock, she suddenly realized that both men were staring at her, expecting some sort of reply. Cassie's cheeks turned the most attractive shade of pink as she replied, "We hit a rather rough spell of road and our axle broke. We made it here," she continued, glancing around the busy stable yard, "but the carriage needs fairly extensive repairs that can't be done until tomorrow." Cassie tried not to stare at Richmond, but it was as if his eyes were beckoning to her. Instead, she focused on a pile of hay to the right of his head. "And there aren't any rooms available at the inn," she concluded, pushing her spectacles up her nose and tucking an errant piece of hair behind her ear.

Richmond smiled at Cassie, his features turning almost boyish. "Let's see what can be done," he said in the soft, caressing voice that she remembered well, since he used it often enough with Pandora. Richmond turned to the gent from the inn. "If the lady needs her carriage repaired today, you will have the work completed for her today," Richmond ordered in a voice that proclaimed he was a member of the Quality.

"Of course, Lord Richmond," the gent from the inn all but stuttered. "I can have it done for you—I mean, the young lady—right away."

"Very good. I'll be by later to check on your progress," Richmond declared in the same lord-of-the-manor voice, then smiled boyishly at Cassie.

"Yes, my lord," the gent replied, then promptly disappeared into the stables to hasten the work.

Cassie's heart was slowly breaking. Yes, it had been six years, and she had changed since then, but she thought he would at least remember her. The vague look in his eyes told her that she was a complete stranger to him. She'd had numerous conversations with Lord Richmond when he was courting Pandora, and now she was just a nobody who couldn't even get a servant from an inn to do her bidding. Of course, none of Pandora's numerous suitors ever paid much attention to Cassie, but she'd thought that Richmond was different. Obviously she'd been wrong.

"Thank you so much for your help, my lord. It was very generous of you to step in," she said in her most courteous voice. She didn't want him to reply, or to inquire about her name or identity. It was better that he didn't know, that they went their separate ways. Before he could reply, Cassie turned and strode purposely toward the inn, never looking back.

If she had turned, she would have noticed Richmond staring at her, a look of confusion on his face.

"Cassie, you have to talk to Mama. I can't wait a whole year for my come out," the young and deliciously beautiful Daphne Wyndmoore whined, her large blue eyes filled with tears.

Cassie stared out the window of the carriage, oblivious to the scenery. The trip wasn't going well at all. First the axle, then the encounter with Richmond, and now Daphne's whining. If Daphne said one more thing about missing the Season in London, Cassie knew she would scream.

"Cassie, you're not attending," Daphne said in a petulant voice.

The sound of Daphne's harping brought Cassie out of her reverie. Daphne had been complaining about missing the Season for the entire trip, and now Cassie was absolutely certain she should receive some sort of medal for enduring her sister's constant complaining.

"I know Mother's being terribly unfair, but you know I can't change her mind. She doesn't pay me any heed, so I certainly couldn't persuade her to change her mind about your Season next year," Cassie replied, trying desperately to placate her rather spoiled sister.

"But, Cassie, I have to go to London. You know it's practically a crime to let my beauty wither away in the country," Daphne replied.

Daphne's proclamation of her beauty made Cassie grit her teeth for the umpteenth time that day. How much longer would it take before they got to Bath? If she had to endure one more comment about Daphne's superior beauty or the injustice that her Season was being postponed, Cassie decided she was going to stop their carriage and push Daphne out into the green and wonderfully scenic rolling hills. Of course, even if she did toss Daphne out of the carriage, some incredibly important peer would no doubt rescue her and take her to London, where she would be hailed as a diamond of the first water. She was incredibly lovely and would more than likely be hailed by the *ton*. Obviously, pushing her out of the carriage was not the best option at all. *If only I can figure out a way to make her stop talking,* Cassie mused, staring at Mary, their abigail, who was sleeping soundly.

"I agree completely, Daphne," Cassie said compliantly, willing her sister to stop talking. There was a vast difference between seventeen and twenty-five, and Cassie really hadn't grasped that fact until they were well into their journey to Bath to visit Aunt Honoria.

The trip had seemed like a good idea at the time. Aunt Honoria wrote Mother that she was feeling blue deviled and thought a visit from the girls might boost her spirits. Actually, the invitation was extended specifically to Cassie, but Mama added Daphne, since the latter was still sulking about her postponed Season.

Daphne was undoubtedly the loveliest female in all of Warwick. Her blue eyes were like pools of water, and mirrored every emotion that passed through her petite form. Her blonde hair fell gracefully around her shoulders like a halo, and more than one sonnet had been written proclaiming Daphne's beauty. She had a talent for watercolors, a perfect singing voice, and a way with the pianoforte. Daphne was utterly and completely perfect. She was also the image of their oldest sister

Pandora. In fact, the two Wyndmoore girls were hailed as the most beautiful women in Warwick. Cassie was the middle Wyndmoore. She had short, brown hair, wore spectacles, and did not have blue eyes that were like pools of water; and did not inspire anyone in Warwick to write sonnets about her. In fact, no one even noticed her. Cassie, at five and twenty, was firmly on the shelf.

Pandora, and now Daphne, the lauded beauties of the family, were both cosseted by their mama, and this time, Mama wanted Daphne to mature some before her Season. Pandora had her Season at the tender age of sixteen and had proved to be a bit . . . uncontrollable, to say the least. Therefore, Mama decided that Daphne needed to settle down before going to London, and a trip to Bath to see Aunt Honoria was just what Daphne needed. Cassie was sent along as a companion to Daphne, to keep her out of trouble.

Cassie continued to stare out the window, her mind drifting back to Lord Richmond. She hadn't seen him in ages. Of course, Pandora never forgave him for ending their relationship. Her elder sister told everyone that she had given Richmond his congé, but Cassie was one of the few people who knew the real story of Pandora's less than respectable behavior.

The scenery was lovely, but Cassie wasn't looking at it. She thought about Richmond and about the rumors that Pandora and the rest of Society had heard about his pregnant mistress who put a period to her existence. It had been quite the scandal at the time, and Cassie didn't know if she should believe the story, but Pandora was adamant: don't ever trust Lord Richmond. And Pandora should know, Cassie thought. Richmond had been in

Pandora's pocket for ages and had once been her closest confidant.

After an interminable amount of time, the carriage finally came to a grinding halt, and Mary came out of the slumber that had engulfed her for the entire trip. The door sprang open to reveal Bath.

"'Ere you go ladies," John Coachman announced, depositing the ladies in front of a magnificent white Georgian town house on Great Pulteney Street.

A heartbeat later, Laughton, Aunt Honoria's aging butler, bustled the road-weary sisters into the parlor to await the arrival of Lady Raverston, their Aunt Honoria. While the girls sat in the parlor, drinking glasses of cool lemonade, Mary supervised the unloading of their trunks and portmanteaus. Most of them belonged to Daphne, who was consumed with the latest fashions. As a spinster, Cassie was disinterested in clothes and did rather resemble a poor relation, at least from a fashion standpoint.

"Isn't this the most interesting house?" Daphne asked in whisper that could be heard in Paris.

Cassie studied the decor. There were traditional landscapes on the walls, Grecian statues in the corners, and a variety of Egyptian artifacts. In theory, the room sounded horrid, but Aunt Honoria somehow managed to make it look original and fascinating without being overdone and gauche.

While the sisters studied the room with interest, Aunt Honoria walked slowly into the room, looking younger than her six and fifty years. Her somber bottle-green gown was impeccably fashioned and proclaimed to the world that she was indeed a member of the Upper Ten.

Before Honoria could utter a word, Cassie jumped to her feet to greet her aunt. "It's so good to see you, Aunt Honoria," she exclaimed and rushed over to her, enveloping her in a hug. Daphne stared at Cassie in utter horror.

Honoria embraced her favorite niece warmly. "And it's wonderful to see you, my dear Cassandra. I'm glad to see that you're not afraid to give me a proper greeting," she said, her hazel eyes staring into a pair that mirrored her own.

A wide smile appeared on Cassie's face, utterly transforming her from a spinster of five and twenty into someone who looked much younger and appeared to be much more carefree. "I'm so very glad you invited us, Aunt Honoria," she said in all sincerity, as Honoria walked her back to the sofa.

"How was your trip?" Honoria asked, sitting down on an ornately carved chair.

"It was horrible, Aunt Honoria," Daphne began. "First the coach broke down, and we had to wait for ages at the most dreadful inn, and it was so dashed hot . . ." Daphne began and just prattled on and on.

Cassie looked knowingly at her aunt. Honoria rolled her eyes to the ceiling and Cassie smiled. Aunt Honoria obviously knew what a trial it was to travel with Daphne.

Honoria let Daphne prattle on for a while before interrupting her. "Before we discuss anything else, I'd like to have Sara show you your rooms. I'm sure you both must be exhausted from the trip, and I do believe that your abigail finally has your trunks upstairs," Honoria said.

Daphne stared at her aunt in shock. Honoria hadn't even bothered to let her finish her sentence.

"Of course, Aunt Honoria," Cassie said calmly, standing up.

"I really wasn't expecting both of you, so your sleeping arrangements are a bit . . . unconventional," Honoria began. Daphne's eyes widened in horror, while Cassie merely seemed curious. "I'm doing some renovations in the east wing, and the bedrooms are closed off. I know you need to have your abigail nearby, Daphne, so I've arranged the main guest room for you," Honoria explained, as the look of horror gradually disappeared from Daphne's lovely face. She then turned to Cassie. "I've been using the west bedroom for my painting, and it is a bit out of sorts. I hope you don't mind being alone there, do you, Cassandra?" she asked calmly.

"I'm sure the room will be fine," Cassie replied in a serious voice, and then, as Daphne looked away, Cassie actually had the temerity to wink at Honoria. Her aunt smiled back. *Aunt Honoria knows I want to be as far away from Daphne as possible,* Cassie realized.

"Very good," Honoria said with a broad smile, and then turned to the tiny young maid with bright red hair peeking out from under her mobcap who had magically appeared at her side. "Sara, show Cassandra and Daphne to their rooms."

The maid gave Honoria a small curtsy. "Yes, ma'am," she replied.

Honoria turned back to the sisters, who were both ready to follow Sara to the nether regions of the house. "Why don't you both get some rest and I'll see you at supper at eight?" she said, waving the trio out of the room.

Daphne's room was so filled with gowns of every color that they practically spilled out into the hallway like some sort of rainbow. There were frothy pastels that befitted a girl of Daphne's age, modest walking dresses, riding outfits, and gowns for every possible occasion that might arise. In fact, in Cassie's opinion, Daphne had at least two or three dresses for every possible situation.

When the sisters, accompanied by Sara, entered Daphne's room, Mary, their abigail, was trying to sort out Daphne's wardrobe. At a mere sixteen, Mary was the latest in a long line of Daphne's abigails. Mary's advantage was an easy disposition that enabled her to endure Daphne's moods, which was a definite asset.

"Isn't the room lovely, Miss Daphne?" Mary exclaimed with a bright smile.

Daphne frowned furiously. Cassie watched her sister glance around the tiny room in dismay and waited for Daphne to protest.

"Are you sure this is my room?" Daphne asked in her haughtiest voice—a voice that definitely bespoke her displeasure with the arrangements.

"Yes, Miss Daphne," Sara replied.

The frown was replaced by a pout as Daphne turned to Mary. "Well, Mary, most of my clothes will have to be stored in Cassie's room. I'm sure it won't be a problem, since she has the wardrobe of a governess. I know she doesn't care about her appearance, but I certainly can't be seen walking around like a quiz," Daphne proclaimed.

Cassie looked down at her gown. It was her favorite shade of gray and reminded her of the sky in the winter. Technically, it was a bit on the large side and did sport a high neck, since Cassie wasn't blessed with the womanly assets of her sisters. If she looked closely, she could see one or two places where the stitching was repaired, but overall, it was a lovely dress. At least to Cassie.

"I'm sure that won't be a problem, Daphne," Cassie

finally replied. "I wouldn't want you looking anything but your best," she concluded, heartily sick of Daphne's vanity.

Cassie's comment immediately calmed Daphne down a trifle, as Cassie had expected. Daphne was nothing if not predictable.

"You're the best sister, Cassie. I knew I could count on you," Daphne said, the smile returning to her face.

Cassie glanced toward the door and wondered what her room was going to look like. Aunt Honoria obviously knew that she needed some time alone and had arranged for her to have some privacy. "Why don't you and Mary concentrate on unpacking. I'll have Sara show me to my room," she said, moving toward the door.

"I'll come fetch you when it's time to eat, Miss Cassie," Mary said brightly.

Cassie smiled at the girl. Mary was wonderfully amiable and a veritable gift from heaven. "Thank you, Mary," she said, and left the tiny guest room with Sara.

The pair trod down the hallways, and, to be honest, Cassie was grateful her room wasn't next to Daphne's. She had heard enough of her sister's complaining to last a lifetime, and some time away from her sibling was just what she needed.

They arrived at a closed door, and when Sara gently opened it, Cassie gazed in and gasped.

The bedroom was three times the size of her sister's. A large, canopied four-poster bed was nestled next to the window, accompanied by a matching wardrobe, a dresser, an escritoire, and a small settee, all done in glistening mahogany. A small table with lion-claw feet sat in the far corner, home to a variety of paints and brushes. An easel with a blank canvas stood nearby. A discriminating person would immediately realize that the bedroom was probably not used for painting at all. The paints were too neat, and the easel wasn't anywhere near the window. Moreover, Cassie knew as a fact that Aunt Honoria had given up painting and turned to doing pencil sketches of the local flora. Of course, Daphne wasn't privy to that bit of information, and would more than likely believe that the bedroom was indeed a studio.

Sara stood at the door and watched Cassie intently. "Is the room to your liking, miss?"

Cassie turned and bestowed a glowing smile on the diminutive maid. "The room is absolutely lovely, Sara. Please thank Aunt Honoria for me, and tell her I'll come down after a bit of a nap. The trip with Daphne was actually quite taxing, and I need some time to rest."

The pert little maid smiled back. "Yes, miss, I can see that you would need some time alone. Begging your pardon, but is your sister always this . . . difficult?" Sara asked pensively.

Cassie sighed. "Daphne is very beautiful, and is at her best when she has many admirers around who notice that fact. She's had a bit of a bee in her bonnet for weeks, since our Mama is postponing her Season until next year. Hopefully she'll attract a few adoring swains while we're in Bath, since that would certainly restore her good humor," Cassie concluded.

Sara nodded sagely. "I understand, miss. I'm sure Lady Honoria will be able to find some young bucks for Miss Daphne. If she can't, I will," the maid added resolutely.

Cassie grinned, her eyes dancing mischievously. "I might have to take you up on that offer," she said as Sara left the room.

Once Cassie was alone, she went over to the window. All of Bath was before her, from the River Avon to the bridge and the forbidding Abbey. It was a magnificent

view that Cassie certainly appreciated. Daphne
wouldn't.

Aunt Honoria was certainly spot on in her room
choices.

Richmond sat in the bustling taproom, drinking a
glass of ale. His father, Hugh Leighton, the Marquess of
Stanton, was in an adjoining room, engaged in a card
game with another peer. Richmond was happy about the
situation. As long as his father was preoccupied with
various activities, he wouldn't ask too many questions
about why his son was going to Bath.

He suspected that his father knew he was working for
Castlereagh and the Foreign Office as an operative, but
until he decided to quit, he wasn't at liberty to discuss
his activities with anyone. It was Castlereagh who had
sent him to Bath. Richmond's father thought it was an
innocent excursion for both of them.

However, Richmond was heading to Bath to check on
the actions of another operative who suddenly appeared
to be rather unstable. Castlereagh, ever the diplomat,
didn't actually say that Lloyd, the agent in question, had
run mad, but he insinuated that something was very
wrong. Richmond's task was simple: appear in Bath
with his father, who was taking the waters, then locate
Lloyd and relieve him of all the sensitive documents in
his possession. And since Lloyd specialized in troop
movements, it was especially important that those documents didn't fall into the wrong hands. Overall,
Richmond considered it a simple assignment that would
take no time or even effort to undertake.

As he continued to sip the amber ale, he thought
about the girl he had met in the stable yard. The young

lady was actually quite fetching in a very subtle way, he thought, and he wished she was staying at the inn for the evening. Then he might have actually had a proper introduction to her, even if she was a servant. In his daydreams, she was a companion, or even a governess. Or a perhaps poor relation. She had bright, lively eyes, and Richmond was certain that if he had bespoken a private room for their dinner, she would have been an intelligent and charming companion. Of course, she was probably too honorable to dally with him, which was a shame, he thought. Now he'd probably never see her again.

As Cassie, Daphne, and Aunt Honoria relaxed in the parlor after their meal, it slowly dawned upon Honoria that her nieces were exactly what she needed to cure her blue devils.

Once again, Daphne was complaining about the postponement of her Season, and Honoria glanced over at Cassie, who was once again ignoring her sister. Truth be told, Honoria was ignoring Daphne as well. *Anyone who survived a trip with this widgeon is a veritable paragon,* Honoria mused, sipping her sherry.

Of course, Daphne did look rather charming in her pink muslin dress adorned with tiny white bows and a few dozen yards of flounce at the hem. *It's too bad Daphne is so boring and bird-witted,* Honoria mused, studying Cassie. Yes, if Cassie wore the right fashions and did something with her hair, she would be transformed into a very enchanting and desirable young woman—a woman who would attract the right kind of man, not the simpering dandies who paraded after Daphne.

When Daphne took a breath during the middle of her diatribe, Honoria took the opportunity to break into her niece's constant stream of conversation to say, "I know you'll both want to get out in the next few days to do some shopping." Honoria glanced at both girls' frocks. Daphne obviously had more clothes than the royals. "Cassie, we must find you some new clothes while you're in town," she declared, staring at the abominable gray dress Cassie was wearing.

Cassie looked down at her dress and blushed slightly.

"Unfortunately, I've been feeling a bit under the weather these last few days, so Sara will take you about until you learn your way around Bath. And I do hope I don't need to tell you to mind your manners and avoid talking to strangers," Honoria added, mostly for Daphne's benefit. She knew that Cassie wasn't one to put herself forward with the gentlemen, which was more the shame, since Honoria thought Cassie was delightful.

"Of course, Aunt Honoria," Daphne replied obediently. "I've tried for the longest time to get Cassie interested in fashion, but she's just simply too stubborn and won't even talk about her clothes," she finished, as if Cassie wasn't even in the room.

Cassie smiled placidly at her sister, and Honoria would have bet the family emeralds that Daphne was quite accurate in her judgment. When she had been Cassie's age, she was busy traipsing across Europe and didn't give a fig for the latest fashions. So she was completely sympathetic to Cassie.

"Daphne is right, Aunt Honoria. I just don't have the time or the inclination to do anything about my wardrobe or lack thereof. Of course, I'm most assuredly on the shelf, so my looks don't really matter," Cassie concluded, a cynical edge to her voice.

"You might be on the shelf, Cassandra, but you don't need to look like a dowd. I'll have Sara take you over to my modiste, and she'll advise you on some suitable gowns. We'll be going out in Society while you're visiting, and I won't have it said that my niece dresses like a servant," Honoria concluded, her hazel eyes boring into Cassie's.

"But, Aunt Honoria, I don't have the money for . . ." Cassie began.

"You're not to worry about the expense, my dear. Have I made myself clear?" Honoria asked firmly.

Cassie was subdued, for the moment at least. However, Honoria could tell from the gleam in Cassie's eyes that the discussion was only temporarily closed. "Of course, Aunt Honoria," Cassie replied in her most obedient voice.

Honoria studied Cassie intently. Something had to be done about the situation at hand, and Honoria was the woman to do it. Cassie had grown up in the shadow of two remarkably beautiful sisters and, as a result, was convinced she had nothing to offer. In fact, Cassie was intelligent, pretty, and very charming. Cassie had much more than her looks to recommend her to a gentleman, while Pandora and Daphne were simply spoiled and beautiful, two traits that weren't a bargain, in Honoria's mind. With the right gowns and a bit of confidence, Cassie could easily compete with her sisters, since she was a much nicer person overall. *Yes, this is the summer I'm going to teach Cassie and Daphne that beauty isn't everything,* Honoria decided.

Chapter 2

"Cassie, I just have to see if they have a ribbon that's the right shade for my new walking dress," Daphne explained as the pair stood in front of one of the many shops in Bath catering to ladies' fashions.

Cassie sighed. She was sure she would scream if she saw one more ribbon today. This was their fourth shop in Daphne's quest for the perfect hue, and Cassie was very tired. *If only Mary or Sara had accompanied us,* Cassie mused. *Even better yet, if only I had stayed home.* However, Mary and Sara were busy in the house, and Aunt Honoria didn't think it would be a problem if Cassie and Daphne went ribbon shopping alone.

Daphne stood at the open door, and tapped her dainty foot. "Are you coming in, Cassie?" she asked impatiently.

If I never see another ribbon again, it will be too soon, Cassie thought, desperately trying to find a way out of visiting the milliner. She glanced across the street and found her solution in the shape of a park. A lovely green, flower-filled park with long wooden benches. Benches that all but beckoned to her. "Go inside and take all the time you need, Daphne," Cassie finally said. "I'll be on the bench across the street," she added, gesturing toward the benches.

An angelic smile appeared on Daphne's face. "All

right. I'll be out when I'm finished," she said pertly, and sashayed into the store.

A somewhat less breathtaking but just as heartfelt smile appeared on Cassie's face as she crossed the busy street and took possession of one of the very welcoming wooden benches. She opened her reticule and took out a copy of *The Iliad* in Greek, which usually discouraged any man from speaking to her. The park was empty except for a graying, nondescript gentleman who was sitting on the bench nearest to her. He seemed harmless enough, and had the look of a poor relation or a peer who had fallen on hard times. Cassie glanced over at him and smiled slightly, her glasses crinkling up on the bridge of her nose.

A new girl in town, the man on the bench thought, studying Cassie intently. *Not a servant, although she dresses like one. No, she's reading, and not many ladies' maids read, more the pity. A governess, perhaps? No, she's with the diamond of the first water who's in the milliner's shop. Probably a companion.*

He craned his neck to see what Cassie was reading, and, as he edged closer, he realized she was reading Homer. In Greek. This was his golden opportunity, and he had to make sure he didn't muck things up.

He still didn't know if he was being poisoned or not. His staff was eating the same food that he was, yet they didn't seem to be suffering from the blinding headaches or the dizziness that rendered him unable to work. Day by day, the attacks were getting more intense, but he wouldn't let the doctors in Bath look at his horse, let alone try to treat him. He was too weak to survive the journey to London to deliver his papers, but he couldn't destroy the work that he'd done in the last eight months. Conversely, he couldn't send Castlereagh a missive asking him to send someone over to collect his information. No, that would be too risky. And would Castlereagh know who to trust? Was there anyone who wasn't working for the French? His documents could be the final blow to the Corsican Devil if they weren't destroyed. If they didn't fall into the wrong hands.

He knew he was being watched. He could feel it. Maybe he was getting old and delusional, but that didn't explain the fact that the hair on his neck stood on edge almost every time he left the house. Someone was watching him. Occasionally he would see a shadow or someone out of the corner of his eye, he was certain of it.

All he had to do was get the papers into the hands of someone who was beyond suspicion. Someone he could trust. Someone who would be intelligent enough to get the papers to Castlereagh without calling attention to the fact that they existed. He didn't trust the post; Castlereagh had even advised him against using it for anything but the most mundane of correspondences. He certainly didn't trust anyone in Bath, a city that was just crawling with Frenchies.

So the thin, graying man on the bench had developed a plan. A plan that might appear risky, but he was sick. And he knew his once agile mind was suffering because of his illness.

He had started to write a diary. In Greek. The diary was a thinly veiled code that could easily be understood by someone of above average intelligence. Once the code was broken, his reader would easily understand where the papers were hidden and what needed to be done with them.

However, he couldn't hand the diary to someone on

the street. He was being watched. He was known in Bath to be a hermit, and it would certainly attract attention if he suddenly began to socialize. He knew his cover was potentially compromised and if he simply handed the diary to someone, it would be devilishly easy for his enemies to get their hands on it and find his work. That simply would not do.

Therefore, he had come up with a plan. He'd leave the diary where someone would find it. Someone trustworthy. Someone who could read Greek. Maybe even a woman. *No one pays heed to a woman, especially if she's quiet,* he reasoned. *Like a governess. Or a companion. They're almost invisible in Society and, if I find the right one, she'll undoubtedly be curious enough to break my code and go to Castlereagh.*

The young lady, who was obviously of a certain age, was reading Greek. That was essential. Her short brown hair and her dress were completely nondescript, and she looked like every other poor relation or companion. Her spectacles were a bit of an identifying feature, which was a problem. But besides that, she filled the bill perfectly. She was bookish, she was beyond the first blush of youth, and she had smiled at him, yet in no way encouraged his acquaintance.

He had gone to the park every day for the past four days, waiting for someone. Sometimes a man was there, watching him. The man on the bench knew when he was being watched; today wasn't one of those days. Today he was alone in the park, and today was his chance.

Cassie looked up as the graying man on the bench next to her walked by. For a brief moment, his troubled gray eyes met hers, and she felt as if he wanted her to do something for him. Which was quite odd, since Cassie knew she wasn't the type of person that strangers, especially men, ever even noticed. Yet the older man on the bench gazed at her intently before he disappeared down the street, which was somewhat disquieting.

Before Cassie could ponder the motives of the gray-haired man, Daphne suddenly appeared in front of her, awash in ribbons and ruffles. "Is that your book, Cassie?" she asked, pointing to the bench next to Cassie.

Cassie looked over at the bench. The man next to her had been reading and had obviously left his book. "No, it isn't. It must belong to the man who was sitting next to me," Cassie said, looking down the busy street to see if she could find the owner of the book. The shabbily dressed man had been swallowed up by foot traffic on the busy street and was nowhere in sight.

Daphne picked up the leather-bound book in her small, delicate hands and began to thumb through the pages. "It's not in English," she said and immediately handed it to Cassie.

Cassie opened the soft brown leather cover and immediately realized it was a journal or diary of some sort. In Greek. She thumbed through a few more pages, looking for the name of the owner. It didn't seem to be there.

"What are you going to do with it?" Daphne asked, sitting down next to Cassie and smiling at a very handsome gentleman who was walking his fluffy white poodle.

Cassie was momentarily perplexed. If she left the book on the bench, the man might come back to retrieve it when he realized it was still in the park. On the other hand, someone else might pick it up and simply throw it out. "I suppose I'll take it back to Aunt Honoria and see if she can help me find out who it belongs to," Cassie said, still looking at the contents.

"Was someone sitting next to you? I didn't see anyone," Daphne said, smiling at a dashing young man driving his phaeton down the road.

"Yes, an older man with gray hair and rather worn clothes was sitting on the bench before you came out of the milliner's. He certainly didn't look to be the type who could read and write Greek, though," Cassie noted, wishing her Greek was a trifle more extensive. She could only read about every third or fourth word, which was terribly annoying. A trip to the lending library for a Greek dictionary was definitely in order.

"I'm sure Aunt Honoria will know what to do with it. Did I tell you I found another hat? One that's perfect for my merino spencer."

"That's good," Cassie muttered, not paying any attention to Daphne's babbling. Something was wrong with the book; it didn't seem to be a diary at all. It was something else. Something that didn't quite make any sense at all.

The book sat inside Cassie's black reticule all day, forgotten. In fact, at the end of the day, the reticule and the book were left in the back of Cassie's wardrobe, out of sight and out of mind.

"We're visiting the Pump Room?" Daphne whined, making it very apparent that a trip to the Pump Room was not her idea of fun.

"I know the Pump Room isn't quite your idea of an entertaining afternoon, my dear, but there will be people your age there," Honoria explained patiently. Every time she talked to Daphne, she needed every ounce of patience that she possessed.

"I'm sure the Pump Room will be lovely," Cassie said

in an encouraging voice. Daphne glared at her but said nothing.

Honoria smiled at Cassie. *If only Daphne were more like Cassie and less like Pandora, this visit would be so much easier.* "I'm sure you'll meet any number of young gentlemen there who will be accompanying their fathers the same way you and Cassie are accompanying me," Honoria said in a level voice.

The reminder put a period to Daphne's complaining—at least for the moment.

"Lloyd stuck his spoon in the wall?" Aunt Honoria questioned Lady Something or Another as Cassie and Daphne sat next to her, sipping their tea. Cassie listened to the conversation, while Daphne concentrated on smiling at every gentleman under the age of five and forty.

Lady Spenser nodded vigorously, her tall primrose turban bobbing ridiculously. "They found him this morning. They're not sure of the cause of death," she whispered, as if she was imparting an important government secret. "It could have been a bad mushroom," Lady Spenser added.

"Does he have any relations?" Honoria questioned.

"They haven't been able to locate them yet," Lady Spenser replied. "I hear the authorities are questioning his staff," she added, glancing around the bustling Pump Room to see if anyone was eavesdropping.

Cassie gaped at the pair, spellbound. Some poor gent was dead, possibly murdered. Why? Was it a grudge? Or was a bedlamite with a liking for poison on the loose? For once, life was actually more interesting than a Minerva Press novel.

"Who was Mr. Lloyd?" Cassie asked pertly, hoping that Lady Spenser could shed some light on this mystery.

Lady Spenser gave Cassie an indulgent smile that proclaimed, *How terrible it must be to be a spinster bluestocking.* "Mr. Lloyd lived on the edge of town and appeared to be living off some sort of meager inheritance. He never came out into Society and was the most curious man. Did you know I actually saw him in public once reading a book? In Greek?" she concluded, a look of shock appearing on her carefully painted face.

Cassie frowned. The dead man had been seen reading Greek in public. "What exactly did Mr. Lloyd look like? I think I might have seen him before," she asked.

Lady Spenser gave her a disapproving look that told Cassie she was being much too curious and much too forward. "Lloyd was rather on the thin side, had gray hair, and didn't pay much heed to fashion. In fact, he rather had the look of a peer who was down on his luck. He wasn't tall, short, handsome, or even unattractive. He was just average. Lloyd was average looking," Lady Spenser concluded firmly.

Cassie fell into an uneasy silence. How many men in Bath could read Greek? She stared at the new white beaded reticule in her lap. Not many. *Mr. Lloyd had to have been the man on the bench in the park,* Cassie realized with a frown. *Now the poor man is dead, possibly murdered, and I have his book.* Cassie stared at the beautiful beads on her reticule, her mind in a whirl. *What am I going to do?*

Lady Spenser's next words brought Cassie out of her reverie. "And have you heard what they've been saying? The tabbies are declaring that Lloyd was a spy. One of ours," she proclaimed, her blue eyes alight with pleasure. It was obvious that Lady Spenser was one of the tabbies and liked nothing more than spreading tales herself, Cassie noted.

Honoria frowned. "Ridiculous. Lloyd couldn't have been a spy. He was so common."

"But that's what made him the perfect undercover agent," Lady Spenser replied, leaning closer to Honoria and dropping her voice discreetly. "No one would believe that someone so ordinary would be working for our government. And who would expect an agent of the government here in Bath, of all places?"

Aunt Honoria raised her eyebrows in disbelief and let the subject of Lloyd's illicit activities drop, and Lady Spenser soon began to point out all of the eligible young bucks in the room. At that point, Daphne's interest was piqued, while Cassie once again drifted off.

Eventually, Lady Spenser left their table, and Cassie continued pondering the story of Mr. Lloyd. It seemed so unbelievable that a spy would be in sleepy little Bath. Then there was the book Mr. Lloyd wanted her to find. Cassie was sure of that. But why?

Cassie glanced over at her sister. For some odd reason, she was batting her eyelashes and waving her delicate feathered fan quite vigorously, even though it wasn't particularly hot. Cassie followed Daphne's gaze.

As usual, Daphne had spotted a man—a man she obviously wanted to meet. A man every single woman in the room obviously wanted to meet.

The gentleman in question was the male version of an Incomparable. He seemed to tower over everyone in the room, yet he wasn't freakishly tall; it was the way he carried himself. His eyes were an exotic shade of brown that made him seem slightly foreign. When he smiled, he revealed the best teeth in all of England. His hair, as blond as the sun, was coaxed into a Brutus. His buff pantaloons covered muscular legs, and his shoulders seemed to strain in the perfectly cut midnight blue jacket he sported. He was a Greek god come to life in the middle of the Pump Room. Cassie looked over at Daphne. She was all but gaping at the masculine vision on the other side of the room.

Finally, after what seemed to be an eternity of Daphne fluttering her eyes and playing with her fan, the gentleman glanced over at her. Her sister responded by giving him her most engaging smile, the one that enslaved the boys back home in Warwick. Cassie almost laughed aloud when the Greek god lifted his quizzing glass and studied Daphne from across the room, making him look rather ridiculous. For a long moment he did nothing, and Cassie was sure that Daphne was holding her breath. Then the Greek god lowered his ornate, gold-rimmed glass and bestowed a dazzling smile on Daphne, who was now fanning herself furiously. *It's like watching a particularly bad play,* Cassie thought, positive that the god was going to request an introduction to Daphne, the beauty.

Moments later, an unknown dowager in a cerise walking dress that showed a bit too much of her womanly charms appeared at their table, the god in tow. Cassie glanced over at her aunt, who didn't seem surprised that the god was now going to request an audience with Daphne.

"Lady Raverston," the dowager began, smiling sweetly at her, "I'd like to present Percival Paige, the Earl of Pembrook. Lord Pembrook is a bosom bow of mine from London," the dowager concluded, her hand resting possessively on Pembrook's arm.

Honoria studied the Corinthian who was causing

Daphne to act like a gapeseed. After a long moment, she obviously decided that there was no harm in introducing him to her charges. "Lady Bonham, Lord Pembrook, these are my nieces, Cassandra and Daphne Wyndmoore."

Cassie glanced at Lord Pembrook. She was invisible to him, as she had expected. But she noticed something else. His smile didn't reach his eyes—and there was something there, something Cassie couldn't quite define. She did know, however, that she didn't like him.

The ever-so-correct Lord Pembrook kissed Cassie's hand, and a chill ran down her spine. It was terribly unsettling.

He then reached over and kissed Daphne's delicate hand, while the lady in question turned a delightful shade of pink. "Lady Raverston, you're blessed to have such a beautiful relation," he murmured gallantly, staring straight at Daphne, who turned an even more delightful shade of pink.

Cassie stared at Pembrook, oblivious to his slight. He seemed to be at least three and thirty, much too old to be slavering over a chit like Daphne, who was barely out of the schoolroom.

As they joined Honoria's party at the small table, Lady Bonham broached the main topic of conversation at the Pump Room that afternoon. "Did you hear about Lloyd? That's all everyone has been talking about this afternoon."

"Yes, of course," Honoria replied in a voice laced with disapproval, and glanced over at the far end of the room. "Lady Bonham, there seems to be a gentleman in a bottle-green coat across the room trying to get your attention," she commented.

Lady Bonham, who was actually quite a bit older than she first appeared and wore almost as much paint as an actress, gazed across the room to discern who was trying to get her attention.

In the meantime, Cassie leaned over and listened to the conversation that Lord Pembrook was having with Daphne.

"It must be so difficult for you to be in Bath, Miss Daphne," he commented in a voice that would melt butter, while devouring Daphne with his eyes.

"Whyever would you say that, Lord Pembrook?" Daphne said prettily.

"You're undoubtedly the most beautiful female in this part of England. You must be besieged by callers," he said, gazing soulfully at her.

Cassie started to feel sick. The most romantic thing anyone had ever said to her was, "You're a sensible one, aren't you?"

Daphne toyed with her fan, obviously basking in Pembrook's attention. Before she could say something witty and charming, Lady Bonham all but grabbed Pembrook's arm and practically dragged him out of his seat. "It was ever so nice to meet you both," Lady Bonham called as she dragged Pembrook across the room.

A furious frown appeared on Daphne's perfect features. "Lady Bonham is certainly ill bred," she said to Cassie. "Lord Pembrook and I were having quite a nice coze until she forced him to leave," Daphne snapped irritably.

Strangely enough, Honoria didn't seem in the least bit upset that Lord Pembrook and Lady Bonham were gone. "An acquaintance with Lady Bonham isn't something that I'd encourage either of you to pursue," Aunt Honoria commented, glaring at Daphne with disapproval.

Once again, Daphne pouted.

* * *

Dinner, which should have been pleasant for all of the ladies, was something of a trial. The conversation, which was dominated by Daphne, consisted of her mooning over someone very specific.

"Aunt Honoria, isn't Lord Pembrook the most handsome man you've ever seen?" Daphne gushed later that evening as the trio supped on a meal of broiled neck of mutton.

Honoria snorted. "He's a dandy. As for his legendary good looks, you should have seen some of the gentlemen around when I had my Season. They were real men, not preening fops," Honoria concluded.

"I think he looks like a Greek god. Don't you, Cassie?" Daphne asked, turning to her sister.

Cassie looked up from her neck of mutton and smiled at Daphne. *It's hard to believe, but it's as if she's just a younger version of Pandora,* Cassie thought reflectively. "Yes, Lord Pembrook is exceptionally handsome, but I don't know if I would try to strike up a closer acquaintance with him," Cassie said mildly, hoping to stir some sense into her sister. There was something she didn't like about Pembrook, and she'd be happiest if Daphne would just forget the handsome peer.

"Of course you couldn't strike up an acquaintance with him, you're already five and twenty! And you're certainly not eligible for someone as . . . perfect as Lord Pembrook," Daphne replied, picking at her creamed asparagus.

"Daphne, you will not speak to your sister that way," Honoria chastised, glaring at her.

"But, Aunt Honoria, it's true! Everyone knows Cassie's on the shelf," Daphne countered, looking at her aunt incredulously.

Honoria frowned. "Daphne, you will not speak to

your sister like she's a pasty-faced ogre while you are under my roof. If you continue to do so, not only will you be sent home, but I will inform your mother, in the strongest terms possible, that you are much too immature to enter Society for at least another two or three years," Honoria concluded.

Daphne dropped her mouth open in shock. Cassie waited for her words of protest, but none came.

"Do you understand, Daphne?" Honoria asked, glaring at her niece.

Daphne stared at her plate. "Yes, ma'am," she said in small voice.

Cassie looked down at her plate, a small smile on her face. *Maybe this trip won't be quite so bad,* she mused.

It was nightfall by the time Richmond and his father arrived at the house that Castlereagh had secured for their visit to Bath, and they both agreed that the trip had gone remarkably well. The roads were fine, the inn was acceptable, and both men were in a good humor.

Richmond was happy because the marquess had actually refrained from lecturing him about getting married. Since they were in a closed carriage for an interminable amount of time, his father could have lectured him on the topic at length. Yet he didn't, a fact that made Richmond eternally grateful.

Instead, his father tried to get him to explain how he ended up with a bullet in his leg. Richmond hadn't told him. The marquess, who was nothing if not persistent, also tried to find out the real reason for their trip to Bath. Richmond couldn't tell him that, either. Overall, the trip had gone very well, and Richmond decided to settle in for a day or two before contacting Lloyd.

Castlereagh hadn't put any kind of time constraints on the mission, and Richmond wanted to be anonymous for at least a day or two.

The house Castlereagh had arranged for the pair was on the far end of Great Pulteney Street, and was wonderfully unassuming. In fact, it looked no different from every other Georgian-style house in Bath, outside of those in the Crescent. That suited Richmond fine.

As he stood in the hallway dusting off the travel dirt, Richmond decided everything was in order. *I must thank Castlereagh for sending me on holiday,* Richmond thought, heading for the parlor.

He was sure that nothing could go wrong.

Chapter 3

"Yes, Daphne, we will be visiting the Assembly Rooms, but not until Cassandra is fitted for some new gowns," Honoria repeated for what seemed to be the hundredth time that morning. They weren't even through with breakfast, and Daphne was already whining about her social life.

"But, Aunt Honoria," Daphne began in a very unflattering grating voice, "Cassie doesn't need any new gowns. It's not as if anyone is going to pay any attention to *her*," Daphne said.

Honoria put down her fork and stared at Daphne, aghast. "Daphne, you will go up to your room and stay there until dinner. At that time, you will come downstairs and apologize to your sister. If you cannot find the proper words to atone for the way you've maligned her, you need not come down until breakfast tomorrow. Do I make myself clear?" Honoria asked, her hazel eyes boring into Daphne.

Daphne's eyes were wide with shock. She opened her mouth as if to say something, then obviously thought better of it and said nothing. She stared at Honoria for the longest time, then finally said, "Yes, Aunt Honoria." Daphne took the napkin off her lap, folded it, placed it on the table, and left the table without uttering another word.

Cassie was dumbfounded. She had never seen anyone actually discipline Daphne or Pandora, and it was quite the shock. Of course, Mama had no problem disciplining *her.* Perhaps that was because she wasn't as pretty as Daphne or Pandora. "Aunt Honoria, Daphne doesn't mean what she what says, you know that. And she is telling the truth," Cassie added, hoping inwardly that Honoria would waver in her punishment. It wasn't Daphne's fault that she had been cosseted since the day she was born, Cassie mused, chewing on a crisp slice of bacon.

Honoria's eyes turned to Cassie. "Cassandra, you are a very charming and beautiful young woman. Not in the same way that your sisters are, but beautiful nonetheless. I will not have anyone in this family undermining your confidence while you are under my roof. Do I make myself clear?" Honoria asked, reaching for the plate of kippers.

Cassie stared down at her meal and meekly replied, "Yes, Aunt Honoria."

"We're going to get you some proper clothes. Right now you're rigged out as if you're some sort of poor relation, or, worse yet, a companion. In fact, we'll go today to see Madame Babette. She'll know what do to with you," Honoria concluded confidently.

Cassie continued to eat her breakfast. *Mama has been trying for years to make me presentable and has finally declared the task impossible,* Cassie thought, staring at her food. *Most gowns look dreadful on me; my hair isn't long, blonde, and curly; and everyone knows I'm a bluestocking. I'm destined to be a failure in Society,* Cassie reasoned. *Why won't Aunt Honoria simply accept that fact?*

* * *

Madame Babette was everything Cassie expected: petite, genteel, and very charming. She also reminded Cassie of the modiste her mama had used when she decided that it was time to rig Cassie out for her Season—the Season where Mama had tried to transform Cassie into a darker-haired version of Pandora. It was a monumental disaster.

As Madame Babette's assistants took her measurements, Cassie remembered the pains her mama took to try to get her up to scratch. First, there were the frilly new gowns. Pandora even helped Mama select them, since it was known that Pandora had a great sense of style. It didn't help. No matter what their seamstress attempted, Cassie did not look even mildly appealing in the frothy pastel gowns with ruffles and flounces. In fact, she looked rather drab and colorless, much to everyone's utter astonishment.

Cassie's Season lasted a little longer than a sennight. That's when Papa stepped in and declared that if Cassie didn't want a Season, he wasn't going to force her to have one. That caused quite a row in the household, but Cassie got to stay home.

"Cassie, why are you so Friday faced?" Honoria asked, bringing Cassie out of her reverie.

Cassie blushed. "It's nothing, Aunt Honoria. I just hate for everyone to waste all of this time and the expense on me. Mama tried it years ago. I'm nothing but a bluestocking and a spinster and it's just folly to pretend I can be anything but that," Cassie said in resignation.

Aunt Honoria and Madame Babette stared at Cassie in horror. Madame Babette recovered first. "Miss Wyndmoore, when your mama tried to make you fashionable, what style of gowns did you wear?" the dainty French-woman asked.

"Mama and Pandora favored lacy and frilly gowns, and that's what they ordered for me," she answered simply.

"And the colors?" Madame Babette inquired.

"Most of them were white, but I also had a few light pastels."

"But you do not resemble your sister, do you?" Madame Babette pointed out.

Cassie cringed. Once again, someone had noticed that she wasn't Pandora, which was a very apparent fact. "Not at all. Pandora and Daphne, my younger sister, are both blonde and fair," she finally replied.

"That was the problem, Miss Wyndmoore. Your mama and her seamstress were still dressing your sister, not you. You cannot wear such fussy styles and white! *Mon Dieu!* You should not wear white at all. You need color to keep your face glowing. Madame Babette will make sure you like all of your new frocks, and you'll look beautiful in each and every one of them," the petite Frenchwoman declared, rather blowing the wind out of Cassie's sails.

Honoria smiled at Cassie. "Madame Babette is right. You're old enough to choose the fashions you like, and Madame Babette will create them for you only if they will compliment your figure. While you're in Bath, you will look as charming as every other young lady, spectacles or not," she declared.

A shy smile appeared on Cassie's face. "I don't have any choice in the matter, do I?"

Madame Babette and Aunt Honoria replied, "No," in unison.

* * *

Richmond sighed as he sat alone in the surprisingly large study of the house they had let in Bath.

His day had not gone at all according to plan. He thought that he would simply search Lloyd's house, find the papers in question, and then enjoy a bit of a holiday. Then, when local Society bored him to tears (as it invariably did) he would return to London for his next assignment.

Well, he did get to search the house and realized that someone had been there before him. In fact, when he had made some inquires with the neighbors, they had indeed seen a gentleman nosing around the property while the servants were at Sunday Mass. After a dozen or so more interviews, he found out an odd coincidence. The handsome Lord Pembrook had asked them the exact same questions a few days earlier.

Why did God curse me with Pembrook? he wondered, filling his glass with port.

Pembrook didn't arrive in London until well after he had returned from an extended visit to his relations in France, after the episode with Pandora Wyndmoore. The ever so charming Lord Pembrook was enormously popular with the ladies, had impeccable manners, and lived like Prinny himself. This was deuced odd, since, according to Castlereagh, Pembrook was notoriously let in the pockets. There was a discreet investigation, and it was concluded that Pembrook received his funds from out of the country—from France, in fact. Castlereagh lived for the day that Pembrook would be exposed as a spy and exiled. That day had not yet arrived.

Richmond sipped his port and stared at the traditional English landscapes that hung on the walls. *This obviously isn't going to be an easy assignment,* he thought wryly. Someone had sent Pembrook to Bath, and more than likely, he was the one who searched Lloyd's house first.

However, Pembrook was still in Bath. *If he has Lloyd's documents, he should have left,* Richmond thought with a frown. *If he's still here, it means that he's not any further along than I am,* he mused.

Richmond was so engrossed in thought that he didn't even notice that his father had opened the door to the study and walked in.

"You certainly appear to be preoccupied," Stanton commented, walking over to the elaborately carved mahogany table that held the decanter of port. He poured himself a glass and sat down in the Chippendale chair across from his son.

Richmond looked up and managed a wan smile. "I'm sorry, I wasn't attending. What did you say, Father?"

"I said that you appeared to be deep in thought," he commented, eyeing his son.

"It's nothing," Richmond replied with a slight sigh. "I've just had some setbacks . . . on a project I'm completing," Richmond said vaguely, running his hand through his thick mane of hair.

"Are you going to be out all day tomorrow?" his father asked calmly, his voice filled with curiosity.

Richmond had more on his mind than whiling away the hours at the Pump Room. After spending what seemed like every waking hour casually interrogating every single person in Bath (primarily dull, gouty peers or eccentric dowagers in turbans), he did come across one lead in the search for Lloyd's book. He learned that Pembrook was looking for a young woman, possibly a companion or a governess, who was seen with Lloyd in the park. The description left much to be desired; he was looking for a female of an undetermined age with spectacles and short light brown hair who was wearing decidedly shabby clothes. *It almost sounds like the young lady I met at the inn,* he mused, staring off into the distance, totally unaware of his father. No one knew the identity of the mystery companion, so the wench in question obviously wasn't from Bath, which was somewhat helpful.

"You're not attending again," Stanton commented.

Richmond looked over at his father, a bit flustered. "Sorry, what did you say?"

"It was nothing important," the marquess replied, studying his son intently.

Richmond stared at the Aubusson carpet, perplexed. He had only one solution. "If you were a woman in service, perhaps as a companion, and you were a stranger in Bath, where would you spend your free time?" he asked in what he hoped was the most casual tone.

He looked up. His father was frowning. Richmond knew it was a dashed odd question, but he was out of ideas.

"Well, I suppose I'd be in the Pump Room in the morning, and out shopping or seeing the sights in the afternoon. Or even the library, perhaps. Or the Assembly Rooms. Why?"

Richmond could feel his muscles tense. The dreaded question. Why? He most certainly couldn't tell his father the reason for the question, but he didn't want to lie to him, either. Finally he said, "It's a long story. I'd rather not go into the details. I just need to talk to a certain unassuming brunette, probably a servant, who was reading in the Park a few days ago. Suffice it to say I'm not planning any nefarious liaisons, I just need to speak with her," he added hastily.

His father smiled. "Actually, a nefarious liaison with

a respectable young woman might do you a world of good."

Richmond stared at the wall. The last respectable young woman in his life had been Pandora Wyndmoore. She left him humiliated and emotionally bereft, so instead, he had turned to women of the demimonde, but that was becoming tedious. For the moment, he was without a mistress. However, he certainly didn't need what his Father termed 'a respectable young woman.' They were usually insipid and useless.

Of course, a nice bookish female was something else altogether. Someone like his lady at the inn. Intelligent, charming, and kind. He could tell she was kind. And charming. If she were eligible, she would have been a welcome addition to his life. "We're in Bath, Father," he began with a smile. "We're more likely to find an eligible match for you than for me," he concluded.

A sigh escaped his father. "I'm never going to be a grandfather, am I?" he asked softly.

Sunlight streamed through Cassie's windows, beckoning her outdoors. Birds chirped, a slight breeze could be felt through the open window, and if Cassie had looked up, she would have noticed that she was missing the most delightful day.

Cassie didn't look up. Her nose was planted firmly in the diary she had found. Which was probably poor Mr. Lloyd's, she reasoned. Cassie leafed through the pages, deep in thought. *I probably should return it when his heir arrives,* she mused, staring at the words inscribed in Greek. *But from what Aunt Honoria says, that won't be any time soon.*

Thankfully, Cassie's papa had been wonderfully liberal.

While Mama spent hours with Pandora and later Daphne, teaching them to play the pianoforte, paint watercolors, do needlepoint, and so on, Papa realized that Cassie had different talents, such as her inclination for mathematics and languages. Greek wasn't her best language, but she was capable, and she thought she could translate most of the diary. The first page read:

> *Once upon a time, a donkey dressed himself up in a lion's skin. As the king of beasts, he was able to learn about the life of the lions and report his findings to the other donkeys to keep them safe. Then one day, his lion's skin slipped off and he was in great danger.*

Cassie stared at the entry. It made no sense. She vaguely remembered reading some sort of fable about the donkey and the lion, but something was wrong with this story. It just didn't sound quite like a fable, and there was no real ending. Was Mr. Lloyd working on a children's book? Did he have a child somewhere? And if he did, why in the world was he writing in Greek? Her mind was in a whirl.

She began to flip through the pages and decided on one thing. The book was definitely filled with children's stories. Why was a man without an heir, a hermit, writing children's stories? It made no sense. Why were most of the townspeople in Bath convinced that Mr. Lloyd was murdered? Who would murder a simple hermit who was writing a child's book? Cassie decided that it was time to quiz Aunt Honoria about the mysterious and enigmatic Mr. Lloyd.

* * *

Once again, the dinner table was perfect. The Dresden china plates, in white with a lovely blue design, were surrounded by shiny silver cutlery and crystal goblets that sparkled as they reflected the candlelight and all but beckoned them to the table.

Cassie and Aunt Honoria sat at the table, ready to eat. Daphne stood in the doorway in a simple, unassuming cream muslin dress and faced Cassie, tears brimming in her luminous blue eyes. "I'm very sorry about what I said this morning, Cassie," Daphne said in a small voice that was little more than a whimper. "I don't mean to be unkind or insulting to you, since you're the very best of sisters. I just sometimes forget that you have feelings, and I don't always think about what I'm saying," she murmured, staring down at the floor, unable to meet Cassie's eyes.

Cassie practically gaped at her sister. Never in all of her life had anyone ever made Daphne—or Pandora, for that matter—apologize to her for being thoughtless. Mama overlooked Daphne's and Pandora's slights to Cassie. Every so often, Papa would scold them when they said something unpleasant about her, but everyone understood. Cassie was not the beauty of the family and had no expectations at all. Consequently, she wasn't the focus of the family.

Before Cassie could collect her thoughts, Daphne added, "So please accept my apology, since I would just die if you hated me."

Cassie glanced over at Aunt Honoria, who rolled her eyes toward the heavens. Obviously, she wasn't impressed with Daphne's performance. But then again, Aunt Honoria didn't realize that this was perhaps the first and only time that Daphne had ever apologized to anyone.

"Of course I accept your apology, Daphne," Cassie said in a level voice, and both girls turned to Aunt Honoria.

Honoria stared at Daphne for what seemed like an eternity. "That was nicely done, Daphne. You may join us for dinner. In the future, please be mindful that you will be punished every time you slight your sister. Do you understand?" she asked firmly.

Daphne took her place at the table on the other side of Aunt Honoria and gulped audibly. "Yes, Aunt Honoria," she replied.

As they began their rather sumptuous meal of roasted veal with a variety of fresh vegetables, Cassie couldn't stop thinking about Mr. Lloyd. As Aunt Honoria chatted about the latest *on-dits,* Cassie's mind kept returning to the book and the man who wrote it. Finally, when Aunt Honoria took a break, Cassie saw her opportunity.

"I'm sorry to be so curious, Aunt Honoria, but did you know anything about poor Mr. Lloyd?" Cassie asked cautiously.

Honoria washed down her meat with a glass of claret. "Not much, I'm afraid. Mr. Lloyd was something of a recluse, you see, so no one outside of his staff knew much about him," she replied.

"Did he have children? Or was he involved with an orphanage?" Cassie asked, trying to sound casual.

Honoria gaped at Cassie as if she were a slow-top. "Children? Orphans? Where do you come up with these things, Cassandra? Mr. Lloyd was a bachelor and a recluse. There are no children, no paramours, no relatives, no friends, and most assuredly no orphans in his life," Honoria concluded.

Cassie chewed contemplatively on her veal. Then why had he been writing a children's book? He had no children, no friends in Bath, and maybe not even any relatives. So why had he been writing a book in Greek? A book that sounded dashed familiar. "Daphne, do you remember the fables that Papa used to read to us when we were small?" Cassie asked suddenly.

Daphne's eyes lit up. "The Aesop stories? Of course I do. That was when Papa was trying to teach me Greek."

"Wasn't there a story about a donkey in a lion's skin?"

"Why are you interested in a children's fable, Cassandra?" Honoria asked, a frown deeply etched on her brow.

Cassie wanted to be honest, but she just couldn't. If she told Aunt Honoria about the book, she was sure that she'd have to return it. And she didn't want to return the book at all. *Mr. Lloyd wanted me to have it,* she thought, certain of that fact. So Cassie told a lie that wasn't quite a lie. "Oh, there was a reference to that particular Aesop story in the book I'm reading, and I couldn't remember how the story ended. Do you recall, Daphne?" she said ever so casually.

Daphne took the etched goblet in her hand and sipped the red liquid. "You know I could never keep all of those stories correct, Cassie."

Cassie chewed on her creamed carrots, deep in thought. The key to Mr. Lloyd's book might be in a book of Aesop's fables. A book that Aunt Honoria most definitely didn't have in her library, since Aunt Honoria didn't have any children of her own. "Do you think I might go to the lending library tomorrow, Aunt Honoria? I know it's a silly matter, but I would like to find out how the fable ended," she concluded, hoping upon hope that Aunt Honoria wouldn't think she was a bedlamite.

"Certainly, go if you'd like. Take Daphne with you. I was planning on making some morning calls that would bore you both to tears," Honoria replied.

Cassie smiled, relief flooding her body. Aunt Honoria

wasn't going to quiz her about the Aesop book. Or ask her why she was so interested in Mr. Lloyd.

She looked over at Daphne, who looked like she was trying to conceal a very attractive pout. Then Cassie remembered. Daphne wanted to spend every waking moment socializing or shopping, and the lending library wasn't on her social calendar.

"I'm sure that Bath's lending library will be filled with eligible gentlemen," Cassie said softly to her sister.

Daphne's pout disappeared and was replaced by a radiant smile. "Do you think so?"

"Possibly. And isn't it better than spending the morning making calls?"

Daphne seemed to consider the idea for a moment. "I suppose you're right," she replied with a slight sigh.

Cassie hid a small smile. Her sister was so desperate to start making her way in Society that she would even try to meet someone at the library. Cassie spent hours and hours at the library back home and had never once met an eligible man there. But then again, this was Bath. Obviously Daphne was so desperate to meet someone eligible that she would even venture into the dreaded lending library.

Cassie stood among the shelves in Bath's modest lending library, a frown marring her delicate features. She was alone in the decidedly miniscule section that carried what was termed 'foreign literature,' and she had managed to locate a copy of *Aesop's Fables*.

But something was definitely wrong. As Cassie read the story entitled 'The Donkey in the Lion's Skin,' she found that it wasn't the story in Mr. Lloyd's children's book.

In Aesop's tale, the donkey finds a lion's skin, dresses up, and frightens people. Every man and beast runs away in terror. Then the donkey brays, giving his identity away to the fox. There was nothing about observing the life of the lions or being in great danger when his costume came off. Mr. Lloyd was obviously not simply retelling the Aesop story. *Something is very definitely wrong,* Cassie thought, staring at the graying pages of the book.

Daphne stood near the huge wooden front door of the library, pretending to look at a Minerva Press novel. Mary was hovering nearby, watching her every move, which was more than annoying. *As if I can get in any trouble here,* Daphne thought, a sigh escaping her pink lips.

She glanced around the library. It was filled with badly dressed dowagers, a few servant types who were either governesses or companions, and a wizened old man or two. Daphne smoothed an invisible wrinkle in her peach walking dress and glanced over at the door, hoping beyond hope that her knight in shining armor would walk through the door. And if not her knight, at least a man who was younger than five and fifty. *How am I supposed to develop a stable of suitors here if everyone in Bath practically has their spoon stuck in the wall?* Daphne wondered in vain.

Then the large carved oak door opened, and Daphne casually looked over her shoulder, a shy yet welcoming smile on her face. Hopefully the man behind the door would be handsome and eligible, unlike everyone else in the library.

The man who walked in was about five and thirty and

had a very slight limp. That made him look a trifle older, and Daphne really didn't care for men who had physical infirmities. His clothes proclaimed that he was a gentleman, yet they lacked the style and dash that Pandora said marked a true man of fashion. This gentleman simply wore all black with a white shirt and white cravat, which did set off his thick dark hair. His features were a bit harsh, his nose a little too prominent, and he was much too tanned to be fashionable. But he wasn't wearing any wedding ring, wasn't rotund, and didn't appear to be drunk. Daphne decided to become acquainted with him.

Richmond stood staring at the young woman in the lending library like a jackanapes in the first throes of calf love. Of course, he definitely wasn't in love with the blond vision in peach standing in front of him. If anything, his first inclination was to turn around and leave. Immediately. For the decidedly young, bewitchingly beautiful goddess holding a book and batting her eyelashes at him was the image of Pandora Wyndmoore. And he certainly didn't want to be reminded of that heartless doxy.

Unfortunately, he was caught off guard by the goddess, and simply stood gaping at her like a sapskull, his brain momentarily frozen. Thankfully, he knew that it wasn't the thing for a young woman to approach an unknown gentleman and start a conversation.

When the goddess and her peach walking dress sashayed over to him, he was stunned.

"Are you interested in borrowing the same book that I am?" the goddess said with an inviting smile on her face.

Richmond snapped out of his temporary paralysis and smiled at the beauty, noticing the curve of her milky white breasts, her bright blue eyes, and the pink flush of her cheeks. *She is a tempting thing,* he thought, *and if her parents don't keep a close eye on her, she'll be seducing men all over Bath.* "No, actually I'm not," he stated politely, then added, "I didn't mean to stare, but you rather remind me of someone I once knew in London." As soon as the words escaped his lips, he cursed himself. *Why did I have to mention that? Now the goddess will actually try to engage me in conversation, and I really don't have the time or the interest in her type,* he decided.

The goddess smiled blandly and batted her eyelashes again, which irritated Richmond. "It's been said that I resemble my oldest sister Pandora. She had her Season ages ago and is now Lady Lyntwoode," Daphne explained with a smile.

Richmond blanched a bit, but kept his voice level. "Then your sister is the former Pandora Wyndmoore?" he asked, hoping upon hope that he had somehow misunderstood the goddess.

The goddess clapped her hands together in delight. "Why, yes! How utterly delightful to find a friend of Pandora's in this rustic setting," she said.

Richmond was less than delighted.

Cassie was glancing around the musty shelves, looking for another translation of the Aesop stories, when Mary, who was trying her best to be an attentive abigail and escort, appeared at her side. "Miss Cassie, Miss Daphne has started a conversation with some dandy who just walked into the library," Mary whispered.

Cassie sighed. "Does Daphne know this gentleman?" she asked calmly, but she already knew the answer. Outside of Aunt Honoria's staff, Daphne had no acquaintances in Bath.

"I don't think so, Miss Cassie."

Cassie picked up the half dozen tomes that she wanted to borrow and replied, "We'd better go see what trouble Daphne's got herself into," and followed Mary through the narrow aisles.

As they reached the doorway, Cassie stopped in mid stride and gaped at the scene unfolding in front of her.

Daphne, looking all the rage in her peach ensemble embellished with tiny seed pearls, had her hand lightly placed on Lord Richmond's arm. *What is he doing in Bath?* Cassie wondered. *And why is he flirting with my sister?*

As Cassie slowly approached the pair with Mary in tow, she wondered if Richmond would remember their meeting at the Pig and Crow inn. *Probably not,* she thought dejectedly. *I spoke with him dozens of times when he was courting Pandora, and he didn't remember that either,* she thought. *Because I'm not Pandora, and I'm not beautiful, so gentlemen don't need to remember me or even pay attention to me,* Cassie thought dejectedly.

The incident with Pandora and Richmond had occurred ages ago, but Cassie would never forget him. He was always the smartest of Pandora's suitors, and Cassie knew that he was much too good for her sister. Richmond wasn't a dandy; he was thoughtful, well-read, and everything she could ever want in a suitor. But he was Pandora's, and, as the plain middle sister, Cassie was always invisible.

Of course, Pandora never forgave Richmond for ending their relationship, and actually pretended that she gave him his walking papers. Cassie knew that Richmond ended the relationship, although Pandora said that Richmond wasn't respectable enough for her. Then there was the story that Pandora told her about the suicide of Richmond's pregnant mistress. Cassie knew that Pandora was free with her attentions, and that Richmond caught her in a compromising position with another man. Pandora simply shrugged off that explanation and told Cassie that Richmond was half French and was probably a spy for them; he was therefore a very suspect person who wasn't up to her standards.

Now that very suspect person was giving her younger sister a breathtaking smile. *This hasn't been a good day,* Cassie thought, approaching the pair.

Chapter 4

Richmond was getting bored. Pandora's baby sister was a younger version of the original. Her main concern and topic of conversation was her own beauty, and she was hard pressed to put together a coherent sentence. *However, it might be amusing to toy with her, just to annoy Pandora,* he thought, then immediately rejected the idea. *The child would bore me to tears in less than a sennight.*

Then, seemingly out of nowhere, the delightful damsel in distress he had assisted at the Pig and Crow appeared with another woman behind her. *What's she doing here?* he wondered. He was even more confused when the Wyndmoore goddess giggled and said in a sugar-sweet voice, "Oh my, I have forgotten my manners, haven't I? Lord Richmond, may I introduce my *older* sister Cassandra," she finished.

Richmond stared at the woman in the drab brown walking dress with the frightfully high neck. *There is no possibility that this female is related to Pandora and her widgeon of a sister,* he thought.

The companion, actually the sister, had wonderful manners. "It's very nice to see you again, Lord Richmond," she said politely.

Daphne glanced over at Cassie and gaped at her. "You

actually know Lord Richmond, Cassie?" Daphne asked in an incredulous tone.

Cassie glanced over at her sister. "Yes, I met Lord Richmond at the inn where we had our carriage repaired," she said and glanced over at Richmond.

Richmond was genuinely stunned. He'd spent hours at the Wyndmoore's house in London, playing adoring swain to Pandora, and he was sure he had never met a younger sister. How could the charming companion he had met at the inn be related to Pandora Wyndmoore? It made no sense at all. "It's a pleasure to see you again, Miss Wyndmoore," he said in his most cordial voice, as he took her hand in his and gently kissed it. *If only she weren't related to Pandora,* he mused.

As Richmond gaped at Cassie and Cassie blushed prettily, Daphne broke the spell. "I suppose you met Cassie while you were in London during Pandora's Season?" Daphne asked.

Richmond frowned. He didn't remember a sister. Of course, he had been so taken with Pandora at the time that she could have had a dozen sisters and he wouldn't have noticed any of them. But since he honestly didn't recall any sisters at all, he smiled benignly at Daphne and replied, "Unfortunately, I can't say that I did."

Before either sister could reply, Mary broke in. "Excuse me, Miss Cassie, we really have to be leaving," Mary said firmly, eyeing Richmond suspiciously.

Cassie gave him a wan smile. "Good day, Lord Richmond," she said abruptly and looked over at Daphne.

"It was very nice to meet you, Lord Richmond. I'm sure we'll be seeing you around town," Daphne said pertly, before Cassie dragged her away from him.

As they headed for the desk with a stack of books, Richmond stared after them. How bloody awful that the charming companion from the inn was related to Pandora Wyndmoore. *If she were anyone else, I would have tried to strike up an acquaintance,* he thought. *Unfortunately, she's a Wyndmoore, and they're nothing but heartless jades.*

"Cassie, what's wrong?" Daphne asked as they walked toward Aunt Honoria's Georgian-style home.

Cassie didn't want to answer. She didn't want to talk about Richmond. She was acting like a fool. More than anything, she wanted him to remember her and the times they chatted while he was waiting patiently to take Pandora to a rout. They talked dozens of times while Pandora was in London, and he didn't even remember her.

It had been different at the inn. She didn't expect him to remember her right away, since it was ages since they'd seen each other. *As soon as he heard my name, he should have remembered me,* Cassie reasoned. *He didn't. Because I'm not beautiful, and I'm not Pandora or Daphne. Because men of Lord Richmond's ilk don't waste their time on women who aren't beautiful.*

"Cassie?"

Daphne's voice finally pulled Cassie out of her rather depressing reverie. "I'm sorry, Daphne, what did you say?"

"I asked what was wrong," Daphne said, frowning slightly.

Cassie stared ahead at the other couples on the street, walking hand in hand. "It's nothing. And you would do well to remember that you shouldn't strike up an acquaintance with every man who catches your eye," she replied, wishing the whole encounter at the library had never happened.

Lord Stanton listened to his son with interest. They were dining alone at home, on turkey in celery sauce (quite tasty) with puree of artichokes (tolerable) and apples with rice (one of his favorites) accompanied by a fairly tolerable burgundy. His son was filling him in on the events of the day.

"You wouldn't have believed it, Father," Richmond began. "Pandora's youngest sister, who must be on the verge of her first Season, is her veritable twin. From her delicate features to her sparkling blue eyes to her complete lack of sensible conversation." Richmond chewed on his turkey. "And Pandora's other sister—I believe the beauty said her name was Cassandra—she's nothing like the other two! How two such lovely creatures can have a sister who's so . . . unlike the other girls in the family is beyond me," Richmond finished, taking a sip of the burgundy.

Stanton sighed. For all the work his son had done for the government, which Richmond still didn't know that he knew about, he was quite the flat. "Tell me again, Derek, what does this middle sister look like?" he asked, hoping that Richmond could see beyond the connection to the infamous Pandora Wyndmoore.

"She's charming enough, in a rather unassuming kind of way. I actually first met her on our way to Bath, at the Pig and Crow. Helped her with her carriage," Richmond replied.

"Is she plain? Pock faced? Fat? Hooked nose? Bad teeth? What's she like?"

"No, not at all. She dresses in a rather unassuming

manner, rather like a governess. Or a servant. She wears spectacles and has short brown hair. Why?" Richmond asked, looking over at his father.

"Have the Wyndmoore ladies been in Bath long?" Hugh asked, hoping that his son would see where he was going with his questions.

"I don't believe so. I do recall the widgeon, Miss Daphne, saying something about their recent arrival. Why?"

Hugh sighed and put down his fork. "You were looking for a young woman in service who was new to the area. She's supposedly drab and brunette. She wears spectacles and reads. Has it occurred to you that this young woman could be the middle Wyndmoore—what's her name? Cassandra? She does fit your description, doesn't she?" Hugh finally said, certain that Cassandra Wyndmoore was the woman his son was trying to locate.

Richmond picked up his crystal glass of burgundy and sipped it thoughtfully. After a long pause, he finally said, "You know, Father, you may be correct. Miss Wyndmoore might be the lady I need to contact. Which is to my advantage, since I know exactly how the Wyndmoore ladies behave."

Hugh stared at his son in disbelief. Richmond had to know that he was courting disaster by predicting that Miss Wyndmoore would react the same way as her spoiled older sister. "When you do talk to the lady in question, it might be good to remember that she is an individual and may not behave precisely like her older sister," Hugh cautioned. Of course, he knew Richmond would more than likely ignore his advice and treat the poor girl like a doxy.

"She is a Wyndmoore, and although I might have

misread her personality when I met her at the inn, I won't underestimate her now. She's a Wyndmoore, and I can't see that she'd be any different than her sisters," he proclaimed.

Once again, Stanton sighed. His son could be incredibly stubborn at times. He just hoped that Miss Cassandra Wyndmoore, who sounded perfectly respectable to him, wasn't too offended by his son's attitude.

After returning from their sojourn to the lending library, Cassie all but disappeared into her room. She forced herself not to think of Richmond, who, on a good day, she would admit that she had loved from afar for years. She'd dreamed of the day when she'd see him again, and that day had come at the inn. He didn't recognize her, but at least he was pleasant to her. In fact, he almost seemed to be partial to her.

Today was a different story, she thought wryly. *He saw Daphne and I became invisible once again.*

Cassie flipped open one of the books from the library, hoping to get her mind off Richmond and the fact that she was on the shelf and he was utterly disinterested in her.

She had translated five or six of the stories in Mr. Lloyd's book and they all appeared to be modified retellings of Aesop's stories. Why would someone take the time to paraphrase Aesop's stories and then reprint them in another book? It wasn't as if the tales were difficult to understand in the first place. The whole idea made no sense at all.

Cassie relaxed on the bed, fluffed up the goose down pillows, and started reading the next entry in Mr. Lloyd's book. It was the story of a coopersmith and his puppy, and the translation seemed a bit too rough to be a direct copy of the Aesop story.

Frowning, Cassie picked up the Aesop book from the library. What would the title of this story be—'The Coopersmith and the Puppy'? Cassie leafed through the library book until she found that very entry. It had to be the same.

But it wasn't. In Aesop's fable, the coopersmith worked all day, while the puppy slept. When the coopersmith ate dinner, the puppy woke up and begged for food. That was the gist of the story.

That wasn't the story in Mr. Lloyd's book. In Mr. Lloyd's book the puppy hid his food in case the coopersmith stopped feeding him. First, there was the tale of the lion and the donkey, and now this. *Why did Mr. Lloyd change these two stories?* Cassie wondered with a frown. *What's he trying to tell me?* Cassie was convinced that Mr. Lloyd wanted her to have the book, but had had no idea what the stories were trying to tell her.

In desperation, Cassie went over to the escritoire in the corner and took out a pencil and some drawing paper. She began to draw up a simple chart, comparing the two stories from Aesop and the two stories that Mr. Lloyd wrote.

She was almost finished when Mary appeared at the door. "How can you see, Miss Cassie? You need some candles," Mary declared and started lighting candles around the bedroom.

Cassie frowned. She couldn't make heads or tails of Mr. Lloyd's stories, but perhaps Mary could give her some insight. "Mary, if I read you two short stories, could you tell me what you think they're about?" Cassie asked, hoping her maid could shed some light on the subject.

Mary started to straighten up Cassie's room. "All

right, Miss Cassie, I'll try my best to understand them," she said simply, fluffing the pillows on the bed.

Cassie read her the story of the lion and the donkey first and watched as Mary smiled at her. "That's an easy one, Miss Cassie. The story is about someone who pretends he's something he isn't. Like a poor man who's pretending to be rich," Mary noted, waiting to hear the next story.

Cassie frowned slightly and started reading the story about the coopersmith and the puppy. Another smile appeared on Mary's face. "These are ever so easy, Miss Cassie!" Mary exclaimed. "That story is about someone who's saving for the day when things start going badly, like when he runs out of blunt," Mary finished confidently.

In reality, Cassie was so caught up in the literal translations that she missed both of those obvious ideas. She asked Mary another crucial question. "Do you think these stories have anything in common?" she queried, wondering how Mary would interpret the stories as a pair.

"Well, the person in the first story is pretending to be something that he isn't, and he gets punished. In the other story, the man is waiting for something bad to happen, so he hides the things that are important to him. Maybe both stories are about the same man, a bloke who's pretending to be something that he isn't and is doing it to help everyone. But he knows he'll be discovered some day, so he hides his blunt or his jewels or his papers so that when he's gone, he may still be able to help everyone. Is that the right answer?" Mary questioned.

A wide smile appeared on Cassie's face, the first in many hours. "Actually, there is no right or wrong answer, Mary. I just wanted to know what you thought," Cassie explained, focusing on Mary's interpretation of the stories. Maybe the stories made sense if they were interpreted the way Mary viewed them. Maybe Mr. Lloyd had been trying to tell her something through the fables. Maybe the book wasn't a children's book at all. Maybe it was something much more important.

Mary moved over to the door. "Will you be coming down for dinner? Lady Raverston is expecting you."

"I'll be down directly," Cassie replied, her mind reeling. *Who was Mr. Lloyd trying to help, and what was he hiding?*

"Mr. Lloyd, the gentleman who died, was a spy?" Daphne asked, her blue eyes wide with amazement.

Cassie began to choke on a piece of the mutton they were eating for dinner and swilled down her glass of claret in one gulp, then continued coughing.

Honoria glanced over at Cassie, frowning. "Are you all right, Cassandra?" she asked, wondering if she should go over and slap Cassie on the back a few times.

Cassie continued coughing and gulped down her second glass of claret. "I'm all right," she muttered, her choking episode thankfully at an end.

When Honoria decided that Cassie wasn't in dire need of medical attention, she turned to Daphne. "That is what Lady Spenser said. You were at the table. Weren't you attending?"

Daphne looked embarrassed. "I'm sorry, Aunt Honoria, I guess I wasn't paying attention."

"Yes, well, it was rumored that Mr. Lloyd was a spy for our government, but there isn't any actual proof. And I wouldn't encourage either of you to start spreading that nonsense around when we're at the Pump Room tomorrow morning," Honoria noted, tasting a forkful of liver and bacon. Cook was at her best since the girls arrived, Honoria decided, and helped herself to another serving.

"Do you think we'll see Lord Pembrook tomorrow?" Daphne asked eagerly.

Honoria rolled her eyes. Daphne was a terrible trial and wasn't ready to be out in proper Society, since she was still a simpering schoolroom chit. "You will mind your manners around Pembrook, my dear. And everyone else, for that matter. He isn't the only catch in Bath, and you'll do well to remember that. In fact, I think he's a sly boots and I'd prefer you didn't associate with him at all," Honoria concluded, glancing toward the door. *Dessert should be appearing soon,* she mused.

A white pallor spread over Daphne's features. "I'm not allowed to speak with Lord Pembrook?" she asked in a desperate little voice that proclaimed her life was over if she couldn't.

Honoria glanced over at Daphne. The chit sounded like she was going to cry. "Of course you can talk to Pembrook. I just don't want you to encourage his suit," she stated, shifting her attention to the currant pudding that appeared in front of her.

Daphne sighed. "Of course, Aunt Honoria," she said in a voice that sounded terribly obedient.

Honoria glanced over at her niece and was convinced that Pembrook was going to be a problem.

The moonlight was streaming through Cassie's room, there was a lovely breeze, and Cassie should have been fast asleep.

She wasn't asleep. All Cassie could think about was Mr. Lloyd's book. What if he really was a spy and the book was some sort of important clue? What was she supposed to do with it? Should she give it to the magistrate? *If Mr. Lloyd had wanted the magistrate to have the book, why didn't he give it to him in the first place?* Cassie wondered. *Why did he leave it in the park for me?*

Cassie turned over and stared out the window into the darkness. It had been a dreadful day. First, there was the encounter with Lord Richmond in the library. He didn't even remember her, which crushed her heart, and then he spent the entire time gaping at her beautiful young sister. *He seemed so different at the inn,* she mused. *Why did his attitude suddenly change? And why can't I stop thinking about him?* she wondered, but there was no answer.

Chapter 5

"Cassie, he's here, he's *here*," Daphne said in a very loud whisper, poking Cassie in the ribs with her elbow.

Cassie glanced over to the other side of the busy Pump Room. Yes, he, meaning the Adonis-like Lord Pembrook, was most certainly here, Cassie noted. He was alone. For the moment. As Cassie glanced around the room, she noticed that every female of a marriage-able age, save herself, was gaping in rapt adoration at Lord Pembrook and his maroon waistcoat, buff pantaloons, and shiny Hessian boots. He cut quite a figure and was undoubtedly the most well-dressed dandy in the room.

It was then that Pembrook caught sight of the girls.

"He's coming toward us," Daphne explained in alt, smoothing the wrinkles out of her pastel pink walking dress. Daphne's hair shone like the sunlight and she looked radiant that morning, rather like a rose in a field of daisies.

Luckily for Daphne, Aunt Honoria, clad in a mature gown of cerise, was talking to the Dowager Countess of This or That and was so engrossed in their conversation that she didn't even notice when the Adonis appeared at their table.

"How very nice to see you, ladies," Pembrook said

smoothly, the smile on his face very false in Cassie's eyes.

Daphne picked up her fan and almost cooed in excitement. "Please join us, Lord Pembrook," she said boldly, and Cassie kicked her under the table. Daphne ignored her. "Are you enjoying your stay in Bath?" Daphne asked, her eyes never leaving Pembrook.

Pembrook sat down in the chair farthest from Honoria, who seemed to be oblivious to the new addition to their table. "Bath is lovely this time of year," Pembrook replied, his eyes never leaving Daphne.

Cassie groaned inwardly. It was a repeat of every other time she had been out in Society. Usually she was at Pandora's side and was completely ignored by whoever was courting her older sister. This time, she was being ignored by the god-like vision who might very well be courting her younger sister. *It's dashed annoying being invisible,* Cassie thought, irritated.

Much to Cassie's surprise, Pembrook, the Adonis, turned to her. "I haven't seen either of you at the Assembly Rooms," he commented.

But before Cassie could utter a word, Daphne broke in. "Oh, we'll be at the Assembly soon enough. Cassie had to have her wardrobe completely redone. It was terribly countrified, you know," Daphne said, leaning in toward Pembrook as she spoke, as if they were bosom bows.

Cassie glanced down at the dress she was wearing. It was the only one Aunt Honoria let her keep: a simple blue muslin walking dress free of any adornment save a bit of Belgian lace at the neck and on the sleeves. It wasn't one of her favorites, but Aunt Honoria liked it, so it would have to do until the modiste did something about the rest of her wardrobe.

Pembrook was speaking again, and Cassie was

mortified when she realized that he was addressing her and that she wasn't attending at all. "I'm sorry, Lord Pembrook, what is it you were saying?" Cassie asked, a very becoming blush appearing on her cheeks.

"I was wondering if you spent a lot of time in the park, Miss Wyndmoore. I thought I saw you there a few days ago, reading on a bench, with an elderly gentleman beside you," he asked smoothly, his eyes boring into Cassie's.

The hairs on the back of Cassie's neck stood on end. Something was very wrong, but she couldn't quite pinpoint the problem. Lord Pembrook was very definitely talking about Mr. Lloyd, the alleged spy. Who would want to know about Mr. Lloyd? Another spy, of course. Pembrook could be a spy for England, Cassie rationalized. Or he could be an agent for the enemy. Cassie wasn't sure if she should deny being in the park and risk Daphne's contradicting her, or just admit it and consequently admit she had Mr. Lloyd's book.

At that moment, Aunt Honoria entered the conversation. "Lord Pembrook, tell me, are you alone today or did you arrive with Lady Bonham?" Honoria asked, casually changing the topic of conversation.

Cassie watched as Pembrook paled a bit and immediately stood up. "I'm alone today, Lady Raverston, but you have reminded me of my other social obligations. If you'll excuse me," he said and dashed across the room as if the hounds of hell were after him.

Honoria smiled. Daphne pouted. Cassie stared into the grainy gray glass of medicinal water that the Dowager Countess of This or That left on their table. *I wonder if it tastes as bad as it looks?* Cassie wondered, staring at the cloudy beverage.

"You know, Daphne, gentlemen aren't attracted to young ladies who are prone to pouting," Honoria commented, and Cassie smiled. Mama certainly hadn't taken the time to discipline Daphne, but Aunt Honoria was another matter indeed.

Derek Leighton, the Earl of Richmond, and his father, Hugh Leighton, the Marquess of Stanton, strolled into the Pump Room in search of one person: Miss Cassandra Wyndmoore.

Richmond was certain that his job was going to be simplicity itself. All he had to do was find out if Miss Wyndmoore was the lady in the Park and if she possessed any documents that had belonged to Mr. Lloyd. Although Miss Wyndmoore had initially charmed him, she was Pandora's sister, so she couldn't be too bright; intelligence wasn't Pandora's long suit. Therefore, he anticipated getting the information from Miss Wyndmoore before his father finished his first cup of tea.

His father was all but gaping at the table where Cassandra, Daphne, and Lady Raverston were seated. "Derek, who is the woman sitting with the two attractive young ladies in the corner?" his father asked, casually motioning to Lady Raverston.

Richmond, once again looking a bit rough around the edges, followed his father's gaze. His eyes fell on Daphne, a vision in pink; Cassandra; and an older woman, obviously their chaperon. "I don't know. The young ladies are Pandora's sisters. Can't you see the family resemblance in the blonde?" he asked, his eyes never leaving Daphne. At one point in time, many years ago, he would have moved heaven and earth for a female like her. Now he was a bit older, and he found incredibly beautiful women to be vain, self-centered, and heartless.

His father was still staring at the older woman. "Yes, of course I can see the resemblance. When you talk to Cassandra, be sure to find out who her chaperon is, will you?" he asked casually.

Richmond frowned. It was dashed odd for his father to inquire after anyone in the Pump Room, especially a female of a certain age. "Of course," Richmond replied, frowning.

Cassie was still studying the cloudy water, certain that she had spotted an insect, when she heard Daphne exclaim, "Lord Richmond, how very nice to see you."

Once again, Cassie recoiled. *Why, oh why, do I have to see him?* she agonized.

"Do you mind if I join you, ladies?" Richmond asked, much to Cassie's horror.

Unfortunately, Aunt Honoria wasn't there to discourage him, and Daphne certainly wouldn't. "Please do join us, Lord Richmond," Daphne said in the voice that proclaimed that she was trying to act as mature as possible. Cassie cringed again. Daphne was trying to act sophisticated, and now Richmond was at their table. She continued to stare at the cloudy water, certain that Richmond would ignore her.

"Both of you ladies look lovely today," Richmond said suavely, and Cassie was certain the compliment was meant for Daphne. Her sister did indeed look lovely. Daphne always looked lovely.

Daphne fanned herself and blushed prettily. "Why, thank you, Lord Richmond. Have you been enjoying your stay in Bath?"

Cassie cringed. Someday, Daphne was going to have to say something other than 'Have you been enjoying your stay in Bath?' and then she'd be in dire trouble, since she knew her sister had minimal conversational skills. Of course, Richmond was intrigued with Daphne, just like Pandora had intrigued him, so he didn't notice that she was a bit of a widgeon.

Her gaze moved from the glass of medicinal water to a potted palm in the corner. She completely ignored Richmond and Daphne until her sister kicked her under the table not so delicately and said, "Cassie, Lord Richmond asked you a question. Do attend."

Cassie shifted her gaze to Richmond only to find his gray eyes staring intently at her. "I'm sorry, Lord Richmond, what did you say?" Cassie asked softly, utterly mortified by her own lack of social skills.

"I was wondering if you've been spending any time in the park recently," he said with a bland smile.

Cassie blanched once again. Pandora had told her in strictest confidence that Richmond was working for the French, and he did have close relations in France as well. There were several options. Pembrook could be working for the French, or Richmond could be working for the French. Alternatively, both of them could be spies, although that didn't seem logical to Cassie. She had only one logical course of action. "No, I really haven't spent any time at the park at all."

Richmond looked stunned at her reply. Cassie was certain that he expected her to admit to being in the park and to having Mr. Lloyd's book as well. She wasn't going to give up her secret quite yet.

"How very strange," Daphne commented innocently. "Not a quarter of an hour ago, Lord Pembrook asked

Cassie about the park as well. Why are you men so curious about where Cassie spends her time?"

A benign smile appeared on Richmond's strong features. "You know how curious we men can be," he replied vaguely. "May I ask where you're staying in town?" he asked, looking straight at Cassie.

Cassie frowned. Why was he suddenly so curious about their situation? "We're visiting Lady Raverston, our aunt," she replied very properly.

"You must come call on us one afternoon," Daphne blurted. "I'm sure Aunt Honoria would love to meet an old friend of Pandora's. Then there are the Assembly Rooms. I'm sure we'll see you at the next rout," Daphne added.

For one brief moment, Cassie and Richmond locked eyes. *He knows I lied,* she thought frantically.

Then she realized that he was looking at her the same way he used to look at Pandora. This was quite unsettling indeed.

Stanton wanted all of the details of his son's conversation with the ladies. He was trying to appear disinterested; he knew that too much interest would cause Derek to suspect his motives. As well he should.

He hadn't seen Lady Raverston, if that was indeed the identity of the lady in question, in nearly thirty years. Her family hadn't actually disapproved of his suit, but they had favored the suit of a very distant cousin. When things became serious, Honoria's parents whisked her off to the continent for a year. She got to study in Greece and Rome and was invited into the very best of houses. He was certain that she had forgotten him.

So when he met Derek's mother and they rubbed

along well, he decided to forget Honoria, do his duty, and marry. The marriage worked out well enough, until Elizabeth died giving birth to their second child. He raised Derek with the help of a variety of nannies and governesses, and lately, he'd wished that he'd spent more time with his son.

Now, all these years later, Honoria was sitting across the room with two very fetching young ladies. Did she have any children of her own? What exactly was her marital status?

"So the Wyndmoore ladies are visiting Lady Raverston. She's their aunt?" Hugh asked in his most casual voice.

Richmond yawned. "Yes."

"I must have forgotten about the family connection," Stanton commented, his eyes drifting back to Honoria. How beautiful she looked, even after all these years. "Are you planning on calling on the ladies?" Stanton asked curiously.

"Miss Daphne, the Vision, hinted that they were going to be at the next rout at the Assembly Rooms. I'll speak with Miss Wyndmoore there and get the information I need," Richmond replied.

Hugh wasn't a betting man, but he would have wagered his very extensive holdings that Miss Wyndmoore wasn't anything like her sisters. Moreover, he guessed that his son wasn't going to get the information he needed easily.

"You look as lovely as the first rose of summer," Pembrook crooned, smiling into Daphne's adoring eyes.

Cassie sat in the corner, doing her embroidery. She detested playing chaperon for Daphne, and although Pembrook said he was there to visit both ladies, he barely glanced at her. His only interest was in the charming and delectable Daphne.

A delightful giggle escaped Daphne's lips. "Why, thank you, Lord Pembrook," she replied, smiling coyly, touching Lord Pembrook ever so slightly on the knee.

"So tell me, when is Society going to be graced with your presence in the Assembly Rooms? You know you're all the rage, and everyone wants to meet Lady Raverston's beautiful young niece," he said, once again completely ignoring Cassie.

"We're planning on attending the next rout," Daphne began, leaning closer to Lord Pembrook. "Aunt Honoria has registered our names with the Master of Ceremonies. It will be such a nice change from all of the rusticating we've been doing since we've arrived," Daphne concluded.

Cassie sighed. Once again, Daphne was trying to sound more sophisticated than her age. *Certainly Lord Pembrook has to see that,* she thought, glancing over at the pair.

Pembrook was staring intently at Daphne with the oddest look in his eyes. Not a look of desire, which Cassie had seen directed at Pandora and later Daphne more times than she cared to remember, but a different look. There was something hard in Pembrook's gaze, which made no sense at all, considering the fact that he appeared to be Daphne's latest conquest.

"That's wonderful news," Pembrook crooned. "Everyone is dying to meet you, my dear," he added. Cassie cringed again. *He shouldn't be so familiar with her,* she thought, but decided to ignore his transgression.

Daphne giggled and coyly twisted an errant lock of hair around her finger. "Really? Is everyone talking about me?"

"Most assuredly. In fact, Lord Kingston mentioned that he saw you about a sennight ago and was utterly captivated. At least he thought it was you he saw in the park. Across from the milliner's," Pembrook said.

Cassie could feel the muscles in her neck tighten. Pembrook wanted to find out if she had been there, in the park, with Mr. Lloyd. He wanted to know about the book, she was sure of it.

"Why yes, I do believe your friend Lord Kingston was right," Daphne said brightly. "That's when I was out buying ribbons."

She might as well tell him about the book too, Cassie thought in frustration. *That's what he wants to know.*

"And was your sister reading while you were making your purchases?" Pembrook asked casually.

Cassie looked up. "I am in the room, Lord Pembrook, so you can address your questions to me," Cassie said sharply.

Pembrook was polite enough to look chagrined. "Well, um, yes, of course. Daphne's beauty is so overwhelming that one tends to forget about anyone else when in her presence," he replied.

"Oh, you are feeding me Spanish coin," Daphne said, batting her eyelashes furiously at him.

For Cassie, there was nothing worse than listening to one of Daphne's suitors. This time, she was glad that her sister's constant demand for praise turned the topic away from her activities in the park.

"Oh, but I'm not. You're undoubtedly the most beautiful female in all of Bath—no, all of England. No, all of the continent," he blurted, and, predictably, Daphne turned the most engaging shade of pink.

"I do think that's doing it up a bit brown, Pembrook," Aunt Honoria said from the doorway.

Cassie smiled as Pembrook turned a deep shade of red. "Lady Raverston, I didn't hear you come in," he said as she glided into the room.

"Of course you didn't. You were too busy slavering over my niece," Honoria said, as Pembrook kissed her hand.

"But you can see how Miss Daphne's beauty could inspire a man."

Aunt Honoria sat down on a chair near Cassie. "No, not really," she muttered, focusing on Pembrook. "You know, Pembrook, I was wondering about some *on-dits* I heard. Did you indeed duel with Lord Paige over his fiancée?"

Cassie grinned as Pembrook and Daphne both turned slightly different shades of white. "The whole episode was greatly exaggerated, Lady Raverston," Pembrook said, rising from his seat. "I'm terribly sorry to rush off, but I do have other business this afternoon," he said quickly.

Daphne looked crestfallen. "You're leaving?"

"Yes, but it was lovely speaking with you, Miss Daphne," he said, and, after a brief bow, he was out the door before anyone could utter another word.

Cassie looked over at Daphne. Her sister was pouting. Again. "It's not fair, Aunt Honoria. You always say something that makes Lord Pembrook bolt out of here before we're done having our coze," Daphne whined.

Honoria picked up her embroidery and ignored Daphne. Cassie grinned as she looked down at her needlework.

"It's not fair," Daphne reiterated. "I know you wouldn't act that way if Lord Richmond came to call on me. You've just taken some sort of awful dislike to Lord Pembrook and it's just not fair," Daphne said, her voice sounding almost shrewish.

Cassie stared down at the flower she was working on

and willed herself not to giggle. If only Daphne knew how terribly childish and unattractive she looked, Cassie thought. Most of her sister's admirers wouldn't be so pleased with their Vision if they knew she had the tendency to behave like a badly spoiled child.

"Lord Richmond? Hugh Leighton's son? He's in Bath?" Honoria asked, her eyes darting to Daphne.

Daphne began to play with a flounce on her mint green morning gown. "Lord Richmond used to be one of Pandora's favorite suitors. We saw him at the library, then the Pump Room," Daphne explained.

"The Pump Room? Where was I?" Honoria demanded.

"Oh, that's when you went to talk to the Dowager Marchioness of Whatever," Daphne replied flippantly.

Honoria glanced over at Cassie. "Is that true, Cassandra? Is Richmond alone or here with his family?"

Cassie was intrigued. *Why is Aunt Honoria so interested in Lord Richmond?* she wondered. "Yes, it would appear that Lord Richmond is in Bath, but I don't know how long he's planning to stay or if he's traveling with anyone at all," Cassie noted.

"Oh," Honoria said in a voice that was decidedly dejected.

Cassie frowned. *Why does Aunt Honoria suddenly sound so sad?*

Ever so slowly, Cassie's Greek was improving. She had finished translating three more stories from Mr. Lloyd's book: "The Stray Dogs," "The Fox without a Tail," and "The Mountain." All of them were practically identical to the stories in her Aesop book, which made the work a bit quicker.

Then she came upon the next story, which was called

"The Miser." It seemed to be another literal translation of Aesop, until she came upon the name Jonathan Lord.

Aesop's fables don't use proper names, Cassie thought, struggling through the translation. The story was about a miser who hid his valuables. In a very specific place, in fact, according to Mr. Lloyd. The lines in question read:

> *Finally, after many days of looking, the miser happened upon the perfect place to hide his treasure: a hollow tree in the cemetery. It was twenty paces due east of the grave of Jonathan Lord, just off the river Avon.*

Cassie could feel her heart beating faster. This definitely wasn't a traditional Aesop story. What could it mean?

Chapter 6

Cassie stared into the cheval glass mirror. Her bosom, which was normally concealed under high-necked gowns, was all but winking at her in the mirror. A great expanse of her milky white flesh was revealed in Madame Babette's gown, and Cassie felt awkward. "I'm not certain about this gown," Cassie muttered, tugging at her bodice. "Isn't it a bit . . . revealing?"

"Not at all, Miss Cassie. You look all the crack!" Sara said brightly.

Cassie continued to stare into the mirror. Sara had somehow coaxed her hair into short, feminine ringlets, which did make her look much younger than her five and twenty years. Then there was Madame Babette's gown. For her first night out in Bath, Madame Babette suggested—and from what Cassie was told, no one ever dared disagree with her—the golden shot silk gown that Madame fashioned in the Grecian style. The gown draped elegantly over Cassie's modest figure, although Cassie thought it draped a bit too dramatically over her bosom. Her feet were clad in golden kid slippers, and Aunt Honoria had even found a golden fan and beaded reticule that matched the hue of her gown perfectly.

"You don't think the gown shows too much of my . . . womanly charms, does it?" Cassie asked with a frown. *It's as if I'm a prize brood mare for sale, and my chief asset is my bosom,* she thought.

"Not at all Miss Cassie. Lordie, it's not like you're dampening your petticoats," Sara replied.

Cassie looked away from the mirror. *It doesn't really matter what I look like,* she reasoned. *As soon as I enter any room with Daphne, I become invisible.*

"You look very lovely," Sara added.

Cassie gave the pert maid a smile. "It's nice of you to say so, Sara. I know you're trying to make me feel good, but I'm well aware that I'm the antidote in the family. My mama has never come out and said so, but she's quite appalled by my lack of good looks and is happy that I choose not to participate in Society," Cassie said candidly.

"But, Miss Cassie, you're not an antidote!"

"You're very kind, Sara. Shall I head downstairs to meet Aunt Honoria?" she asked.

Sara smiled again and seemed to gulp. "Miss Cassie, may I ask how well you see without your spectacles?"

Cassie stared at the abigail. *Why would she ask about my glasses?* "I have a hard time seeing things that are far away," she replied vaguely. "Why?"

Sara stared at the floor and nervously twisted her fingers around her apron. "If you don't have your spectacles on, would you bump into people?"

"No, I wouldn't actually bump into people, although I might have a hard time recognizing them across the room," Cassie said.

"Lady Raverston thought it might be a good idea for you to leave your spectacles at home just this once," Sara said quickly, without taking a breath between words.

A deep sigh escaped Cassie's lips. *Don't they know that they're wasting their time? I can never be Pandora or Daphne or even a diamond of the second water, if there is such a thing.*

However, since it was at Aunt Honoria's request, Cassie took the spectacles off and handed them to Sara. "I know what everyone is trying to do, and it won't help. Glasses or not, I'm still the antidote of the family," she said in voice tinged with resignation.

Sara took the glasses and smiled brightly at Cassie. "Thank you, Miss Cassie. And maybe you'll have a lovely time at the rout," she added for good measure.

Cassie forced a slight smile that looked more like a grimace. "I'll try. But I'd much rather be home reading."

"You have to go out once in a while," Sara said evenly.

Cassie sighed. "I suppose," she replied in a lackluster voice and headed downstairs.

Honoria was pacing the parlor. Would Cassie ever emerge from her bedroom? She fully expected Daphne to linger in her room until the very last moment, but certainly not Cassandra. *I hope she doesn't get a case of the jitters and try to cry off,* Honoria thought. *That won't do at all. If only she didn't spend so much time comparing herself to her sisters, she'd be much better off.*

She was standing at the window, gazing out into the yard, when the door burst open and Daphne appeared like a whirlwind.

"I'm ready to leave," Daphne announced, a vision in her white satin gown trimmed with seed pearls. Her golden blonde hair was arranged in long, artful ringlets, and, as always, she was the image of a goddess.

Honoria sighed. *Why does Daphne have to be so damnably beautiful?* she wondered. *Once again, she's going to outshine Cassandra and throw her sister into the doldrums.* "We're waiting for your sister," Honoria said, conveniently forgetting to mention how lovely Daphne looked.

"Don't I look enchanting tonight?" Daphne said, staring down at her gown. "I think I look even lovelier now than I did last month, when we attended the Smithford's rout."

Honoria raised an eyebrow. It was apparent that Daphne was just as vain as her oldest sister Pandora was. "I suppose you look presentable," Honoria muttered, disinterested.

At that point, the door to the parlor opened and Cassie emerged, rather like a butterfly. Honoria gasped at the transformation of her elder niece and exclaimed, "Why Cassandra, you look delightful!"

Cassie was scowling. She looked over at Daphne, and then appeared to sigh. "That's very kind of you to say, Aunt Honoria," Cassie replied.

Honoria went over to the side table and began to look through her reticule. "I thought you might like to wear some jewelry tonight, Cassandra," she said, pulling out an impressive gold necklace fashioned with dozens of emeralds. Before Cassie could object, she walked over to her and fastened them around her neck.

"Why, they look lovely," Honoria noted with a smile. The green jewels sparkled around her neck, giving Cassie a regal air. "I couldn't wear these, Aunt Honoria," Cassie protested.

"Nonsense."

"But how about me? I can't go out without any jewelry," Daphne protested.

Honoria turned and gave Daphne a placid smile. *Spoiled chit,* she thought. "Daphne, my dear, you're not even out yet, so it wouldn't be appropriate for you to be seen in any jewels outside of pearls," she explained in a level voice, moving toward the door.

As the girls followed her, Daphne looked over at Cassie jealously. "The only reason Aunt Honoria is letting you wear them is to help make you more presentable," she hissed.

Cassie sighed and didn't bother with a reply.

Richmond leaned against the wall of the Assembly Room, frustration written on his countenance. *Things are not going well tonight,* he mused.

He had a plan. A very simple plan that he was certain would work. He knew how to charm the Wyndmoore women, and Cassandra Wyndmoore was obviously no different from her sisters. All he had to do was find somewhere that he could be private with her and ply her with kisses. Then she'd simply tell him everything she knew and his problem would be solved.

Except there was nowhere in the Assembly Rooms that he could be private with Miss Wyndmoore. Therefore, he had to devise an alternate plan. Which was dashed inconvenient, since he knew his first plan was foolproof.

Pembrook was across the room, holding court in a large group of fashionably attired young ladies. Once again, he looked like Adonis surrounded by a court of nymphs, Richmond thought wryly, watching Pembrook smile at every attractive female. *Yes, Pembrook certainly has a way with the ladies.* However, Pembrook wasn't in Bath for its social offerings. Richmond was certain that Pembrook was there to locate Lloyd's documents and hand them over to the Frogs.

From the corner of his eye, Richmond could see that a new party had entered the room. He continued to focus on Pembrook. But when the man in question turned and focused all of his attention on the newcomers, Richmond followed his gaze, then smiled.

This time, Richmond wasn't going to be at a total loss when confronted with Pandora's baby sister. Pembrook gazed at Daphne Wyndmoore, who was accompanied by Lady Raverston and a stunning, yet unknown, female. *If the younger Miss Wyndmoore is here, obviously her older sister can't be far behind,* Richmond reasoned.

As the party moved through the room, Richmond found he couldn't take his eyes from the unknown miss walking a step behind Daphne. She was clad in a gown of golden silk that hugged her body suggestively, but without being vulgar. Her skin was luminescent, and she carried herself with the natural grace of a royal. When she turned and spoke to Lady Raverston, a smile appeared on her face that shone like the glow of a thousand candles. She was beautiful in a quiet and elegant way, and Richmond found that he couldn't take his eyes off her.

"Cassie, Lord Pembrook is here!" Daphne exclaimed in glee.

Cassie scanned the room and did indeed spot Lord Pembrook surrounded by female admirers and talking with some young bucks on the other side of the room. As usual, he looked absolutely perfect. "I'm not surprised," Cassie replied. The Assembly Rooms were filled with people, and without even realizing it, Cassie found herself looking for Lord Richmond. At first glance, it appeared that he wasn't there. Or, perhaps he was there, and she just couldn't find him.

"Come along, girls, I have some friends I'd like you to meet," Honoria said, and they began to work their way through the crowd.

Cassie couldn't help but notice that every male that they encountered seemed to stop whatever they what they were saying to gape at Daphne. Once again, she was rendered invisible by the power of one of her sisters' beauty.

"I won't have to dance tonight, will I?" Cassie asked reluctantly. She didn't want to dance with anyone, with the possible exception of Richmond, and he was already taken with Daphne.

Honoria looked over at her and frowned. "Of course you're going to dance. And you'll have a lovely time tonight," she added.

It sounded like an order to Cassie.

"Derek, you're not attending," his father said, as Richmond continued to gaze at Pembrook.

Richmond slipped out of his trance. "Sorry, Father, what were you saying?"

"I asked if you had found an opportunity to speak with Miss Wyndmoore yet. She's over in the far corner with Lady Raverston," he said, motioning to the three ladies.

Richmond followed his gaze and frowned. "I have to speak with Miss Cassandra Wyndmoore, not Miss Daphne, the widgeon."

"Derek, your Miss Cassandra is standing right next to her sister," his father said in a voice that proclaimed that Richmond was obviously a slow top.

Richmond stared at the girl in the golden dress. The hair was different; she wore no spectacles; but, yes, amazing as it seemed, she was Cassandra Wyndmoore. "Damn me, I didn't recognize her without her glasses and her dowdy gowns. That is Miss Wyndmoore, isn't it? How remarkable," he finished, amazed at the transformation.

As the men gazed at the trio of ladies, Lady Raverston left for a moment, and Stanton commanded, "Take me over and introduce me to the girls."

"You want to meet the Wyndmoore jades? Why?"

His father gave him a stare that would have made lesser men cringe in horror. "My reasons are none of your concern," he replied curtly.

Richmond shrugged slightly. His father rarely wanted to meet women of that age, so this was a trifle mysterious. "Of course I'll introduce you."

Cassie's lively hazel eyes were fixed on a gentleman in a puce striped waistcoat, which was perhaps the most vulgar piece of clothing she had ever seen in her entire life. Daphne was droning on and on about Lord Pembrook and all the other men who were trying to make her acquaintance. Or something similar to that. Cassie had actually stopped listening to Daphne quite a while ago and was wool gathering when she heard Daphne exclaim "Cassandra!" in a shrill voice.

Cassie looked away from the puce waistcoat and was horrified to realize that Lord Richmond and an older gentleman were addressing them.

Daphne smiled smugly and said, "Cassandra, Lord Richmond has come by to introduce his father. Lord Stanton, this is my older sister Cassandra," Daphne said, once again sidestepping propriety a bit.

Cassie smiled at the older gentleman, who looked quite different from his son. While Richmond's features were harsh, and his eyes penetrating, Lord Stanton had gentle gray eyes that sparkled with mirth and foretold an easy-going nature. She immediately liked him. "It's so very nice to meet you, Lord Stanton," Cassie said politely.

"It's a pleasure to make your acquaintance," Richmond's father replied. Before Cassie could say a word, the band struck up a waltz. "May I have the pleasure of this dance, Miss Wyndmoore?" he said cordially. "That is, if you don't mind being seen dancing with one of your elders," he added with a smile.

Cassie turned a very charming shade of pink and smiled back at him. Her smile took Richmond's breath away. "The pleasure is mine, Lord Stanton, but I must warn you, I do tend to have two left feet," she said softly.

He smiled back at her and took her hand in his. "I'm sure you don't."

The pair headed out to the dance floor, and Cassie was surprised to find that, with Lord Stanton leading, her waltzing wasn't as bad as she remembered.

"My son tells me that you're staying with Lady Raverston," Stanton commented.

"Yes, she's our aunt," Cassie replied, concentrating on her steps.

"I knew her ages ago in London. How is she doing?"

Cassie frowned slightly. It had seemed odd for Lord Stanton to ask her to dance, since she was certain that he wasn't interested in her. Now he was asking about Aunt Honoria, and Aunt Honoria was definitely eligible. "She's doing fine, but it's been a few years since Uncle Jonathan, Lord Raverston, passed on. I think she's lonely," Cassie added, throwing caution to the wind.

They continued dancing in silence, and when the waltz ended, Cassie decided it was her turn to help Aunt Honoria. "Lord Stanton, may I take you over to Aunt Honoria? I'm sure she'd be delighted to see you again," she said.

Cassie was surprised to see him blush ever so slightly. "That would be lovely," he finally said, and they headed over to Honoria and Daphne.

Honoria actually blushed for the first time in many, many years. There, standing in front of her looking gallant and handsome, was Hugh Leighton, Lord Stanton. The Hugh Leighton that, at one particular moment in time, she had wanted to marry.

He looked so very handsome tonight, she thought, studying him. His black coat was obviously from Weston, and his snow-white cravat was tied simply, which made him look even more elegant than the preening fops in the room. His eyes sparkled when he talked to her, and Honoria felt her heart lurch. *If only things had been different*, she thought with a sigh.

She looked over at Cassie and Daphne, who were chatting about some gentleman wearing a dreadful striped waistcoat. They were completely oblivious to her conversation with Hugh, Lord Stanton, which suited her quite well.

"It's so nice to see you after all these years," Stanton said smoothly.

She blushed again. *He's so charming,* she thought, *just as I remember.* "Yes, it is," she replied, suddenly devoid of conversation.

"You and your late husband never spent much time in London," Stanton noted, his eyes never leaving her.

"He never cared for London," Honoria admitted. "We did travel extensively on the continent, which was nice. But then we settled in Bath, and he got ill," she said simply.

"I'm so sorry," Hugh said, leaning closer to her. "Would it be too personal to inquire if you have any children of your own?"

Once again, a slight color stained Honoria's cheeks, which was quite astonishing, since she knew she never, ever blushed. "No, I don't have any children. But I have heard about your son," she replied, adeptly changing the subject.

Stanton smiled, which made him appear more handsome to Honoria, if possible. "Ah yes, Derek. He's a good son. A bit headstrong, though. He was involved with your niece Pandora at one time."

Honoria raised her eyes heavenward. "I do hope he has more common sense now."

"I think so. That was years ago, and I am hoping that he settles down soon."

Honoria leaned forward so that Cassie and Daphne wouldn't hear their conversation. "I'm hoping to find someone for Cassandra," she admitted in a soft voice. "She's the real catch in the family, but no one can see that."

Stanton gazed into her eyes, and she could feel her heart beating in her chest. "I can," he replied simply.

The evening was turning out very different from how Cassie had imagined. She had actually enjoyed her dance with Lord Stanton and danced with a few other men who seemed to be quite charming. They weren't as young or as handsome as Daphne's growing legion of swains, but they were nice.

Then Aunt Honoria introduced her to Lady Buckminshire and her charge Olivia, a young lady who was incredibly shy and bookish. Cassie immediately drew Olivia out of her shell, and soon the two were chatting like bosom bows.

In fact, Cassie was looking forward to having tea with

Olivia when a shadow fell over the pair. Olivia looked up and her pallid complexion paled a bit more as she gazed at the very imposing Lord Richmond.

"Good evening, ladies," Richmond said politely and turned to Cassie. "Would you care to join me for tea? I believe it's going to be announced momentarily."

Cassie stared up at the dark-haired lord pensively. *Why is he being so cordial?* Cassie had dreamed of the day that Lord Richmond noticed her as a person, and it appeared that day was upon her. Yet something was wrong. The smile didn't reach his eyes, and, as she studied him, she thought he looked somewhat vexed.

Before Cassie could reply, Olivia said, "You must join Lord Richmond, Cassandra; Mama expects me to have tea with her and Mr. Wilkerson."

Cassie sighed slightly. She really didn't know why Richmond was singling her out, but his interest didn't seem genuine at all. Unfortunately, she couldn't think of a reason to refuse him, so she replied, "It would be my pleasure to join you at tea."

Richmond stared openly at Cassie, almost in awe of her utter transformation. First he had known her as the charming companion who caught his attention at the inn. Then he found her to be the unexceptional sister of Pandora and Daphne. And now—now she was someone else once again. Not a goddess like her sisters, but someone even more enchanting. A female with immaculate manners, an easy charm, and beauty that she didn't even realize she possessed. Nevertheless, she was a Wyndmoore, and he'd been duped by her ilk before. Richmond sipped his tea and continued to study her. "Did you enjoy your dance with my father?"

"Your father is a very accomplished dancer and a charming partner," she replied politely.

"Really?" he commented. "My father dances . . . infrequently. He paid you quite a compliment by leading you out."

"Your father has a previous acquaintance with my Aunt Honoria, and even as we speak, they're having tea with my sister Daphne," she said simply.

Glancing over his shoulder, Richmond confirmed her words. His father was indeed having tea with Lady Raverston and the Vision. His father and Lady Raverston.

That wasn't the issue at hand. He needed to find out about Lloyd's book and complete his mission for Castlereagh, and it was always better to start on questioning sooner rather than later. "So tell me, Miss Wyndmoore, how have you been spending your free time? I haven't seen you around Bath that often."

"I've been working on translating a bit of Greek literature I picked up," she said casually.

Richmond's eyes never left her. As soon as the words came out of her mouth, he could see her cringe. *She doesn't want me to know about the book she has in Greek. She must realize it's Lloyd's book,* he reasoned, and tried to coax the information out of her casually. "Oh, really? I personally don't have any affinity for Greek. I rather excelled in Latin and French."

Cassie looked down at her tea. "The tea is lovely, isn't it?" she said calmly.

He smiled at her. *She wants to change the subject. She definitely has Lloyd's book.*

On the other side of the room, Daphne was in high alt. Ever since she was a child and had watched Pandora's suitors parade through their house, she had dreamed of the day that she would have a handsome man dangling after her. And not just any handsome man, but the most handsome man in all of England, a man who was more handsome than all of Pandora's suitors combined.

Lord Pembrook was that man. Everything about him was perfect. From his shiny Hessians to his blond hair to his sparkling eyes, he was the image of a Greek god come to life. He was smiling at her.

"Miss Daphne, you're undoubtedly the most beautiful woman in the room," he practically purred, leaning toward her.

Daphne glanced at Aunt Honoria, who stood just a few feet away talking with Lady Whatever. She was oblivious to the fact that Daphne was spending time with Lord Pembrook, which was a very fortunate circumstance. Daphne was convinced that as soon as Aunt Honoria noticed Lord Pembrook, she'd frighten him away once again.

"You're bamming me, Lord Pembrook," Daphne cooed and swatted him playfully with her fan.

Pembrook smiled and took her gloved hand in his. "But I'm not, Miss Daphne. Your overwhelming beauty is something that words can barely describe."

Daphne blushed prettily. "Oh, Lord Pembrook," she replied.

Pembrook leaned closer to her, and her heart was all aflutter. "Miss Daphne, do you think I might call on you next week? Is there a time when we could be . . . private?" he asked, running his hand through his perfect blond locks.

She stared into his warm brown eyes and forgot all about propriety. The most handsome man in England wanted to be alone with her, and she would move heaven and earth to make it happen. "On Wednesday, Aunt Honoria and Cassie are going for a fitting. I'll be home alone," she said softly, gazing at him worshipfully.

"I'll call on Wednesday then," he replied in a silky voice, his eyes never leaving her. "Waiting to see you that long will be like an eternity, though," he added.

"Oh, Lord Pembrook," Daphne murmured, blushing again.

She never noticed that his smile didn't reach his eyes.

Cassie and Richmond stared at Daphne and Pembrook.

"Does your aunt approve of Pembrook?" he asked casually.

Cassie sighed. *Will the tea ever end? Why is he trying to be so solicitous? I know he's not genuinely interested in me.* "Not really. But I think Daphne is rather taken with him. Why?"

"Pembrook is on the fringe of the *ton*. He isn't accepted by the high sticklers and has a bit of a dubious reputation," he said calmly.

Cassie glanced around the room. It appeared that everyone was looking at Daphne and Lord Pembrook. *Gads, she's making a cake of herself,* Cassie thought.

Before she could reply to Richmond's comment, the band struck up another waltz. "Would you care to dance, Miss Wyndmoore?" he asked cordially.

Cassie frowned. *Why is he being so nice to me? He couldn't actually be attracted to me, that's out of the question.* Once again, she couldn't think of a reason to say no, so she replied, "Yes, of course," and they headed out to the dance floor.

As they began their set, Cassie noticed something odd. Lord Richmond was holding her a trifle too close for propriety. In fact, he was holding her much too close for propriety. Cassie could feel his hand on the small of her back, gently pressing her closer to him, and if she were of a romantic sentiment, she could have closed her eyes and imagined that the handsome and dashing Lord Richmond really wanted to be with her, the unexceptional Cassandra Wyndmoore.

As he guided her across the floor, she wished she could lose herself in the moment and enjoy the feeling of his strong, muscular form against her.

"Pandora used to relish telling the story of her name. Am I correct in assuming that you're named after a character in Greek mythology?" he said softly.

Cassie could feel her heart lurching in her chest. *Isn't this what I always wanted?* Yet something felt . . . wrong to her, but she couldn't pinpoint it quite yet. "Yes, Papa was in his Greek phase then. I'm lucky not to be a Venus or an Aphrodite," she said, concentrating on her steps.

"You didn't answer my question. Who was Cassandra?" he said in a deep, sultry voice.

He actually sounded curious. "Cassandra was a Trojan princess who was eventually given the gift of prophecy," she answered simply, trying in vain not to tread on his shiny Hessians.

"And can you foretell the future?" he asked seductively.

Cassie looked up at him, frowning. *If it was anyone else, I'd say he was actually trying to set up a flirtation,* she mused, utterly confused. However, everyone knew that Lord Richmond was quite particular about his women, and the more beautiful the better. *I'm not beautiful,* she added mentally. "I think not, Lord Richmond," she said in the voice she used to discourage impoverished curates who imagined she might be a pliable wife.

She waited for him to ask her about the book. *That has to be what he's after,* she decided, convinced that he was feigning interest in her. However, he never mentioned Mr. Lloyd, or the book, or anything else for that matter. In fact, they danced the rest of the set in silence, until the music stopped and he led her back to Daphne and Aunt Honoria.

"Do you have any social engagements next week, Miss Wyndmoore?" he asked.

"Not that I'm aware of," she answered cautiously.

"Then would you be interested in going for a drive with me?"

Cassie stared at him as if he'd run mad. *This is so unsettling,* she thought, frowning. *I've spent a good portion of my formative years dreaming of Lord Richmond, and now he's actually seeking out my company.* Unfortunately, Cassie, who always thought of herself as an imaginative person, couldn't think of a good reason why she couldn't go out on a drive with him. "If you'd like," she said in a terribly noncommittal voice.

In her heart, she knew he was only after Lloyd's papers.

"You danced with Cassandra Wyndmoore," Stanton noted, gazing over his glass of port at his son.

Richmond sipped his glass of port. "Yes, I did."

"Were you able to talk to her?" Stanton asked. He knew Richmond worked for the government, but he pretended ignorance. He also suspected that this discussion with Cassandra Wyndmoore had something to do with the reason they were in Bath, but he didn't know why.

"No, the time wasn't right. I'm going to take her driving, though; we'll talk then," Richmond said, staring once again at the landscape on the wall.

"She seems charming," Stanton noted. *Almost as charming as her aunt,* he thought with a smile. He had been worried about seeing Honoria again. It had been years since they had last met, but when he saw her tonight, it was as if it were yesterday. She was still the same vibrant, intelligent woman that he had almost married. Now fate had brought them together once again.

"She's no different than her sisters," Richmond said harshly.

His father frowned. "Aren't you being just a trifle judgmental, Derek? Miss Wyndmoore seems perfectly respectable."

Richmond sighed. "Pandora seemed perfectly respectable as well."

A deep frown marred Stanton's brow. *This isn't going to go well at all for Derek, especially if he continues under the misconception that all of the Wyndmoore sisters are the same,* he mused.

Cassie sat alone in her room, staring out the window. It was well past midnight, and although her nightdress was on and she should have been exhausted, she wasn't.

As she gazed out at the full moon, all she could think about was the night at the Assembly Rooms. Why was Richmond being so solicitous? She didn't have any answers.

Of course, she knew about the legendary Richmond charm. When he had been courting Pandora, she gave Cassie every single detail of their romance. Cassie knew almost everything about Richmond, from his preferences in horses (he didn't care about matched pairs, but instead wanted their gaits and temperaments to complement each other) to his ideas on fashion (he was disinterested) to gambling (a diversion but not a passion). She knew he enjoyed long walks in the moonlight and dreamed of a day when he'd have his own family. That's what he'd told Pandora.

Now he wants something from me, she mused. *Something that he can't have.*

Cassie turned her gaze to her trunk, where Lloyd's book was hidden. She wasn't certain if Richmond was a spy; she had always thought it unlikely, and reasoned that Pandora just fabricated that information to discredit his character. He did have relations in France, though, and he was certainly acting suspiciously. So there was a chance that he was working for Boney. As a loyal English subject, she wasn't going to take any chances.

Then there was the waltz. Most of the time, Cassie was the practical one in the family: she worked on Papa's accounts with him; she managed the staff at home, since her mama wasn't interested; and she remembered every single detail about their servants. Cassie wasn't romantic. At all.

Except for Lord Richmond. The first time she saw him with Pandora, she had felt that there was something special about him. He wasn't the most handsome of Pandora's suitors, but for a time he was the most well-heeled. Cassie always made sure she 'accidentally' left her needlework in the parlor where Richmond waited for Pandora and tried to talk to him as much as possible. Mama was always busy with Pandora, so she didn't even notice Cassie's interest. No one noticed Cassie's interest, not even Richmond. However, she enjoyed his company, and even enjoyed listening to him talk to her papa when he came for dinner.

Then Lyntwoode had appeared. Fabulously wealthy yet terrifically boring Lyntwoode. When he appeared,

Pandora was determined to marry him, and when Richmond was no longer a part of her life, Cassie was certain that she was more depressed about the situation than Pandora.

First, there was the chance meeting at the inn. Now, it almost appeared that Richmond wanted to get to know her. From what she observed, and she did keep her eyes on him most of the evening, he didn't dance with many available females. In fact, he almost singled her out by waltzing with her and taking her to tea. It was as if he wanted to get to know her.

Except that Cassie knew he didn't want to get to know her at all. *He's only after the book,* she decided with a sigh. *Everything else is just an act.*

She got up from the chair at the writing desk and climbed into bed. She knew it would be long time before she fell asleep.

Chapter 7

"Look, Cassie, I must have received flowers from every eligible gentleman in Bath," Daphne proclaimed triumphantly, waving her hands at the plethora of flowers sitting in Aunt Honoria's parlor.

Cassie looked up from her reading and smiled indulgently. It was always best to simply agree with Daphne at certain times, or else she'd go on and on interminably, which was much, much worse. "I'm not surprised. You were one of the most sought after young ladies in the Upper Rooms last night," she replied, looking back down at her book.

"*One* of the most sought after ladies?" Daphne asked. "I was undoubtedly *the* most sought after lady," Daphne concluded haughtily, fingering a rose from the bouquet that Lord Pembrook had sent.

Before Cassie could think up a suitably mild reply that would make Daphne stop babbling about her popularity, she was interrupted by a voice from the doorway.

"Are you gloating again, Daphne?" Aunt Honoria said as she strode into the parlor.

Daphne paled. "Oh, no, Aunt Honoria. I was just telling Cassie how lovely the flowers looked," she said innocently.

What a liar, Cassie thought, trying to concentrate on

the Minerva Press novel she was reading. The book was rather predictable, but she found it quite relaxing.

Honoria, wearing a modest blue gown, settled herself on the settee and glared at Daphne. "Daphne, you're a poor liar. I heard everything you said to Cassandra. I warned you about your behavior," Honoria said sternly.

Daphne sighed loudly and looked down at the floor, her bottom lip trembling as if she was going to cry. *It's the look she always gives Mama, and Mama gives in,* Cassie noted to herself.

Honoria wasn't as easily swayed as their mother. "You will spend the rest of the day in your room, Daphne, writing a one-hundred-word essay on the evils of vanity. You will have this essay ready for my inspection before dinner," Honoria announced, as both Cassie and Daphne looked at her in shock.

"But, Aunt Honoria, that's not fair! What if one of my new gentlemen friends calls this afternoon? I have my social responsibilities, you know," she added passionately.

Honoria seemed to consider the request for a brief moment. "You're right, Daphne. You do have responsibilities, as do I. Your essay will be two hundred words. Now go to your room," she said sternly.

Daphne opened her mouth to say something, then obviously thought better of it and headed silently to her room, wearing an air of defeat.

"Daphne doesn't do these things on purpose," Cassie interjected, putting down her novel.

Honoria frowned. "Your sister has been cosseted all of her life and genuinely believes that the world revolves around her. Your mama asked me to set her on the right path, and I'm doing that to the best of my abilities. If Daphne wants to make a suitable match some day and lead a productive life, she has to realize that she is not the center of the universe," Honoria concluded, ringing for tea.

Cassie sighed slightly and picked up her book. Aunt Honoria was right, and Daphne did deserve to be disciplined. However, it was rather unnerving to see it happen.

As she stared at the words in front of her, Cassie's thoughts kept returning to Mr. Lloyd's book. *I should tell Aunt Honoria about it,* she mused. *She'll know what to do.*

"Thank you for bringing over Lord Stanton last night," Honoria said in a bit of a stilted voice, almost as if she was somewhat . . . embarrassed. "We were great friends when we were younger, and it was nice to see him again."

"Do you know Lord Richmond, as well?" Cassie asked ever so casually, her plan suddenly coming to a screaming halt. If Aunt Honoria was friends with Lord Stanton, she might tell him about Cassie's book. In addition, if Aunt Honoria told Lord Stanton, then he would tell Lord Richmond. And Richmond might be a spy, so Cassie definitely didn't want him to know about the book at all, even though she knew he suspected she had it in her possession.

"Not at all, I'm afraid, but I'm sure he's perfectly respectable."

Cassie was nonplussed. Of course Aunt Honoria would say that Richmond was perfectly respectable.

One of Aunt Honoria's mobcapped servant girls appeared with their afternoon tea, but Cassie hardly noticed her, since she was busy thinking about Richmond. The potential spy.

"Would you care for some tea, Cassandra?" Honoria asked.

"Of course. Do you think Lord Stanton will be calling on us?" she asked distractedly.

Honoria smiled as she handed Cassie a delicately flowered teacup and saucer. "He did mention that he would stop by. And you do realize he sent both of us flowers," she said, pointing to two huge arrangements of the loveliest wildflowers that Cassie had ever seen.

Cassie lit up. She did like Lord Stanton, even though his son was probably a spy. Aunt Honoria seemed to favor him as well, and she certainly needed male companionship. "That was very kind of him. You know, Lord Stanton is one of the nicest people I've met in Bath," she said honestly.

Honoria smiled. "When I was much younger, Lord Stanton and I had an agreement, although he wasn't Lord Stanton at the time. Unfortunately, my parents didn't approve of his suit, although I can't imagine why. When I came back, I was engaged to Raverston and he was married to Richmond's mother," she explained.

Everything was falling into place for Cassie. She had sensed that there was more to Aunt Honoria's relationship with Lord Stanton, and her aunt had just confirmed that fact. Cassie worried about her being alone, and now Lord Stanton had arrived. Maybe if she helped them along, Aunt Honoria and Lord Stanton could make a match of it. *It would serve them right,* Cassie thought with a smile. *Aunt Honoria means to find me a match while I'm in Bath, I'm sure of it. But maybe I'll find someone for her!*

Honoria drained her delicate white and blue teacup and placed it on the table. "Have you finished the book that Sara says you're slaving over day and night?"

Cassie cringed. *Does everyone know about the book?* She tried to appear nonchalant, but her heart was pounding. "Oh, it's nothing, Aunt Honoria. I'm just trying to brush up on my Greek," she said lightly.

"I didn't invite you here so that you could spend all of your time alone in your room," Honoria chided.

"I know," Cassie conceded. "I'll try to get out more, I promise."

"I'll make sure you do, young lady," Honoria replied, playfully shaking her finger at Cassie. "There's no reason that you should not be as popular as Daphne while you're in Bath," she concluded.

Cassie groaned inwardly. When would Aunt Honoria and the rest of the world realize that she was destined to be in the shadows while beauties like Daphne and Pandora captured the attention of every male within miles? *It's going to be a long visit,* Cassie decided, sipping her tea.

Daphne paced the sitting room, waiting for Lord Pembrook. He had said he would come. He had promised he would. She glanced up at the ormolu clock on the mantel. Aunt Honoria and Cassie were due back from their visit to Madame Babette's in an hour, unless they happened upon an acquaintance or stopped for an ice.

The hands of the clock mocked her. Pembrook wasn't going to come. Pandora had been teasing her for years about being a country rustic, and this was her chance to show everyone that she was lovely enough to capture the handsomest man in Bath.

Daphne fell onto the couch. *This visit has been nothing like I expected,* she thought. Whenever she visited their home in Warwick, Aunt Honoria was always the most congenial of relations. Now that they were in Bath, Daphne found herself to be continually alone in her room, thinking about her vanity, writing essays about it or, worse yet, apologizing to Cassie. If she was in her bedroom being punished, she wasn't out meeting eligible gentlemen.

Eligible gentlemen were the reason that Daphne was in Bath. She was tired of the sonnet-writing local gents in Warwick whom she had known since childhood. She was seventeen, and she was ready to meet a Corinthian. Lord Pembrook was a Corinthian, and he was even more handsome than Byron was. Even the gossips around Bath admitted that Lord Pembrook was more handsome than Byron was. And she had caught his attention. At least Daphne thought she had.

However, it didn't look like he was going to call, which was a dashed shame. It was a tragedy! If he came at any other time, she was certain Aunt Honoria would say something dreadful to him that would make him take his leave almost immediately. Aunt Honoria had a habit of doing that.

Daphne wanted to be alone with him. Pandora had told her that the easiest way to a man's heart was with kisses. Once a man was ensnared, Pandora assured her that a lady's kisses could get her flowers, gifts, and jewelry. *I'd like some jewelry,* Daphne decided. If Aunt Honoria were home, she wouldn't be alone with Lord Pembrook. If he came today, all she had to do was get rid of Sara, since Mary had accompanied Cassie and Aunt Honoria to Madame Babette's. Lord Pembrook was perfectly respectable, and she certainly didn't need a chaperon for someone of his caliber.

She stared at the clock for the longest time, watching the hands slowly move. *He's never going to come,* she thought dejectedly. Then a miracle happened. Laughton, Aunt Honoria's stately and rather dull butler, appeared at the door of the parlor.

"Lord Pembrook is here to see you, Miss Daphne.

Shall I inform him that you are not at home?" he asked in a very stately and serious voice.

Daphne turned her large blue eyes on the aging butler. "I'll see Lord Pembrook. Please send him in," she said, trying to hide a triumphant smile. *He's here,* she thought, her heart singing. *He does care for me!*

A deep frown lined Laughton's brow. "I'll inform Sara that you'll be needing a chaperon. Once she arrives, I'll send Lord Pembrook in," he said stiffly as he exited the parlor.

Daphne began to think quickly. She wanted to be alone with Pembrook, and that meant that she needed to get rid of Sara. But how? Daphne began to pace the room once again.

Then it hit her. She needed to send Sara on an errand. An errand that would take an impossibly long time. That would give her the chance to be alone with Pembrook. All she had to do was think of the right errand . . .

Sara took her time coming into the parlor, and, after an interminably long period of time, Laughton brought in Pembrook. He looked as handsome as ever, from the tip of his blond head to his shiny Hessians. Daphne was sure that he was the most handsome man in all of England, if not the world.

"Miss Wyndmoore, how lovely to see you," he said, kissing her hand gently.

"Good afternoon, Lord Pembrook," Daphne said, blushing.

The pair went over to the sofa and sat down. Pembrook sat a bit too close to Daphne, but she didn't mind. "You look ravishing today, as usual. But you must be tired of hearing how beautiful you are," he said, his eyes never leaving her.

Daphne blushed again but said nothing.

"Where is Lady Raverston? And your sister? Are they at home today?" he asked smoothly.

"No, they're both at the modiste."

He flashed her a sparkling smile. "I'm so glad we have some time *alone*," he said.

Daphne glanced over at Sara. They were not alone, although it appeared that Pembrook would prefer some privacy. Daphne took a chance. "Yes, well, did I mention that I found the pearls I was telling you about at the Assembly?"

Pembrook frowned but replied, "Oh, really?"

"Would you like to see them?" she asked, staring at him intently.

He gaped at her for a few moments, confused.

Daphne glanced at Sara, who was gazing out the window, then actually winked at Pembrook.

He smiled. Daphne knew he finally understood. "Yes, I'd adore seeing them."

Daphne turned to Sara, who was sitting in the corner, her watchful eyes on both of them. "Sara, go up to my room and fetch my pearls. They're in the trunk in my wardrobe."

It was Sara's turn to frown. "Miss Daphne, I don't think . . . "

Before Sara could finish her protest, Daphne interrupted her. "I don't care what you think, I need them now. Go!" Daphne ordered in her most regal voice.

Sara paused for a moment, then left the room. Pembrook immediately arose and closed the door behind Sara.

"Oh, Daphne, it's so good to see you," he said rather melodramatically, taking his seat on the sofa next to her.

She blushed prettily, as he expected. "I'm sorry it

took so long to get rid of Sara," she said apologetically, practically beaming.

"But you did get rid of her, you minx," he said with a grin.

"Yes, I did, Lord Pembrook. What is it that you need to ask me about?" she asked curiously.

He bestowed a radiant smile upon her, a smile that no gently bred lady could resist, especially one so young. "Percival. You must call me Percival, my dear."

She blushed, as if on cue. "Of course, Percival. What can I do for you?"

"I'm in such a quandary, my dear," he said dramatically.

"Really?" she said, leaning closer towards him

"I've been doing some work for our government. It's all very hush-hush, of course, and they sent me to Bath to fetch a book from that dreadful Mr. Lloyd. But it disappeared before he died, and I don't have the foggiest idea of where to look," he concluded.

"What kind of book?"

"Well, I'm not quite certain. It was in Greek, though," he added.

Daphne frowned. "My sister Cassie and I found a book in the park the other day. It's all in Greek. Do you think it could be Mr. Lloyd's book?" she asked innocently.

Pembrook looked completely surprised. "You must be teasing me, Daphne! You cannot mean to say that you have the very book I need?"

"No, really, Cassie has some sort of book she found that's in Greek. Do you really think it's the book you need?" she questioned, her eyes widening.

"It very well may be. Do you think I could take a look at it?" he said with his winning smile.

"Of course, let me go fetch it," she said, and disappeared from the room.

* * *

A quarter of an hour later, Daphne returned to the parlor, dejected. "I'm so sorry, Percival. I couldn't locate the book," she said, sitting down on the sofa next to him. *I can't believe I failed him,* she thought. *It was such a simple task—all I had to do was bring him Cassie's book and I couldn't even do that.*

He smiled slightly and took her hand in his. "That's quite all right. I know how things can get misplaced in a house this large. Will you contact me if you find the book?" he asked, gently kissing her hand.

Daphne felt her senses reeling. Lord Pembrook, Percival, was sitting much too close to her, and she thought she might swoon. That would be a bad thing. "Of course, Percival," she replied with a smile. *He doesn't care about the book at all, he cares about me,* she decided. *Pandora will be green with envy when I come back to Warwick engaged to the handsomest man in London!*

"I noticed that Richmond is friendly with your sister Cassandra," he noted, smiling at her.

"I think he feels sorry for her," Daphne said, leaning closer to him. "Lord Richmond used to be a bosom bow of my sister Pandora," she explained.

Pembrook gazed at her, and she could see the concern in his warm brown eyes. "I certainly wouldn't ever presume to tell you who to associate with, but Richmond doesn't have the most sterling reputation around London," he said simply.

Daphne's eyes widened. "Really? I heard he was of the best *ton*."

Pembrook shook his head slightly. "He was at one time, but he's been involved in any number of scandals. He destroyed his own reputation when he was found in

Dover, helping some Frenchmen," he said in a voice laced with concern.

Daphne was utterly scandalized. "He's a traitor?" she whispered.

"That's the rumor. But Richmond is close friends with the wives of many government officials, so he'll never be investigated, if you know what I mean."

"Oh my," Daphne said in shock. "I'll certainly keep clear of him, and as for Cassie, I'm sure he doesn't have any real interest in her," she added as he stood up to leave.

"And you will tell me if you find your sister's book? It's tremendously important. To England," he added, gazing into her eyes.

She stared back at him in alt and almost swooned when he leaned over and kissed her lightly on the cheek. *It's my first real kiss,* she thought, unable to concentrate on anything but the handsome peer in front of her.

"Good afternoon, my dearest Daphne," he said with a smile.

"Good afternoon, Percival," she said, watching his handsome form saunter out of the parlor. Bath was definitely her favorite place in the world.

"The veal is excellent," Richmond said, helping himself to another generous portion.

Stanton sipped his glass of hock and studied his son. Derek had never really recovered from Pandora Wyndmoore's betrayal, and now he fully expected her sister to be of the exact same cut. Except that any fool could see that Cassandra was as different from Pandora as two people from the same family could be. Yet Derek didn't want to see that, Stanton would bet his prize bloods on

that. "So, Derek," he began, sampling the creamed potatoes, "did you enjoy your tea with Miss Wyndmoore?"

Richmond paused for a long moment and considered his words carefully. "Miss Wyndmoore seems to
be a proper enough spinster. She seemed to be a bit
taken with you, though, Father," he added, almost as
an afterthought.

Stanton grinned at his son as he picked the mush-
rooms out of the stuffing on his plate. "I think not. I was
a good friend of her aunt's many years ago, and Miss
Wyndmoore was kind enough to help me renew my
acquaintance with her," he said, eating a bit of stuffing.
"I did find Miss Wyndmoore to be a very taking young
lady. Or perhaps not so young. Her life might have been
quite different if she wasn't overshadowed by her sisters," he commented, finishing his meal.

"Miss Wyndmoore is quite attractive in her own
right," Richmond said defensively, and Stanton smiled
slightly. "She shouldn't have to be compared to her sisters," Richmond concluded.

Stanton grinned. *My son can be so predictable at
times,* he mused. "But, Derek, aren't you comparing
her to Pandora? Shouldn't you judge her as her own
person?" he said provocatively.

Richmond held up his glass of hock in a mock toast.
"Touché, Father. It's very . . . difficult for me to judge
Miss Wyndmoore objectively because of my . . . time
with Pandora. But I will try. I suppose I owe her that,"
he added.

A contented smile appeared on Stanton's face. Maybe
Derek did have a chance with the lovely and charming
Cassandra Wyndmoore. Maybe, if Honoria decided to
help, there would be a wedding in the offing. Maybe
grandchildren weren't out of the question.

* * *

"Daphne Wyndmoore, I told you I didn't want you socializing with Pembrook," Aunt Honoria said harshly, a scowl firmly set on her face. "Yet you invited him into my home and then conveniently got rid of your chaperon. You should know better than that," she concluded, pacing the study. Honoria was angry with Daphne. Very angry indeed.

"I'm sorry, Aunt Honoria," Daphne said in her most contrite voice and stared at the pattern in the carpet.

"Then, after getting rid of Sara, you spend over a quarter of an hour with him in the parlor behind closed doors! Do you have any idea of the impropriety of that action, young lady?" she sputtered, her hazel eyes dancing with fire.

"Nothing happened, Aunt Honoria. We were just talking," Daphne explained.

"Nothing happened. Well, Daphne, nothing will be happening in your life for a long while. In fact, I should send you home to your mama and tell her that you're as incorrigible as Pandora," Honoria said, utterly frustrated with her wayward niece.

"Please don't send me home, Aunt Honoria, please."

Honoria sat down across from Daphne, and she was still angry. Very angry. "I will be writing your mother regarding this whole episode and your total lack of morals and propriety. She will decide if you're to return home. As your punishment, you will not be allowed out of the house for a sennight. You will not be allowed to receive any callers or to join us in the parlor if we have visitors. There will be no routs. On the evenings that Cassandra and I leave, you will be confined to your room, where you will read the Bible. Do I make myself clear?" she concluded, staring at Daphne.

"Yes, Aunt Honoria," Daphne said meekly.

"Now go to your room. Sara will bring you up a Bible. I don't expect to hear a word from you until supper. And don't bother complaining to Cassandra. She will not convince me to be more lenient with your punishment."

Daphne never looked up as she padded across the carpet and headed toward her room.

Honoria glared after her. What was the girl thinking? It wasn't the thing to be alone with any man, especially one who had a dubious reputation like Pembrook. He could easily have taken advantage of her innocent nature, and then there would have been hell to pay. Thankfully, Laughton had the presence to stay near the door and listen for anything untoward. However, someone had to try to thrust some common sense into the chit before she ended up like Pandora.

Honoria walked over to the window and looked out into the garden. The leaves on the oak tree rustled in the wind, and her flowers were just starting to bloom. It was a lovely time of the year. *It's too bad that Richmond was involved with Pandora,* she mused. *He would have made an excellent match for Cassandra.*

Cassie's eyes were red and bleary. Mr. Lloyd's book was in her hands, and, if she had looked at the clock on the desk, she would have noticed that it was very late indeed. Thankfully, Aunt Honoria wasn't stingy about her candles, since Cassie had used more than a few in the past few nights.

All she could think about was Richmond and their waltz. She hated that her mind kept returning to him, so she tried to think of anything else. Which meant that she kept thinking about Mr. Lloyd's book. None of the stories mentioned a specific person with a first name and surname except 'The Miser.' It mentioned a name, plus very specific directions from the grave. It was unlike any Aesop story she had ever read, and she knew that she was eventually going to have to find out if Bath did indeed have a cemetery. She was sure that it did, which would mean a trip there sometime in the near future. *It's all very strange,* Cassie thought with a yawn.

Her candle was getting low once again. It was very late, so Cassie began to put everything away. *Is there a cemetery in Bath?* she wondered. She didn't recall seeing any since they were in town, but that certainly didn't mean one didn't exist. All towns had cemeteries, and Mr. Lloyd seemed to be giving out some very specific information.

As she did every night, she hid the books and her papers down at the bottom of her portmanteau under the gowns that Aunt Honoria had forbidden her to wear. She was certain they'd be safe there, and that no one would think to look for anything important under a stack of dowdy, unfashionable gowns.

Cassie blew out the candle and curled up in her bed. *I suppose I'll take a walk with Mary tomorrow,* she reasoned. *Maybe we can find the cemetery.*

As she tried to fall asleep, her errant thoughts once again returned to Lord Richmond. *He seemed so different back then,* she mused. *Even at the inn, he seemed to be a different person. It was almost as if he wanted to make my acquaintance back then. Now he smiles at me, but he doesn't seem sincere.*

She was convinced that Richmond and Pembrook were both after the book. Logically, that meant that only one was probably a spy. If both were spies from France, they would be working together, unless they were working for different factions of the French government—if there were rival spy factions, which in itself seemed strange to Cassie.

Logically, only one of them was a spy for France. One of them might be a spy for England. Pembrook, a slave to fashion, seemed too superficial to be a spy. Richmond was more intelligent and did have relations in France. Therefore, he was motivated. In addition, Pandora had warned Cassie that Richmond was a turncoat.

So it was logical that Richmond was working for France. Yet there was something that she didn't trust about Pembrook, and Aunt Honoria said he wasn't of the best *ton*. She couldn't simply hand over the book to either one of them.

Cassie knew she had to sort out the intrigue, one way or the other, and decide whom to trust.

Chapter 8

"Good afternoon, Lord Richmond," Honoria said, studying Stanton's son. He was quite different than she had expected. She had imagined he would be dressed to the nines, with manners and charm to match. In fact, she rather expected to see a younger version of his father.

Richmond surprised Honoria, to say the least. His dress was stylish, but he most certainly wasn't a dandy or even a top-of-the-trees Corinthian. He was clad in a simple black jacket atop a white shirt with a silk cravat, tied in a Mathematical. He carried himself with confidence, but wore an air of indifference, or even perhaps distraction. His hair was slightly wild, and it looked as if his valet had tried to coax it into place without much luck. Yet he was Stanton's son, so he was welcome in her home.

"Good afternoon, Lady Raverston," Richmond said affably. "It's my pleasure to finally make your acquaintance. Is Miss Wyndmoore at home?" he inquired.

Honoria motioned him to a chair and seated herself on the settee. "I suspect that Cassandra is in her room," she began with a slight smile, "but I'm not certain if she's at home." She wasn't sure if Cassie wanted to see Richmond, and it was never good to make oneself too available to a potential suitor, most especially one who had a history with her sister.

That statement earned her a smile from Richmond. "I'd like to take your niece for a drive in my phaeton," he explained. "I asked her about it at the Assembly Rooms, and she seemed . . . amenable."

Honoria continued studying him. What could he have ever seen in Pandora? Of course, Pandora was beautiful, but he seemed serious and well-spoken. Pandora was flighty, beautiful, and mindless. *But then again, men don't always desire what's best for them,* Honoria reasoned. Wouldn't it be logical that if he had been interested in Pandora, he should be interested in Daphne? Honoria tried a different tactic. "I'm sure that Daphne would welcome the chance to go for a drive with you if Cassandra isn't available," she commented, her eyes never leaving his face.

"I'm sure Miss Daphne would enjoy a drive, but I came to inquire after Miss Wyndmoore, and if she is indeed unavailable, I'll be on my way," he answered succinctly.

Ah, so he does know his mind, Honoria thought. *He isn't totally without bottom, although he was birdwitted enough to fall in love with Pandora.* She stood up and said, "If you'll wait for a moment, I'll have Millie bring in some tea, while I inquire about Cassandra's plans for the afternoon."

"Of course," he replied as she sauntered out of the parlor.

Cassie was alone in her room, working on a missive to her papa. Everything she wrote sounded so dull and provincial that she pondered just ripping it up. The only thing interesting that had happened in Bath was Mr.

Lloyd's book, and she was certain that she couldn't tell her papa about that.

As Cassie wracked her brain, trying to think of something entertaining to write, there was a knock on the door. "Yes?"

Much to her surprise, Aunt Honoria appeared. "Cassandra dear, put on your new green walking dress. Lord Richmond is here to take you driving," she announced in a rather regal tone.

Cassie blanched. Richmond? Here to take her for a drive? Why? "Driving? With Lord Richmond? I wanted to go for a walk with Mary today. Do I have to go, Aunt Honoria? Can't you tell him I'm not at home?" Cassie said without taking a breath.

Honoria frowned. "I think not, young lady. You can go walking with Mary any day, and I see no reason why you shouldn't accept Lord Richmond's offer. I expect you to be down momentarily," she said, leaving the room before Cassie could utter another word of protest.

Cassie sighed and went over to the wardrobe for her green walking dress. Part of her wanted to give the book to Lord Richmond so he'd stop the charade, because Cassie was certain his attentions were just that—a charade. What was bad was the fact that part of Cassie enjoyed those attentions, even though they were utterly untrue.

Lord Richmond and Aunt Honoria were so engrossed in their conversation that they didn't notice the door of the parlor creak open slowly.

Cassandra stood there for a moment or two in silence, staring at Richmond. He looked even more handsome than when she had danced with him at the Assembly

Rooms. Oh, not in the same way as Lord Pembrook, or even Lord Lyntwoode, Pandora's husband, but in a unique way. When Richmond walked into a room, he didn't look like every other dandy. His hair was a bit too long, his boots might have a bit of a scuff on them, and he didn't seem to be a slave to fashion. From the day she had met him, she thought of him as a man of action, a man who could get things done. Of course, the whole situation with Pandora was dreadful, and she knew that he had ended the relationship because Pandora was seeing Lyntwoode behind his back.

She took a deep breath and entered the room. "Good afternoon, Lord Richmond," she said politely, nervously pushing the glasses up her nose.

Richmond rose, walked over to her, and took her hand in his. "Good afternoon, Miss Wyndmoore," he said and ever so gallantly kissed her hand.

Cassie stared at him in disbelief. *What is he doing? Why is he pretending he's interested in me?* On one level, it was nice to have Lord Richmond acting like a lovesick pup, but Cassie knew it was a charade.

"Would you care to take a drive this afternoon?" he asked gallantly, giving her the same smile she had seen him give Pandora numerous times.

Cassie was not impressed. "I suppose a drive would be a nice diversion," she replied blandly, glancing over at Aunt Honoria.

"Have a grand time," Honoria said with a wide smile.

When they left the room, Cassie was not smiling.

Cassie clung to the side of Richmond's precariously balanced phaeton, mentally willing him to slow down. Lord Richmond was quite the accomplished whip, but she was used to their carriage in Warwick and their horses as well. Richmond's steeds were lively and well matched, and could obviously take him across the country in a moment's notice, if required.

Since Cassie was literally afraid she was going to tumble out of the phaeton at any moment, her conversation was nonexistent as they drove down Great Pulteney Street, over the bridge, and headed out into the country. *I thought Pandora said he was a great whip,* Cassie mused, as she concentrated on keeping her balance. *I think he's trying to kill me.*

Richmond glanced over at her, and apparently realized that he was going a bit too fast for her liking. He gradually slowed down the pair and remarked, "The phaeton isn't mine. I actually borrowed it while I was in Bath."

The horses finally settled into a tranquil walk, and Cassie was actually able to concentrate on something other than her balance. "Oh," she said, trying to concentrate on anything but Lord Richmond, who was sitting much too close to her.

"Have you been enjoying your time in Bath?" he queried innocently.

Gads, he sounds like Daphne, she thought with chagrin. "It's been . . . lovely," she replied blandly.

"Have you met many of the locals?"

Cassie stared at the scenery. She had heard Richmond talk to Pandora many times. He had been interested in politics and capable of having an intelligent conversation. She didn't remember him being so . . . bland. She sighed. "I've met some," Cassie said vaguely. *I wonder when exactly he's going to ask about Mr. Lloyd.*

The horses ambled on, and he continued his line of conversation. Or perhaps it was more like questioning. "Have you tried the waters at the Pump Room?"

Cassie sighed. *He never used to talk like that to Pandora,* she mused. *He talked to her about his ambitions, his horses, his property, and told the must amusing anecdotes. Of course, that was when he was talking to Pandora.* All she deserved was *Have you tried the waters at the Pump Room?* "No, I haven't," she replied succinctly.

"The weather has been lovely, hasn't it?" he continued, oblivious to the fact that she was barely talking to him.

"Yes, it has."

Every banal question was grating on Cassie's nerves. The charming and delightful Lord Richmond was obviously a thing of the past. This was the new bland and boring Lord Richmond who was interested in her only because of her connection to Mr. Lloyd. He had been more charming at the inn. *I have to put a stop to this,* she thought. *But how?*

"Did you enjoy your evening at the Assembly Rooms?" he said in the most affable voice, as if he really were curious.

I know he's not interested in me, Cassie decided, *and it's just a waste of my time to let him keep dangling after me. I'm tired of listening to him try to make polite conversation with me. He's not even listening to my answers. He's just talking for the sake of talking.*

Cassie stared at the meadow. *If I keep answering him in monosyllables, this drive might go on forever. If I try to be polite, he may decide that he wants to continue seeing me so he can find out more about Mr. Lloyd's book. Well, I'll just do something drastic and get rid of him once and for all,* she decided. "I suppose. Daphne and Pandora love routs and such; I'd rather be home, reading a book or studying. Then there are the account books that I keep for Papa and trades- men to attend to," she said firmly. *There. That will most certainly drive him away.*

"Really?" he asked ever so properly.

Damanation! He didn't even react to her shocking revelations. "Oh yes, I'm quite busy at home. I don't even have time to socialize, and haven't been in Town for the Season for ages," she said. *There! That should give him an aversion to me and end this charade.*

"I find the Season a bit tedious myself," he admitted.

"But, Lord Richmond, I imagine you have your pick of ladies on the Marriage Mart, I would think that's quite . . . well . . . enjoyable," she concluded awkwardly.

"If I have to dance with one more pasty-faced heiress who needs my money, I'll put a period to my existence," he proclaimed.

Cassie couldn't help herself. She giggled. "It can't be that bad."

"It's that bad."

They drove in silence for a while, while Cassie tried to discern a new tactic. She had tried to shock him. That didn't work. He was used to ladies in proper Society, and, for the most part, ladies in proper Society were never direct and rarely said what was on their mind. Therefore, she tried a new tactic.

"I know why you asked me out for a drive," she proclaimed.

"I asked you out on a drive because I find your com- pany enjoyable," he replied.

Damn him! Would nothing fluster him? She tried again. "You asked me out on this drive to find out about a book that belonged to Mr. Lloyd that you think I have," she announced.

Much to her surprise, Richmond stopped the phaeton

on the side of the road under a grove of trees, and stared at her as if she had run mad. "May I ask what you're talking about, Miss Wyndmoore?"

Cassie gazed at him impassively. Finally, they were getting somewhere. "I'm not stupid, Lord Richmond. I'm fully aware that Mr. Lloyd was supposedly a spy, and that he had a book in his possession that you, as well as Lord Pembrook, want. Both of you seem to think that I have the book. Well, I don't, so you don't have to invite me out driving or have tea with me or spend any time at all with me, because I don't have what you're looking for," she concluded breathlessly.

Richmond leveled a steady gaze at her and said nothing.

"I'm sorry if I've offended you with my plain speaking, but I am a spinster who's on the shelf, so I do believe that I'm allowed some liberties," she added.

He had an odd expression on his face, and she was utterly unprepared for his next move. He leaned over and kissed her.

Cassie was stunned. *What's he doing? Why in the world is he kissing me?* she wondered, as her body melted against his. She was awash in a sea of sensation, and, without even realizing it, she wrapped her arms around him and drew him closer to her. It was another dream come true. First the waltz and now a kiss from the only man who had ever set her heart on fire.

They kissed for what seemed a blissful eternity. It ended when he leaned over and whispered into her ear, "You're not on the shelf, and I know you have Lloyd's book."

Cassie pulled away from him in shock, her heart shattering into a million pieces. *I was right; this is all about Mr. Lloyd. His interest was obviously a charade to get his hands on the book so he can turn it over to the French.* "Please take me back to Aunt Honoria's," Cassie said in a voice that sounded much more like a command rather than a request.

"Miss Wyndmoore, I . . ."

Cassie turned to him, her temper fully riled. "Lord Richmond, you forget I know exactly how you behave. In fact, if you'll stretch your obviously meager memory, you might even recall that I walked in on you and Pandora during one of your very frequent trysts. I know Pandora is generous with her affections. I am not," she concluded, turning her head and staring at the hindquarters of his blacks.

Richmond was speechless for quite a long while. After what seemed to be an eternity to Cassie, he simply snapped the reins and they started back toward town.

She was fuming. It was all about the book. He wasn't interested in her at all. However, she had known that from the start. First the questions from Pembrook. Then his questions. *Mr. Lloyd's book must be terribly important for Lord Richmond to try to seduce me,* she mused.

There had been a time when she would have done anything to feel Richmond's lips pressed against hers. She dreamed of wrapping her arms around his muscular form and hearing him mutter her name in the throes of passion.

However, he was a scoundrel. Pandora told her that. This time, Pandora was obviously right.

They continued the drive in silence until they pulled up to Lady Raverston's home. Cassie began to get out of the phaeton without waiting for help, when he grabbed her arm.

"I didn't kiss you to get information out of you," he said, his eyes boring a hole into her very soul.

"I have no information to give you, Lord Richmond," she said coldly. Before he could reply, she jumped out of the phaeton and all but ran up the stairs to the front door.

Richmond drove down the street, cursing his idiocy. He was certain Cassie had the book. In fact, he had even thought of breaking into Honoria's house to try to locate it.

Burglary wasn't always the best plan, though. For one, he didn't particularly enjoy breaking into the homes of law abiding citizens and, two, he was certain that Cassie had the book well hidden. Even if he did break in, he wasn't sure that he'd be able to locate it.

Then there was the fact that he had actually kissed her without any real provocation. Well, her blazing eyes and her heaving breast were quite an enticement, and he had never seen anyone more desirable than she in that moment when she'd had the audacity to tell him that she had discerned his real motives. Proper ladies never even thought of contradicting him in any way and were generally the most agreeable creatures in the world. Miss Cassandra Wyndmoore wasn't intimidated by him and wasn't afraid to voice her thoughts. She wasn't afraid to provoke him, and actually seemed to relish being so frank.

She was, of course, correct. About everything. He did take her out to find out about the book. Actually, he wanted more than to find out about the book. He planned to casually bring the topic about, then ask her to see it. If she let him see it, he could determine if it was what he thought it was.

Most women wouldn't pick up a book abandoned on a bench in the park. He knew from his source that's how she found it. How Lloyd had known that she would guard it so passionately was beyond him.

In the end, though, she still had the book. He couldn't even ask her about it now without looking like a complete blackguard who had ulterior motives—even though he was a blackguard with ulterior motives. He couldn't even complete a simple assignment from Castlereagh and was being thwarted by a charming bluestocking.

He let his horses amble around town as he contemplated what had just happened with Miss Wyndmoore. He did kiss her to get the information about the book. He planned that ages ago; she was a Wyndmoore, and he knew how the Wyndmoore females reacted to a simple kiss.

Yet this Wyndmoore female did not melt in his arms and proclaim her devotion. Well, she did seem to enjoy the experience, at least until he mentioned the book. That was a dashed bad move, he admitted to himself.

He had certainly enjoyed kissing her. Much, much more than he'd expected. Much more than he ever enjoyed kissing Pandora. Or his mistresses. In fact, if she hadn't stopped him, he probably would have tried to compromise her virtue right there in the phaeton. That would have been disastrous, because the phaeton was quite precariously balanced.

He sighed and headed toward his residence. *What did she mean about walking in on trysts with Pandora? I most certainly don't remember that,* he mused. He didn't even remember meeting Cassandra before. She obviously did. Now the charming bluestocking had the upper hand.

Daphne watched her sister push the very appetizing pigeon pie around her plate without really eating a bit of it. This was odd since Cassie liked pigeon pie. Daphne knew that as a fact.

Then there was the drive. Daphne heard from Mary that Cassie went on a drive with Lord Richmond, yet she hadn't said a word about it. Of course, it was possible that Cassie had already discussed it with Aunt Honoria while she was all but locked in her bedroom.

Cassie didn't look happy. Daphne was sure of that. Since she wasn't going to routs or morning calls or shopping, she wanted to know what had happened with Lord Richmond. In glorious detail.

"I hear you went driving today with Lord Richmond," Daphne said, watching Cassie's reaction.

Cassie never looked up from her plate. "Yes," she replied, pushing more of the pigeon pie around on the plate.

"The weather looked lovely," Daphne said, trying to draw Cassie out. It was dashed inconvenient to be punished.

"Yes, it was."

"Where did you go driving?" Daphne said. *What's wrong with Cassie? Why doesn't she want to talk about Richmond?*

"Oh, we took a road out of town. I'm not quite sure where we went," Cassie replied, finally eating a forkful of creamed turnips.

"Lord Richmond is quite handsome, isn't he?" Daphne said gamely. *Surely, Cassie has something to say about the drive,* she thought with chagrin.

That comment made Cassie smile. "He's not nearly as handsome as Lord Pembrook."

Daphne smiled back at her, contented for the moment. Obviously, the drive Cassie had taken with Richmond was boring. So boring that Cassie had nothing to say about it.

"Did you enjoy yourself?" Honoria asked.

Cassie looked back down at her plate. "Lord Richmond and I don't really get on well," Cassie muttered.

Daphne frowned. *Lord Richmond? Cassie doesn't get along with Lord Richmond? How odd. Cassie usually gets along with everyone, except exceptionally handsome men, and Richmond isn't that handsome.*

Honoria frowned. "You don't get on well with Richmond? Why?"

"We just don't rub well together, Aunt Honoria, and I don't really think he's sincere about pursuing a friendship with me."

"Is he a wastrel? Honoria asked.

"I don't think so," Cassie replied.

"A slow top?"

Daphne smiled slightly. Lord Richmond would just die if he knew that Aunt Honoria was asking if he were a slow top and a wastrel!

"No . . ." Cassie replied hesitantly.

"Are his manners offensive?" Honoria said, her frown deepening.

Cassie sighed. Loudly. "We just don't get on, Aunt Honoria, that's all," she said in resignation.

"I heard he's a spy," Daphne announced in a triumphant voice.

Two pairs of eyes stared at her.

"What?" Honoria said with a frown.

"I heard that Lord Richmond was a spy for the French," Daphne announced.

"Ridiculous. I've known Stanton for years. It's simply out of the question, and I won't have you repeating that sort of slander about his son," Honoria announced.

Daphne glanced over at Cassie. She didn't seem surprised that Richmond might be a spy at all. This was odd, since the information from Lord Pembrook was obviously confidential.

"Did you know Richmond when he was courting Pandora?" Honoria inquired.

"Of course. I spoke to him on more than one occasion, and I was actually quite upset when he . . . I mean Pandora . . . when they ended their relationship. Lord Richmond doesn't remember me, though," Cassie said as an afterthought.

Daphne's jaw dropped to the floor. "He doesn't remember you?"

Another sigh escaped Cassie. "Not at all."

"Why on earth not? What's wrong with him?" Honoria demanded.

"It was a long time ago, Aunt Honoria," Cassie replied calmly, and then put down her knife and fork. "May I be excused?" she said imploringly.

"Of course," Honoria replied as Cassie left the room.

Daphne stared after her, a frown on her face as well.

"At home, Cassie gets along with everyone," Daphne said for good measure.

Honoria continued to frown. "I'm sure she does. But the question is, why doesn't she get along with Richmond?"

Daphne ate a forkful of pie. "Maybe she's not telling us everything about the drive."

"Indeed," Honoria replied.

"You mean you actually met the chit while you were romancing her sister and you don't even remember her?" Stanton said in utter astonishment.

Richmond stared out of the window of the study. This was dashed embarrassing. He had been acting like a flat ever since he got to Bath and found out that Cassandra was a Wyndmoore. "Yes. In fact, she claims that she even interrupted a . . . romantic moment I was having with her sister. I don't recall the specific incident, but it is possible," he admitted, feeling very foolish.

"Let's examine what you've just said. You've insulted Miss Wyndmoore by not remembering her. You've also blackened your own character by dallying with her sister, a female of questionable morals. Now, in a moment of complete indiscretion, you tried to seduce her, insinuating that *her* morals are questionable. Is that an accurate representation of the situation, Derek?" Stanton asked tersely.

Richmond couldn't look at his father. He felt as if he was back in school and was being scolded for some sort of transgression. "Yes, Father, I suppose that is the situation," he replied in resignation.

Stanton got up from the overstuffed chair and began to pace the study. "Did you at least find out the information you wanted to know from Miss Wyndmoore before you began to molest her person?"

"I simply kissed her. I didn't molest her person. And no, I didn't find out the information I wanted. It appears she doesn't trust me," he concluded.

Stanton fell back into the chair. Richmond knew his father was disgusted with him. He was disgusted with himself. Finally, after an interminable silence, Stanton said, "Of course, I don't mean to tell you what to do, but a nicely worded apology to Miss Wyndmoore would be apropos if you would like to remain on speaking terms."

Richmond stared at his father. *It's as if I'm seventeen years old and I can't get myself out of a brangle, so he has to tell me what do,* Richmond thought. It was a very lowering thought indeed. "Yes, I know," he said softly.

He also decided that come hell or high water, he would get the information from Cassie Wyndmoore. She might have the upper hand now, but that would soon change, he decided.

Daphne was tired of being trapped in her room. Her trip to Bath was supposed to be a gay romp where she met hordes of handsome, eligible men. Instead, she had spent most of her time reading the Bible. Daphne devised a plan. She sat at the zebrawood escritoire in her bedroom and began to write a letter.

My Dear Sister,

I'm writing you from Aunt Honoria's residence in Bath. Mama sent me into exile for some unknown reason, and now I'm trapped here! Of course, I am the most stunning female in Bath, but then again, it is Bath. There are a few eligible men here, most notably Lord Pembrook, who is paying me some marked attentions, if I do say so myself. But I need your help in bringing Lord Pembrook up to scratch. Cassie is of no use at all when it comes to men and would rather spend her time reading. Your former inamorata Lord Richmond is in town with his father, and I'm sure both of them would welcome a chance to become reacquainted with you. Aunt Honoria has more than enough room, and, Pandora, it's so terribly boring here, I know I'll just wither away and simply die if you don't come immediately!

Daphne stared at the white linen paper and smiled. *Pandora will come,* she thought smugly. *If not to help me,*

then she'll come to get away from her dreadfully dull hus-
band and to see her former flame, Lord Richmond.

When the paper dried, Daphne folded it carefully and
placed it into an envelope. Aunt Honoria was being ever
so uncooperative, so Daphne had to take matters into
her own hands. She needed someone on her side, someone who knew how important it was to keep a budding
romance alive. Someone experienced with men. Someone who wasn't afraid of authority figures. Someone
like Pandora.

She dripped a bit of sealing wax onto the envelope and
stamped it shut. Now all she had to do was bribe Mary
into posting the letter without telling Aunt Honoria.
Which would be easy, since she knew Mary was partial
to chocolates and she had a box of Mary's favorites.

Pandora just had to come to Bath and rescue her!

Chapter 9

Cassie knew she had to get to the cemetery, but it took a while for her to find out where it was located and to figure out a reason for the visit. Gently bred young ladies, no matter what their age, didn't simply hare off to cemeteries for no reason.

To get out of the house, Cassie fabricated a cock and bull story about the famous adventurer Jonathan Lord who was buried in Bath's cemetery. When she asked Mary to accompany to her to the cemetery, Mary was hesitant at first, but Cassie embellished the story a bit. Shortly thereafter, the ladies were off on their stroll to the grave. No one would question the story if asked, even Aunt Honoria.

It seemed like they were walking forever, but finally they reached the stone arches of the cemetery and could hear the rushing of the river in the distance.

"Do you know where the grave is located, Miss Cassie?" Mary questioned, her eyes scanning the headstones.

Cassie frowned. *There must be hundreds of people buried here,* she thought, staring at the countless headstones. The cemetery ran along the bank of the river and was fairly devoid of trees. Except for one area in the west, where there was a small grove of trees.

"I really don't know exactly where to look," Cassie admitted, staring at the trees. That seemed to be a good starting point, since it was somewhat secluded and Mr. Lloyd had said the gold was twenty paces from a tree. So the grave was obviously somewhere near a tree, and there were only trees in one area of the cemetery. "Let's try over there," she said, pointing toward the trees.

Three quarters of an hour later, after looking at dozens upon dozens of headstones, Cassie and Mary stood in front of the headstone marked Jonathan Lord, born 1633, died 1690. It was an incredibly common grave, one that was like every other unattended grave at the cemetery. Cassie knew she would never have noticed it if she wasn't looking.

"Not much of a grave for an adventurer," Mary commented, glancing through the trees toward the entrance of the cemetery.

Cassie smiled. "I think his relatives wanted him to remain anonymous," she said and began to study the trees.

The passage said that the treasure would be in a hollow tree twenty paces due east of the grave. *Is that from the front of the grave or the back?* Cassie wondered, staring at the trees. And there were more than a few; the grave of Jonathan Lord was in some sort of small grove of trees devoid of all but a few graves. A grove that was very secluded and actually quite private. A perfect place to hide something, since one couldn't be seen from the road.

Cassie stared up at the sun. *Which way is east?* she wondered, as she stared at the sun then at the trees.

"Is everything all right, Miss Cassie?" Mary questioned.

"Yes, of course, Mary. I think I'm going to sit down under one of the trees for a moment, to rest," she

added, convinced that Mary must think her a huge
addlepate.

With her heart beating in anticipation, she stood at
the front of the grave, turned, and began walking into
the trees, counting off her steps. Mary tagged behind
silently, a look of confusion on her face.

Seventeen, eighteen, nineteen, twenty, Cassie counted
to herself and indeed found herself in front of a huge
tree of unknown lineage. This wasn't surprising, since
they were in a grove filled with trees.

The tree was large and sturdy and, as Cassie tried to
pretend she was looking for the best place to sit, she noticed it was hollow. Mr. Lloyd's book said that
something would be in a hollow tree.

Unfortunately, there was a problem. Cassie couldn't
simply reach into the hollow portion of the tree without
arousing Mary's curiosity. Although Mary was discreet,
she wasn't that discreet, and Cassie didn't want to answer any questions at all from her abigail. Then there
was the problem of getting the box home. Cassie was
sure they weren't being followed, and that they were
completely alone in the cemetery. But who wouldn't notice Cassie and her abigail lugging home a box of gold?
Surely that would cause endless speculation and might
even put them in danger.

Cassie did need to find out if there was a box in the
tree, though. Once again, she lied to Mary. "Would you
mind picking some wildflowers for Aunt Honoria while I
catch my breath?" she asked in her most congenial voice.

Mary wrinkled her brow once again but complied.
"Of course, Miss Cassie," she said and started toward
the other end of the grove of trees, her back to Cassie.

As soon as Mary was a discreet distance away, looking
for wildflowers, Cassie sprang into action. She stood up

on her tiptoes and thrust her slim arm into the hollow of the tree, willing herself not to squirm too much.

Thankfully, the inside of the tree was mostly dry, and Cassie tried not to think about the strange and unpleasant things that she felt. Her hand went through a dreadfully thick cobweb, she could feel some dirt, then more dirt, and some other things that felt quite nasty. That's when she almost screeched, but that would have attracted Mary's attention, so she kept reaching inside of the tree until she felt something that was metal. Like a box.

She could feel her heart beating wildly in her chest as she took her hand out of the tree and dusted it off on her gown. She would have to visit the cemetery alone to retrieve the box. She couldn't risk letting Mary—or anyone else, for that matter—see what she had found.

Dinner was uneventful. Cassie knew that she had to go back to the cemetery after dark. She didn't particularly want to go to the cemetery alone after dark, but it was the only way to safely retrieve Mr. Lloyd's metal box.

After dinner, she played cards with Daphne. Lady Honoria retired, then Daphne, then finally Cassie.

Cassie waited under her covers for the house to fall silent. One by one, she heard the servants retire until it appeared that everyone was asleep. It seemed to take hours.

Well after midnight, Cassie crept out of bed and opened the curtains to reveal the full moon. There wasn't a candle in the room, so looking through her portmanteau was quite the challenge. But it was something she had to do.

On a whim, Cassie had brought along one of her more unconventional items of clothing. In fact, it wasn't even her own. Deep down at the bottom of her belongings were a pair of breeches and a large white shirt. One of their stable boys had left suddenly, and Cassie found his clothes stashed in the back of the stable. Fortunately, they fit, and Cassie decided that they might come in handy some day.

Today, or rather tonight, was that night. As she slipped on the breeches, she hoped upon hope that no one would notice her on the street that night. As far as she knew, there wasn't an Assembly going on, so she thought the streets would be fairly deserted. She hoped they would be.

Bath was silent as Cassie made her way through the streets to the darkness of the cemetery. She cursed every Minerva Press novel she had read, and almost jumped out of her skin when she heard an owl hoot. Cassie wasn't precisely afraid to be in the cemetery alone at night, but even with the full moon, it seemed to be dreadfully dark, and it was as quiet as . . . well, death.

To make matters worse, everything looked different at night. Cassie was sure she wouldn't have any problem locating the grave. She was wrong, and it took forever for her to find the headstone. Actually, it was less than three quarters of an hour before she found the grave of Jonathan Lord. And the tree with the box inside.

It took all of Cassie's courage to plunge her hand back into the tree, since she wasn't too pleased at what she had felt that day. She was convinced that the hollow tree was filled with worms and bugs, and the fact that it was the middle of the night made her even more squeamish. But there was no other way, so she plunged her hand in; tried not to think about the squishy, crunchy, and moist things that her hand was feeling; and instead tried to get the box out as quickly as possible.

After some intricate pulling and jimmying, Cassie managed to get the small metal box out of the hollow of the tree. As the moonlight streamed down on her, she stared at the dirt-laden box, wondering what was inside. *It's not heavy enough to be gold,* she reasoned, as she slipped it under her shirt, glancing around the cemetery. She was alone.

Cassie walked briskly through the cemetery, and breathed a sigh of relief as she got back onto the main street. She half expected some wayward young buck to appear on his horse and harass her, but the streets were silent. So silent, in fact, that Cassie was convinced that she was the only person in the whole city who was actually awake.

Her heart was still racing when she got back to her bedroom and slipped back into her nightgown as if she had never left. The stable boy's clothes were hidden back in her portmanteau, and she was ready to open the box and uncover Mr. Lloyd's secrets.

As she sat on the bed with the box in her lap, engulfed in moonlight, she wondered what would be inside. Money? Perhaps. Money was always a welcome gift. She felt guilty about trespassing on Aunt Honoria's goodwill and wished she had some of her own pin money. A box full of money would be quite nice.

She opened the lid carefully and peered inside, her heart beating rapidly. Cassie was sure that Mr. Lloyd wanted her to have the box—if he hadn't wanted her to find the box, he never would have made sure that she found his book. And she was sure he wanted her to find the book.

Inside the box were papers, a thick stack of papers wrapped with a piece of twine. Cassie sighed. There was nothing inside that would transform her life. Just papers. She squinted at them in the moonlight. Mr. Lloyd's carefully hidden papers appeared to be nothing but random names of places, dates, and numbers, all written, once again, in Greek.

She sighed and wrapped the papers back up. *They have to be something important,* she reasoned, *or else Mr. Lloyd never would have hidden them.*

Cassie scanned the room, looking for a suitable hiding place. The portmanteau, where she was hiding the book, was too obvious. This needed to be an exceptional hiding place, a hiding place where no one would think to look.

Her eyes fell on Aunt Honoria's thick maroon drapes. At the bottom, there was a seam that had come open. Cassie padded over to the drapes and kneeled down to examine them. If she ripped the seam a bit more, she could fit the papers inside the drapes and they'd be virtually invisible. So she tugged at the seam. It gave way, and she slipped the papers inside. *No one will find them there,* she decided as she crawled back into bed.

Stanton paced Honoria's parlor floor nervously. Generally speaking, he wasn't prone to having fits of nerves, but Derek was acting deuced odd lately, and he was sure that the request from Honoria to join him for tea was to discuss his son.

He had no idea what to do with Derek. He wasn't a bad son, but Derek was certainly acting irresponsibly lately. First haring around Bath on some sort of mission for Castlereagh that Derek thought he didn't know about, then molesting the very charming and very eligible Miss Wyndmoore, which was totally uncalled for, since anyone could see that Miss Wyndmoore was nothing like her sisters and was indeed quite respectable.

Stanton was staring out the window, wondering how he could explain his son's scapegrace behavior, when he heard the door open.

Honoria looked the way he always remembered her, vibrant and smiling and absolutely lovely. Her hazel eyes sparkled, and when she walked into a room, she was always the most beautiful woman. At least in his eyes.

"Good afternoon, Hugh," Honoria said, beaming like a ray of sunshine.

Stanton couldn't help but smile. When he was with her, it was as if the years just disappeared. "You look as ravishing as ever, Honoria," he said, lightly kissing her hand, his eyes lingering over her chestnut morning dress.

They sat down next to each other in two of Honoria's most comfortable Chippendale chairs near the window. "Millie will be bringing in tea shortly," Honoria said calmly. "But this isn't purely a social call. I asked you to come by to discuss your son Derek."

A look of worry crossed Stanton's face. What else had Derek done? Had he omitted telling him about another horrid transgression? He studied Honoria. She looked serious. This was not good news, he decided. "Yes?"

"After Cassandra's drive with your son, she came back very out of sorts, which isn't like Cassandra. When I questioned her about it, she had very little to say, except that Lord Richmond isn't interested in her friendship. Do you know what happened?"

At that moment, Millie appeared with the tea and some

pastries. Honoria poured for both of them and patiently awaited Stanton's reply.

He nibbled on a pastry, wondering what exactly he should tell Honoria. Millie departed, and Stanton decided on the truth. "Truth be told, Derek committed several transgressions."

"Really."

He sighed. "Unfortunately. First, he offended Cassandra by not remembering her at all. From what your Cassandra says, they met several times and conversed at length while he was courting Pandora. He doesn't recall her at all."

"Oh my. And he wasn't . . . bright enough to gloss over the omission?" she said with a raised eyebrow.

Stanton winced. "No. Then there's the fact that Cassandra apparently walked in on Derek and Pandora while they were having a . . . romantic encounter."

Honoria sipped her tea. "That's regrettable. So Cassandra thinks he's a rake with low morals."

Stanton looked out the window. He looked at the floor. He looked at Honoria's odd furniture. He looked everywhere but at Honoria. "Unfortunately, there's more. While they were out driving, Derek rather lost his head and . . . well . . . kissed your niece. She was horribly offended and appeared to misunderstand his intentions," he said quickly, glad to get that bit of information out into the open.

Honoria had no trouble gazing at him. "What exactly were his intentions? Is your son planning to seduce my Cassandra? I won't allow that. Pandora might have been a bit on the wild side, but Cassandra is not. I won't tolerate anyone, not even your son, treating her like a light skirt," she declared.

A slight blush crept into Stanton's cheeks, and he

nervously tugged at his cravat. "I spoke to Derek about his behavior, and he is sending her a letter of apology, which should arrive today. I don't think he means to seduce her, and I certainly won't allow him to treat her like a doxy," he added for good measure. Of course, he knew he had no actual control over the way Derek treated his female companions, but the words sounded good.

"If your son doesn't mean to seduce her, then his intentions are honorable, and it's obvious that Cassandra isn't particularly eligible. If he's looking to set up his nursery, he'd be wiser to look at Daphne. She's young, malleable, and would never voice an opinion on your son's lifestyle," she said in a cutting voice.

Stanton groaned inwardly. Honoria was convinced that Derek was a rake and a seducer. He was certain that outside of the horrid incident with Pandora, Derek always behaved properly and wasn't rakish at all. Even if he was a rake, he certainly knew Derek's attitude regarding women like Daphne. "The beauty? Daphne? I think not. Derek might be acting . . . inconsistently lately, but she's a simpering fool and would drive him mad in a sennight. Your Cassandra would be a much better choice for him. He's really not a rake at all, and is simply guilty of a lapse of judgment."

Honoria studied him carefully, and he squirmed a bit in the chair. "Are you insinuating that your son was overtaken by Cassandra's beauty?"

"Perhaps. She really is quite lovely and very charming. In fact, she's very much like you," he added with a mischievous grin.

He finally coaxed a smile out of Honoria. "I don't want him toying with her."

Stanton relaxed slightly in his chair. She was smiling

at him again. That was a good sign. "I'll make sure he behaves himself. Do you think a picnic might be in order?" he asked, leaning forward a bit. A picnic would be a good place for Derek to get to know Cassandra, and he was certain that Cassandra was the perfect woman for his son. Plus, it would give him a prime opportunity to continue his attentions toward Honoria.

She smiled again. "That sounds like a charming idea. I do so enjoy picnics."

He grinned. "I remember. And perhaps, if everything falls into place, there might be an engagement to announce in the coming months."

Of course, he never explained whose engagement he had in mind.

Cassie stared at the missive in her hand in utter confusion. Lord Richmond had sent her a very prettily worded apology and was practically begging her forgiveness for his rash actions.

When he was involved with Pandora, they'd had disagreements. He'd never sent Pandora an apology. Ever. Cassie knew this because Pandora was always harping to her about it, certain that Richmond was too stubborn and arrogant to apologize. Now it was several years later and Cassie had a letter of apology in her hands. A letter that her very desirable and charming older sister never received.

Why was he bothering to apologize? It made no sense. *I'm not Pandora Wyndmoore, the toast of London,* Cassie reasoned. *I'm not even Daphne Wyndmoore, the beauty of Warwick. I'm a drab spinster. Why is he even bothering?*

There was only one possible explanation. He was a spy. For the French. And he wanted the papers that had

been in the box in the tree. The papers that she still
hadn't translated since there was always someone underfoot. If it wasn't Mary, it was Sara or Daphne.

If Richmond was after the papers, he needed to be in
her good graces. He couldn't get any information from
her if she wasn't speaking to him.

It was the only logical explanation.

Daphne sighed slightly. Once again, she was beating
Cassie in a game of cards. Cassie was ever so bright, but
she had no luck at cards, Daphne mused. She played her
next card and glanced over at Aunt Honoria.

It had been ages since Daphne had been out of the
house on a social call. She wasn't even allowed to be
present when callers showed up to visit with Aunt
Honoria. It was most vexing, and Daphne was actually
trying to improve her behavior so she could at least
leave the house and stop reading the Bible, which had
to be the most preachy book she ever read.

"Are you girls interested in an outing?" Honoria said,
looking up from the pencil drawing on her lap.

"An outing? Will I be allowed to attend, Aunt Honoria?" Daphne asked eagerly, losing all interest in the
card game.

Honoria smiled at her. "Yes, I think so, Daphne. Your
behavior has improved vastly, so you can come along.
We'll be attending a picnic on Wednesday. It's all been
arranged," she explained.

"A picnic? Where?" Daphne asked eagerly. *If Aunt
Honoria will tell me where the picnic is, I can secretly
invite Lord Pembrook,* she reasoned.

"I know a wonderful spot near the river. It will be a
nice change for all of us," Honoria replied.

Daphne frowned. Near the river wasn't a specific answer. "You mean the river near Madame Babette's?"

"No, on the other side of town, closer to the blacksmith," Honoria replied.

Daphne smiled. She could simply write Percival a note, explaining that she had been indisposed for several days and then hint that he'd be welcome at their picnic. They'd run into him accidentally. Once she saw Pembrook, she'd be able to get their courtship back on track.

If things go well, maybe I'll be Lady Pembrook before I return to Warwick, Daphne thought with a smile, directing her attention back to the card game.

Cassie sat alone in her bedroom, a lone candle flickering on her nightstand. Once again, her heart was racing.

She finished translating the first page of the papers in the box, and she was as white as the sheets on the bed. It was numbers. Numbers of French troops. Where they were moving. When they would arrive there to fight the English. As she leafed through the somewhat crumpled papers, she realized that they were the French troop movements for the next three months. At least that's what they looked like to Cassie after she translated them.

Cassie stared at the papers in disbelief. Mr. Lloyd, who may or may not have been murdered, was a spy. He had in his possession troop movements that were of critical knowledge to the English government. How he got this information and why he was in Bath, of all places, was a mystery. However, he did have the information, and Cassie was certain that he had wanted her to find it. She had been reading a book in Greek that afternoon in the park, so Mr. Lloyd knew she could read the language.

What am I supposed to do with this? Cassie wondered with a frown. To whom should she send the documents? She couldn't simply show up in London and hope she located the right person. She was a female, and government officials didn't ever seem to be interested in talking to females. Even females bearing top-secret documents.

The post was also out of the question. Pembrook and Richmond could have agents posted there, and if she sent something to an official-sounding address in London, it could be intercepted. Consequently, that wasn't the best plan of action.

Why didn't he tell me what to do with the papers? Cassie wondered, as she folded them up and put them back in their hiding place in the fold of the drapes. *He told me everything else. What should I do with them now?*

She fell back onto the bed and began leafing through her translations of Mr. Lloyd's stories. As she read each one of them again, her answer came in 'The Wolf and the Donkey.' It was like every other version of the story, except in Mr. Lloyd's version, the donkey goes to Ree Castle and meets a tall blond man.

Cassie stared at the page. *I can't believe I didn't notice it the first time,* she thought with chagrin. Ree Castle. Or Castlereagh, the Foreign Secretary. All Cassie had to do the next day was find out if Castlereagh was indeed a tall, blond man, a fact Aunt Honoria would be certain to know.

Honoria attacked her rasher of bacon with relish. True, it was sometimes annoying to have a house full of guests, but it did stimulate the appetite.

Daphne still hadn't made her morning appearance, but Cassie sat across the table from her, looking tired and rather preoccupied. "Is anything wrong, Cassandra?" Honoria asked, her voice laced with concern.

Cassie managed a wan smile. "Not really. I was wondering, you keep up on the gossip out of London, don't you?" she asked, once again pushing the food around on her plate with disinterest.

"To some extent. Why?"

"I was reading something the other day that was referring to a tall blond, man in government, but they didn't give his name. Do you know who that could be?" Cassie asked.

Honoria chewed on a piece of bacon thoughtfully. "Blond, tall? That would probably be Castlereagh, the Foreign Secretary."

"Oh," replied Cassie, picking at her kippers. "What time does the post go out, Aunt Honoria?" she asked, suddenly changing the topic

Honoria gazed at Cassie with a frown. *Why is she asking about Castlereagh? That's a deuced odd question. And now the post? Is something amiss?* "In the late afternoon. Why?"

Cassie smiled brightly, the first smile she had given all morning. "Well, I have an awfully long letter to Papa I'd like to send out today. Would you frank it for me?"

"Of course, my dear," Honoria replied, not entirely convinced that all was right in the world.

"Thank you so much, Aunt Honoria," Cassie said, and looked as if a lead weight had been lifted off her shoulders.

* * *

Cassie reread the letter she had written to her Papa.

Dear Papa:
    Enclosed is some paperwork I accidentally found while I was in Bath. I know this sounds incredible, Papa, but it must be hand delivered to Viscount Castlereagh, the Foreign Secretary, right away. The papers are of a very sensitive nature, and once you read them, you'll understand why they must be taken to London immediately. Thank you so much for your help, Papa. I'll write again soon.

Cassie signed her name with a flourish and sighed. Her part of this whole mess was over. *Papa will be able to get them to London, and everything will be all right,* she reasoned.

Unless the letter never got to him.

Chapter 10

"Cassie, you can ride along with Lord Richmond in his phaeton," Aunt Honoria declared, as Cassie winced.

She knows I don't want to be alone with Lord Richmond, Cassie thought, trying to avoid Aunt Honoria's eyes. "Daphne hasn't been in his phaeton yet. Perhaps she'd enjoy a ride," Cassie said in desperation.

"Daphne is too young to drive alone with Richmond," Aunt Honoria replied, as if Daphne and Richmond weren't both standing in front of her.

"But, Aunt Honoria, I'd like to . . ." Daphne said and then abruptly changed her mind and said nothing.

Honoria smiled benignly at Daphne and then turned to Cassandra. "Then it's settled. You'll drive with Lord Richmond while we drive with Lord Stanton," she declared.

Cassie sighed. It wouldn't have been so bad but once again, Lord Richmond looked so . . . handsome in a swarthy, non-English kind of way. Today he had on a pair of buckskin breeches, polished Hessians that gleamed in the afternoon sun, and a dark blue waistcoat that fit his figure to perfection. His hair was tousled, as usual, and he seemed to be trying to be cordial to her.

As Aunt Honoria, Daphne, and Lord Stanton headed off, Cassie sat silently in Richmond's phaeton, staring at the flanks of his horses. Cassie knew something about horseflesh, and they were lovely animals. Nevertheless, she didn't want to say anything lest she encourage him to start speaking about their last . . . encounter.

They trotted along in silence for a while, until Richmond casually remarked, "Are you going to speak to me, Miss Wyndmoore, or are you going to make me feel like a heel all day?"

Cassie sighed and looked out at the road. The weather was delightful, and there were beautiful wildflowers springing up everywhere, it seemed. The road through town wasn't particularly busy, and everyone she noticed looked quite happy and contented. She wasn't happy and contented. She was being forced to go on a picnic with a rake who had tried to seduce her for government information. A rake who was possibly a French spy. Finally, Cassie sighed. "I suppose I'll have to speak with you or I'll receive a scolding from Aunt Honoria, and I do hate to disappoint her, since she is one of the only relations who even notices me," she finished candidly.

Richmond smiled at her. Cassie looked at the road and never noticed. "That can't be true. You're the most charming female in your family."

He's trying it again, she thought, feeling quite agitated. *He's going to spend the entire picnic trying to seduce me to get Mr. Lloyd's information. Well, I won't have it!* "My Lord, let's call a truce. If you don't give me any Spanish coin, I won't spend the entire picnic pouting and ignoring you," she said in her calmest voice.

"I wasn't giving you Spanish coin, but I'll honor your truce. If you start to pout and ignore me, I'll be forced to spend the afternoon listening to your sister, which indeed is a fate worse than death," he said a bit melodramatically, and then smiled.

Cassie peeked over at him and back. *Gads, he can*

be charming when he wants to be! "Daphne isn't so bad. All you have to do is just pretend to listen to her. I've been doing it since she was born."

"Then you must have the patience of a saint," he commented.

Cassie grinned. "Ah yes, Saint Cassie the Deaf," she said and was rewarded by a chuckle from Richmond. It was so easy to forget that he was a spy. And a rake. And someone who was just trying to use her.

Daphne looked around nervously as they spread out the blue plaid blankets and the bulging wicker picnic baskets. Aunt Honoria, looking quite attractive in a hunter green walking dress, was talking quietly with Lord Stanton. Lord Stanton was in the most cordial of moods, and Daphne was certain that Lord Stanton had fixed his interest on her aunt. As Daphne studied her Aunt and Lord Stanton, she decided that Aunt Honoria wasn't immune to his charms. She blushed delicately every now and again, and even went so far as to giggle and hit him gently with her fan. Daphne had never seen Aunt Honoria giggle, so she was certain that she was developing a *tendre* for Lord Stanton.

Daphne then glanced over toward Cassie. Richmond was trailing behind her sister like a puppy, and Cassie appeared to be completely ignoring him. This made no sense at all to Daphne, since Richmond was quite the eligible *parti,* while Cassie, well, wasn't eligible at all.

Daphne craned her neck to look down the dusty road. Pembrook knew where they were having their outing, and should have arrived by now. Yet he wasn't there, which annoyed Daphne considerably. If he didn't arrive at their little party, he was definitely going to be in Daphne's black book.

A dirty, sobbing young boy carrying a wilted bouquet of flowers walked up to Lady Raverston's front door and knocked. Laughton appeared in all of his stately glory and talked with the boy for a few moments; the boy wailed even louder, gesturing to his leg. Laughton let the bedraggled urchin into the house and closed the front door.

"Did you enjoy your time in France?" Cassie asked Richmond distractedly, watching Lord Stanton and Aunt Honoria from the corner of her eye. They smiled at each other, and every now and again, Lord Stanton leaned over and put his hand on Aunt Honoria's knee. *If I'm not mistaken, Lord Stanton has a* tendre *for Aunt Honoria,* Cassie mused.

"I spent almost every summer of my childhood there," Richmond replied, sampling the cold chicken in front of them.

"Do you have relations there?" she asked, staring at his blue-black hair. *Proper Englishmen never have such incredibly luxurious hair. It must be his French blood*, she thought.

"Yes, my grandparents still live in the country outside of Marseilles. I see them quite often, as well as my various assorted aunts, uncles, and cousins. I think you'd like it, " he added.

A million questions ran through Cassie's head. She wanted to ask him how he could travel to France while the two countries were at war. She wanted to ask him if his relations were safe from the fighting. She wanted to know the last time he was there. She wanted to know if he sympathized with Boney.

Unfortunately, she couldn't ask him any of those questions. Then he would know that she knew he was a spy. A spy for the French. So instead, she picked up a chicken leg and nibbled on it delicately.

"Do you see your relations much?" he said amiably.

"I suppose we see enough of them. Once Daphne is out, I expect she'll be spending more time with Pandora. We see most of our relations during the holidays, which is nice," Cassie said blandly.

"You don't see Lady Lyntwoode often?"

Cassie raised an eyebrow. *Goodness, he's still not over Pandora,* she thought. *In fact, if I say the wrong thing, he's going to spend the entire afternoon asking about her.* "We're not particularly close," Cassie finally answered.

Richmond finished his piece of chicken and wiped his hands on a crisp white napkin. "I'm not surprised. I would think that Lady Lyntwoode would be . . . taxing for someone of your temperament."

Cassie raised an eyebrow and looked over at him. Was he being insulting? "I beg your pardon?" she said, in a slightly haughty tone.

She was shocked to find a hint of pink staining his rugged, suntanned cheeks.

"I'm terribly sorry, Miss Wyndmoore. What I meant to say was that Pandora, Lady Lyntwoode, seems to be rather . . . superficial and only concerned with gossip and fashions, and it doesn't seem to me that you'd have much in common with her," he said, almost stuttering.

Cassie smiled slightly. "How little you know me, Lord Richmond. I rode in closed carriage from Warwick with Daphne, who spent the entire time talking about gossip and fashions."

He raised his glass of port. "Then I salute you, Miss Wyndmoore, for that's more than I could have tolerated."

"It wasn't so bad," Cassie added.

The conversation came to a standstill, until Richmond broke the silence. "So tell me, Miss Wyndmoore, what are your plans for the future?"

Cassie looked over at him as if he had run mad. "My plans? What do you mean?"

"Well, it would appear that Daphne means to marry, and I imagine that Lady Lyntwoode will eventually have a child. What are your plans?" he asked.

Cassie stared into the distance. It was very curious that Richmond should ask her about her future plans. No one was ever interested in the plans of a spinster. "I don't have any particular plans, Lord Richmond."

"What will you do when Daphne marries? Will you stay at home with your parents?"

"I don't know," she answered candidly.

"And when your parents are gone, what will you do? Where will you live? The future isn't so far away, Miss Wyndmoore, and things can be difficult for an unmarried lady," he observed.

Cassie was suddenly uncomfortable. No one, outside of her father and Aunt Honoria, ever asked about her plans. It was very disconcerting. "I know your plans," she announced, trying to divert the conversation.

"Oh, really?"

"Yes. You'll take your place in Parliament, have a brilliant career, and spend the holidays in the North country with your family."

Richmond's mouth dropped open in shock. "How did you know that?"

Cassie smiled. "You told Pandora. Pandora told me. She used to talk to me about her suitors quite frequently," she admitted.

Richmond seemed to digest that information. There was another long pause before he commented, "You still didn't tell me what you want, Miss Wyndmoore."

Once again, she smiled. "I think that some day I'd like a home like Aunt Honoria's. It's not too small, not too large, it's not drafty, and the rooms are very cozy."

Before Richmond could reply, Daphne walked over and sat down next to Cassie on the blanket. Once again, she looked lovely in a peach walking dress that was adorned with tiny embroidered flowers. "I thought we might run into Lord Pembrook today," she said, her bottom lip jutting out in a pout.

Cassie frowned. "Lord Pembrook? Why?"

"Oh, when I was speaking to him, he mentioned that he often drives by this area during the day. I thought he might stop by," Daphne said, craning her neck to see if Pembrook was anywhere in the vicinity.

Richmond frowned at her as well, but said nothing.

That's when Cassie realized there was another option. Perhaps Pembrook and Richmond were both French spies, working in tandem to increase their odds. However, with the sun shining in his face and his hair glistening, Cassie realized that she didn't want Richmond to be a spy. In fact, she wanted him to be her suitor in earnest.

She knew that would never happen.

Richmond was very adept at playing the suitor. If Cassie hadn't known any better, she would have been convinced he was sincerely interested in her after their drive home. He was attentive, he was interested in her, and she was sure it was all a lie.

So she retreated to her bedroom, only to find the door closed. This was odd, because she always left it open.

She walked into the room and stopped. The contents of every single drawer in the room had been emptied onto the bed. Her clothes were strewn everywhere, her portmanteau was on its side and its contents were thrown across the floor. The mattress was even on the floor.

"Laughton!" she called, hoping to rouse the butler. He appeared at her side almost instantly. "What happened?" Cassie said, gesturing to the room.

"Someone has obviously been in your room," he said in a strangely comforting, level voice. "If you'll return downstairs with me, Miss Cassandra, I'll inform Lady Raverston and she'll decide what is to be done," he said gravely.

"My clothes, my papers, everything's been gone through," Cassie murmured as she followed Laughton downstairs.

They entered Aunt Honoria's study, Cassie blindly following Laughton in a fog. He closed the door firmly behind him, walked over to a cabinet, and brought out a bottle of claret. He poured the dark liquid into a sparkling crystal glass that appeared out of nowhere and handed it to her. "Drink this," Laughton ordered, and she gulped it down quickly. "I'll let Lady Raverston know what's happened," he said and strode out of the room.

Cassie held her hand out in front of her. It was shaking. *It's the book,* she thought wildly. *They broke into my bedroom to get the book. Richmond must have told them that we were going to be away for the day and that's when they made their move.*

It was all so unreal. A stranger had been in her room, touching her things, while Richmond charmed her with his amusing anecdotes. It was the perfect plan, and Cassie was sure the book was gone.

If they don't read Greek, it might buy us some time, Cassie thought wildly. *In addition, maybe they won't be able to figure out the code. Maybe they won't even think of going to the cemetery.*

She didn't even want to think about what would happen if they went to the cemetery and found the box was gone.

Richmond sat alone in his study, a lone candle casting eerie shadows on his angular features.

I've been making a mull of things, he mused, sipping his port. The first time he had met Cassandra, he had thought she was guileless and charming. Then he learned she was a Wyndmoore, so he'd assumed she was a doxy and tried to seduce her. *Perhaps I was right the first time,* he assured himself. *Perhaps she is genuinely guileless and charming.*

Then there was the issue of Lloyd's book. Cassie knew that he knew that she had it. She obviously didn't trust him enough to give it to him. And he didn't blame her. However, he certainly couldn't tell her that he worked for the English government as a covert agent. So now he had the added problem of trying to get the book from her when, in fact, she wasn't going to part with it. The most he could do was suggest that she send it to Castlereagh, but that was a risky plan. Richmond was sure that Pembrook had men at the post, and that anything going to Castlereagh from Bath wouldn't make it out of the city.

He sighed and stared out the window into the blue-black night sky. The picnic had gone so well. Cassie was amusing and relaxing and the most congenial companion. She never talked about her clothes or fashions or even gossiped that much. Instead, they'd talked about books, politics, and their families. She was the complete opposite of Pandora, which was everything he wanted in a female—except that she didn't trust him. This was a problem. He was certain that she wasn't even aware that he was interested in her, which was a novel concept to him, since Richmond was quite sought after on the Marriage Mart. Yet here he was, showering his attentions on an untitled spinster, and she was completely unaware of what was happening. Truth be told, he had been somewhat unaware that it was happening himself. One moment, he was trying to find out information about Mr. Lloyd's book. The next he was laughing at her stories about life in Warwick. She enchanted him and suddenly his assignment wasn't his major concern.

He drained his port and decided that he needed to write a letter. A letter to Castlereagh that explained he was at an impasse. He knew Cassie had the book, and as long as she had the book, he knew Pembrook didn't. He could ask Lady Raverston for the book, but he was certain that she was unaware that Cassie had it in her possession. He could ask Daphne, but he was terribly certain that Cassie wouldn't confide in her.

He stood up, took the candle in hand and walked over to the escritoire. It was time to write Castlereagh and apprise him of the situation.

"And you've looked through all of your belongings, miss? And that's the only thing missing?" the graying, overweight magistrate with the pockmarked skin asked, writing something down in a small book in his hand.

"Yes sir, only the book in Greek. I'm not certain, but I think it might have belonged to Mr. Lloyd, the gentleman who died," Cassie said with a sigh. It was terribly unsettling to have a stranger go through all of one's possessions, and she was still a bit frazzled.

Frazzled, but lucky. The book was gone, but the thief left all of her notes—her translations of Mr. Lloyd's versions of the Aesop stories. *I'm glad I put them with my letters to Papa,* Cassie thought. *I don't even want to consider what would have happened if they had found my notes and realized the box was gone.*

"Your jewelry wasn't touched?" he asked for the third time.

"No sir. Just the book," she said wearily.

"Why would someone break into a home in the middle of the day and ransack just one room? What was in the book?" he asked with a frown.

Cassie lied. "It was a book of children's stories in Greek," she replied simply. It wasn't a full lie, only a half lie.

"Is there anyone you might suspect, miss?" he asked automatically, and the expression on his face told Cassie that he was certain she had no idea who might have done this.

"Yes. Yes, there is," she said firmly.

His furry gray eyebrows disappeared into his hairline. "There is?" he asked in amazement. "Who?"

Cassie took a deep breath. "Lord Richmond and Lord Pembrook have both been curious about this specific book, and I think one of them broke in, or had someone break in, to get it."

The magistrate snapped the book shut and chuckled

slightly. "Miss, you have a rich imagination. A swell like Lord Richmond or Lord Pembrook breaking into a house for a children's book! What folly!" he exclaimed as he walked out the door.

Cassie sat alone in the study, engulfed in a feeling of doom. Whoever took the book was going to end up in the cemetery. When they got there, they would know that she had the box. Then they would come to find her.

Cassie knew she couldn't confide in Aunt Honoria. She was great friends with Lord Stanton, and would never believe that his son was working for the French. As for Pembrook, Cassie knew that while Lady Honoria didn't care for his company, she would be hard pressed to convince her aunt that he was a spy for Boney. As Cassie thought about the situation, it seemed dashed unbelievable to her.

In the end, Cassie could only think up one logical course of action: try to leave Bath earlier than expected. And hope that they didn't look in the tree in the cemetery.

"Aunt Honoria, how wonderful it is to see you," Pandora Wyndmoore, now Lady Lyntwoode, cooed as she hovered around Honoria's chair in the parlor.

Honoria gaped at her niece. Pandora was, of course, as beautiful as ever, her long blond hair coaxed into perfect ringlets, and her blue eyes sparkling like the afternoon sky. Her hourglass figure was fitted into a beaded baby blue gown that displayed too much bosom for the afternoon, or for traveling, and Honoria shuddered at the thought of her niece in even more revealing evening gowns. "My, what a surprise," Honoria finally managed to say, staring at the bevy of trunks that surrounded Pandora. "What brings you to Bath?"

Pandora giggled, an almost musical giggle that Honoria was sure drove men mad with desire. "Why, my favorite aunt, of course!" she said with a smile.

Honoria frowned. Why in the world would Pandora show up on her doorstep? She knew very well that she wasn't Pandora's favorite relative. In fact, she was certain that Pandora didn't care a fig about her. So why was she here? "Are you planning on staying in Bath?" Honoria inquired, all too certain that Pandora would be staying at her house for an extended period and that there was nothing she could do about it.

"Why yes, Aunt Honoria! I've been so bored at home, and, well, Giles, you know he hardly pays any attention at all to me, and when I heard Daphne was here with you, I just couldn't stay away," Pandora replied breathlessly, winding a curl around her middle finger.

"Why didn't you write first?"

"And spoil the surprise? That wouldn't be any fun at all! And I so wanted to spend some time with my little sister Daphne."

Honoria frowned. *If I had wanted Pandora here, I would have invited her,* she fumed. Now her niece was here and propriety proclaimed that Honoria had to be her host. However, she didn't have to make things easy for Pandora. "Well, then, how lovely. You know Cassandra is here as well?" she asked coldly.

"Cassandra? Oh, I don't think I'll be seeing much of her. I'm sure she'll be busy working on your household accounts or ministering to the sick or sitting alone in the parlor reading. That's all our little mouse seems to do."

That answer caused Honoria to furrow her brows even more. The arrival of Pandora was not a good sign, especially with Richmond showing a marked interest in Cassandra. "How long do you plan on staying?"

"I don't really know. I do want to spend some time with Daphne, she's at that . . . difficult age and needs someone with more . . . maturity to guide her," Pandora replied airily.

Honoria could feel her teeth grinding. "I'll have to make arrangements for a room for you. Until then, why don't you go upstairs and say hello to Daphne? Her room is the first door at the top of the stairs. I'm sure she'll be in alt that you've arrived," Honoria declared, a hint of sarcasm in her voice.

"Yes, that would be lovely. And have your girl see my abigail. I'll need my clothes out before dinner so I can change," Pandora ordered before she glided out of the room.

Honoria was not pleased. She could have put Pandora in the room that Cassie had abandoned since she was so unnerved by the robbery. She decided on a more fitting plan. She was going to put Pandora in the smallest bedroom upstairs, and she was going to make sure her staff took their time in getting her settled in.

Honoria was obligated to be her host, but she wasn't obligated to be happy or particularly cooperative.

I'm invisible again, Cassie thought, chewing reflectively on a bit of roast pigeon. It was dinner, and Pandora and Daphne were in a spirited conversation that, as usual, didn't include her. *If only I could go home,* she mused. *Now that Pandora is here, I know Aunt Honoria won't let me leave. She doesn't want to be alone with Pandora and Daphne.*

Cassie sighed and continued to eat, ignoring the rest of the table, until she heard a very telling comment.

"Really? Cassie went out driving with Richmond? How extraordinary," Pandora said, in an incredulous voice, as if the idea of Cassie being seen in public with Richmond bordered on the unnatural.

"Yes, they did, and had a wonderful time," Honoria replied.

Cassie cringed. *They're talking about me as if I'm not here,* she thought, ready to break into the conversation with a sarcastic comment.

"Really?" Pandora said in the same astonished voice.

"Oh yes. He genuinely seems to enjoy her company," Honoria replied, and once again, Cassie cringed.

"Actually Aunt Honoria, I'm sure he was just being polite," Cassie interjected, hoping upon hope to put this conversational topic to an end.

"Well, of course he was, silly," Pandora said in a soothing voice. "Derek always had impeccable manners, and I'm sure the only reason he's spending any time with you is because of the connection we had."

"Pandora, I really . . ." Honoria began and then drifted off.

Cassie decided that now was the time to change the course of their chat. "Daphne, have you told Pandora about Lord Pembrook?" she asked, hoping upon hope that Daphne would go into some sort of lecture on the virtues of Lord Pembrook.

As if on cue, Daphne began rattling on about Lord Pembrook, and Pandora hung on her every word. Thankfully, Richmond was forgotten and Cassie didn't have to be reminded again that he wasn't interested in her.

She already knew that, and it was breaking her heart.

Now Pandora was in town, and Cassie was certain that a visit with Aunt Honoria wasn't the reason Pandora had appeared. Cassie was certain that the real reason was Richmond.

"Your house was robbed?" Stanton said incredulously as he sipped his cup of tea.

Honoria delicately nibbled a scone, her gray, high-necked walking dress reflecting her mood perfectly: gray and somber. It was nice to have Stanton around to discuss the incident, even though he had called at the dreadfully early hour of eleven in the morning. "Well, not precisely. Someone entered the house while we were at the picnic and searched Cassie's room. All of her jewelry and pin money was scattered around the room, which I found odd. And the only thing they did take was a small book written in Greek that Cassie had found in the park," Honoria explained.

"What did the authorities say?" he asked in a very serious tone.

Honoria sighed. Stanton looked so handsome in his buff colored breeches, and when he frowned, he looked so . . . formidable. "Well, they came to the conclusion that a young urchin with an injured leg who was delivering flowers to Daphne was the distraction that allowed the intruder to enter the house. They think that it was an isolated incident and that we won't be bothered again," Honoria concluded.

"Didn't they find the whole incident rather odd?" Stanton asked curiously.

"Well, I suppose they did, but since no one was injured and nothing of value was missing, it didn't seem to concern them overly," Honoria admitted.

"And the book? Why was it the only thing taken?"

Honoria shrugged. "I really have no idea. Cassie said she thought that it had belonged to Mr. Lloyd, the poor gent who died. She even went as far as to suggest that Pembrook might have taken it. That girl and her imagination."

They sipped their tea in silence for a while, until Honoria decided it was time to tell him the other news. "Pandora arrived yesterday."

Stanton started coughing violently. "Pandora is here? Why on earth is she in Bath?"

"Oh yes. From what I can ascertain, I believe that Daphne wrote Pandora some sort of missive beseeching Pandora to come and save her from my evil clutches."

"Your evil clutches?" Stanton said with a slight smile.

"Ah, yes. When Daphne misbehaves, I punish her, which is a new concept to Daphne. Hopefully Pandora will misbehave and I'll be able to send her home to her husband."

"Am I to assume that marriage hasn't settled Pandora?" Stanton asked curiously.

Honoria sipped her tea. "Pandora will never settle down, and there's every chance that Daphne will soon follow her footsteps. Thank goodness Cassie isn't like that."

They sipped their tea in silence for a few moments, until Honoria decided she needed to confront Stanton about her other . . . misgiving. "There's something else I need to clarify with you, Hugh."

The lines on his forehead became deeper. "What?"

"I don't know why, but Cassandra seems to think that your son engineered the theft of her book."

"Why?" he asked incredulously.

Honoria shrugged. "I don't really know. The magistrate informed me that Cassie was convinced that the book was stolen by either your son or Lord Pembrook, since both have been making inquiries about it. I've also heard gossip that he's a spy for the French."

Hugh slumped in his chair. "Please believe me, Honoria, Derek is as respectable as the next swell, and I certainly don't believe he'd be involved in a robbery. And he's certainly not a spy for the French."

Honoria melted as she gazed into his eyes. "I just wanted things to be out in the open, Hugh," she said softly.

"And now they are," he said, gazing back at her with a look that proclaimed he was utterly smitten with her.

At least, Honoria thought it was a look that proclaimed he was entirely smitten with her.

Richmond had been following Pembrook for days, and when his father casually mentioned that Lady Raverston's house had been burgled and the only thing that was stolen was some sort of book, Richmond knew what happened. Pembrook obviously had the book and was sure to head out of town.

Therefore, he spent the entire day watching him, waiting for him to leave. Yet Pembrook didn't leave. He went to the Pump Room, made some morning calls, took a young chit driving, and did everything that a man about town would do in an afternoon.

Then he headed toward the cemetery. Richmond discreetly followed along, pleased that he was still able to do simple undetected surveillance.

He was fully aware that he had botched things with Cassie. If he hadn't treated her like a doxy, she might have come to trust him, and might have eventually given him the book. Instead, he'd tried to seduce her, and now he wasn't sure if she'd ever trust him.

Richmond watched with interest as Pembrook approached a tree and, much to his amazement, reached inside the trunk. As if he was looking for something. Which he obviously was.

He frowned as he continued to watch Pembrook. He stuck his entire arm down into the tree, and seemed to be quite agitated. After a long while, he took his arm out of the tree, dusted off the flecks of dirt, and stalked away from the grave, enraged.

Richmond assessed the situation. Pembrook had the book, and that very well might have led him to the cemetery. If the book had the troop movements in it, Pembrook would have simply left Bath. Which he hadn't done.

Richmond could envision Lloyd hiding the papers in the cemetery. If Lloyd had visited the grave regularly, anyone who was watching him would simply decide that he was visiting a relation and take no notice of him when he went there. It wasn't a bad plan.

Except now the papers, which were more than likely hidden in the tree, were gone. Only one person could have found them: Cassie. If he figured out that Cassie had the papers, then Pembrook would come to the very same conclusion.

A conclusion that could put her very life in danger.

Chapter 11

"What? I was behind the robbery at Lady Raverston's house?" Richmond said in shock, staring at his father.

Stanton casually gazed around the Pump Room to see if any of the dowagers noticed that his son was speaking a bit too loud and was on the verge of causing a fracas. "Derek, do lower your voice," he said firmly, looking around the room.

Richmond raised an eye sardonically and looked quite displeased by the turn of events. "If my memory serves me correctly, I believe I was with Lady Raverston and her nieces when the incident occurred, so how could I be responsible?" he asked, his voice laced with sarcasm.

"Obviously the gossips think you're a clever man."

"Obviously, I'm not," Richmond said. Then, realizing the statement he'd made, he smiled a bit. "I'm not behind the robbery," he said simply.

"Oh, I know that. Did you also know that you're a spy for the French?"

Richmond's heart lurched in his chest. Was his cover compromised? "A spy for the French? I'm not that clever, either," he added in a casual tone of voice.

He was rewarded by a smile from his father. "Yes, I knew both ideas were ridiculous, and hopefully I've set the record straight."

"Thank you, Father."

"I do suppose you know the other news at Honoria, Lady Raverston's, as well," Stanton said calmly. He was certain that his son knew nothing about the return of Pandora, and actually expected him to botch his courtship of Cassandra. Stanton was certain his son was courting Cassandra, even if he wasn't aware of it yet.

When Richmond didn't answer, and instead stared like a gapeseed across the Pump Room, Stanton followed his eyes and gasped.

Standing on the other side of the room was a vision in blue. From her perfect blonde curls to her tiny kid shoes, Lady Lyntwoode, formerly Pandora Wyndmoore, commanded the attention of every man in the room. Her sky blue walking dress, which was adorned with yard upon yard of Belgian lace and tiny seed pearls, showed a bit too much of her bosom to be respectable, but no man in the room was complaining. She looked so lovely that it almost made Daphne seem invisible.

Daphne was dressed in much the same manner as Pandora, wearing a frothy pink concoction with lace and tiny embroidered roses on the hem. Her cheeks were almost as pink as Pandora's, but she lacked the same carriage and confidence as her older sister, and appeared to be a bland copy of the original.

Honoria, wearing a respectable blue merino gown, followed the pair, and Cassie trailed behind her. They both looked miserable.

"Damnation, that's Lady Lyntwoode. Did you know she was in Bath?" Richmond said, turning away from the ladies.

Stanton smiled. "Yes, I was going to tell you."

"Damnation. She's the last person I want to see," Richmond replied, looking directly at his father.

"Don't you want to go over and pay your respects?" Stanton said with a slight smile, certain of the answer.

"I think not. Cassandra, Miss Wyndmoore, doesn't look too pleased with the situation though. She must be miserable being in the same house with both Pandora and Daphne."

Stanton smiled. His son was able to see beyond the beauties and notice that Cassie was unhappy. Maybe Derek wasn't as thick headed as he had imagined. "If I were her, I'd bolt back to Warwick on the first mail coach. Having both sisters with her must be trying beyond belief," Stanton said, watching the men around the room. Every male eye was on Pandora, and almost immediately, young bucks besieged their table. While Pandora and Daphne chatted with their adoring swains, Cassie sat apart from the table and appeared to be deep in thought.

Cassie was, in fact, deep in thought. She noticed Lord Richmond, looking ever so handsome in his black jacket and buckskin breeches, sitting on the other side of the room with his father. She also saw the naked longing on his face when he caught sight of Pandora, who was obviously his one true love. That made her even more depressed. Even though he was probably a spy for the French, and probably arranged the burglary of her room, she still had . . . tender feelings for him. *He never was really interested in me,* she decided, her mood sinking even lower.

Thankfully, a diversion in the guise of Lord Pembrook appeared to pay court to Daphne. Cassie knew that Pandora always had to be the center of attention, and even though she was married, she expected every man to focus on her. *This will be interesting,* Cassie thought, as she turned her attention to the drama unfolding beside her.

"Miss Daphne, you look like an angel sent from heaven to prove to us mere mortals that truth and beauty do indeed still exist," Pembrook cooed, and Cassie was hard pressed not to giggle.

As expected, Daphne blushed prettily. "You're a flatterer, my lord," she said with a smile.

Before Pembrook had a chance to reply, Pandora butted in. "Daphne, you must learn to mind your manners. You don't want everyone in Bath to know you're a rustic who hasn't even been out, do you?" Pandora said with a cunning smile.

Daphne's mouth dropped open in shock.

Pandora turned to Pembrook. "You must excuse my sister Daphne. At times, her manners can be quite . . . wanting. She should be polished enough to perform an introduction, but she is so terribly young, I'm sure she just got excited about being out in Society and forgot her lessons. I'm Lady Lyntwoode, her sister," Pandora said all in one breath, and Daphne continued to stare at her.

"Lord Pembrook, at your service," he said smoothly, kissing her hand lightly.

"It's a pleasure to make your acquaintance, Lord Pembrook," Pandora said, devouring him with her eyes. "I just arrived in Bath recently. Perhaps you would be so kind as to introduce me to some of your friends. It's been trying to be at home with my aunt and my sisters, as I'm sure you can understand," she said in a lilting voice.

Cassie glanced over at Aunt Honoria, waiting for her to put up some sort of objection. Aunt Honoria continued to sip her water and remained silent.

"Of course, Lady Lyntwoode. It would be my pleasure to introduce you to our local Society," Pembrook said, whisking her away from the table toward a group of eligible bucks.

"Aunt Honoria, Pandora just left with Lord Pembrook! And he's my suitor, not hers!" Daphne wailed.

"Pandora is an adult, and if Lord Pembrook wants to introduce her to his acquaintances, that's his prerogative, my dear," Honoria said in a calm voice.

"But he's supposed to be here with me," Daphne whined.

Cassie wasn't sure who annoyed her more, Pandora for slighting Daphne when she hadn't even given her an opportunity to introduce her properly or Daphne for whining about Pembrook. Before she could say something to Daphne that would calm her down a bit, a shadow fell onto their table. It was Richmond.

"Good morning, Lady Raverston, Miss Wyndmoore, Miss Daphne," he said gallantly.

Honoria smiled at him. "Lord Richmond, how nice to see you. Is your father with you this morning?"

"Yes, he's at the table near the window," Richmond replied.

Honoria stood up and looked expectantly at Daphne. "Come along, Daphne, we're going to say hello to Lord Stanton," she said firmly.

"But, Aunt Honoria, Lord Pembrook . . ." Daphne began, then trailed off when she saw the look on her aunt's face. "Of course," she said meekly.

"Do excuse us," Honoria said, and the pair headed toward Lord Stanton, leaving Cassie alone with Richmond.

He sat down next to Cassie and she sipped her tea. She also realized that she didn't have anything in particular to say to him. She wanted to ask him why he wasn't with her sister, but that would be impolite. She wanted to tell him that he should just leave Bath, because he wasn't going to get Lloyd's papers. Ever. That wouldn't be very polite either. She also wanted to tell him how handsome he looked when the sun hit his blue-black hair, but that certainly wouldn't be very polite or ladylike. In the end, she decided to say nothing at all.

"You're very quiet today, Miss Wyndmoore. May I ask if something is troubling you?" he asked in a voice that actually sounded concerned.

Cassie looked up at him. In the light of the Pump Room, his eyes were the color of the sea. "I haven't been resting well after the robbery. It's rather . . . disconcerting to have a stranger go through your things."

"My father mentioned it to me. What did the magistrate say?"

"They don't seem to be concerned and think it was an isolated incident." Out of the corner of her eye, Cassie could see Pandora. She was heading directly toward them, a dozen admirers in tow.

Richmond leaned forward and took her hands in his. "Would you let me take you for a drive tomorrow? It might help you get your mind off all the unpleasantness."

He seemed so sincere that for a brief moment, Cassie almost believed that he wanted to spend time with her. Then she remembered. Richmond might have the book, but he didn't have the box from the cemetery. Which he undoubtedly needed. That was why he wanted to spend time with her. "I don't think so," she said in what she hoped was a firm voice.

He smiled back at her, an engaging, boyish smile that made her heart melt. "I know I'm not the best companion, but if you go driving with me, you'll be free from Pandora and Daphne, at least for a short while."

She couldn't help but smile back. *Even if he spends the entire drive trying to interrogate me, it will still be better than spending the afternoon with my sisters,* she decided. "That is true, my lord. Tomorrow afternoon will be fine," she said with a smile.

As Pandora and her entourage, which was actually moving quite slowly, neared the table, he stood up to leave. "I'm sorry, Miss Wyndmoore, I must take my leave," he said with a regretful smile.

"Aren't you going to stay and say hello to Pandora?" Cassie asked, once again confused. He loved Pandora. Why wasn't he waiting to talk to her?

He leaned closer to her and said softly, "To be honest, I'd like nothing more than to avoid your sister for as long as possible, although it's terribly impolite to say so. You won't give me away, will you?" he asked in a conspiratorial voice, his eyes sparkling with mirth.

Cassie couldn't help but grin at him. *Gads, he can be charming,* she thought. "Of course not," she replied with a grin.

"Until tomorrow then," he said, kissing her hand lightly, then disappearing into the crowd.

Scant moments later, Pandora and her entourage appeared. "Was that Richmond, Cassie? Was he here talking to *you?*" Pandora asked.

"Excuse me?" Cassie said, feigning confusion.

"Lord Richmond. Was he just here?" Pandora said, tapping her shoe on the floor impatiently.

"No," Cassie replied, just to be contrary.

Pandora stared at her. "I know Richmond was here asking about me, so don't lie to me, you little mouse," she hissed as she sat down and crossed her ankles ever so properly.

Cassie smiled slightly. She wasn't sure why she believed him, but she was certain that Richmond didn't

want to see Pandora. That made her quite happy, at least
for the moment.

Richmond was glad he had made the date to go driving with Cassie. He wanted to keep close tabs on her,
since he was certain that she had Lloyd's documents,
and as long as she had them, she was in danger.

He was cooling his heels in the parlor when the door
burst open. He expected Cassie. He was wrong.

"Oh, my darling Derek, it's so wonderful to see you
after all these years," Pandora proclaimed as she burst
into Honoria's parlor.

Richmond stared at Pandora and wondered what had
ever compelled him to enter into a romantic liaison with
her. Of course, she was beautiful, and long ago, that was
much more important to him. Now all he saw was a vulgar, vapid female who was, as usual, showing too much
of her bosom. "Good afternoon, Lady Lyntwoode," he
said coldly, rising and giving her hand a very perfunctory
kiss.

She smiled at him seductively and stood much too
close for his liking. "I've missed you so, Derek," she
cooed seductively, guiding him onto the settee. "And
you must call me Pandora! You never used to be so for-
mal and proper," she added with a smile.

Richmond was annoyed. Highly annoyed. "It would
be unseemly to call you by your given name. How is
your husband?" he said stiffly, inching away from her
on the settee.

"Lyntwoode? He's rich but useless. Not like you,"
Pandora cooed, moving closer to him.

He tried to change the topic. "I'm waiting for your
sister Cassandra."

"It's so kind of you to take pity of the poor little mouse. She's become quite the quiz, you know, and Mama has all but given up on her," Pandora commented in a voice laced with sympathy.

Richmond knew she wasn't sympathetic at all, and was simply trying to curry his favor. He was about to give her a good dressing down when Cassandra sauntered into the room.

"Lord Richmond, Pandora," Cassie said dryly, looking from one to the other.

Richmond's eyes settled on Cassie and took in every inch of her appearance, from her short brown hair, which was once again coaxed into some sort of ringlets, to her emerald green dress that accentuated her figure perfectly, to her luminous eyes. This time she wasn't wearing her spectacles, much to his regret; he thought they made her look charming. "Good afternoon, Cassandra. You look lovely today," he said honestly, rising to kiss her hand.

"Cassie does try, doesn't she, Derek? It's too bad she didn't inherit the family beauty," Pandora finished acidly.

Before Cassie could reply, Richmond turned and glared at Pandora. "Beauty is only skin deep, Lady Lyntwoode, but I'm sure that's a concept that you'll never grasp," he said, and then turned to Cassie. "Are you ready to leave?"

"Of course," Cassie said as he whisked her out of the parlor and away from her dreaded sister.

"You do look all the crack today, Miss Wyndmoore," Richmond said, guiding the phaeton down the narrow streets toward the edge of town.

Cassie let herself relax a trifle. She was becoming accustomed to his phaeton, and today he was driving at a much more leisurely pace. "I always thought you were the most charming of Pandora's many admirers, and it appears that you haven't lost your touch," she said, noticing how masculine he looked in his buff breeches and his dark blue jacket. His hair was still too long to be stylish, and looked a bit unkempt today, but she thought that look favored him. *It's too bad he's a spy and not really interested in me,* she thought with a sigh.

"Is Pandora always so . . . disagreeable to you?" he asked, glancing over at her.

Cassie gazed absently at the shop they were passing, and watched the young girls on the corners selling oranges. They looked so very, very young. "Pandora was very cosseted at home, and tends to become quite prickly if she isn't the center of attention," she explained simply, enjoying the warmth of the summer sun on her skin.

"It must have been very difficult growing up with your sisters."

She shrugged. "Not really. You see, Papa took quite a liking to me, so I had privileges that were never even offered to Pandora or Daphne. And Daphne is a bit more . . . easily led than Pandora, so we get on better."

"Because Daphne is closer to your own age?"

Cassie turned to him and chuckled. "I think not, Lord Richmond. If you must know, Daphne is eight years my junior," she said, her eyes dancing with mirth.

"That most certainly cannot be true, Miss Wyndmoore. You are bamming me!"

"I am not," she said, enjoying the scenery.

They drove in silence for the longest while, and Cassie almost forgot the reason that he asked her out for a drive.

"You are being careful, aren't you, Miss Wyndmoore?" he asked.

"Careful? Why do I need to be careful, Lord Richmond? We're in Bath, not on the battlefield," she pointed out.

He coughed. "Yes, well, your room was burgled, so perhaps you should be on guard."

"On guard?"

"Yes," he said firmly. "On guard. And you will tell me if anything . . . unusual happens, won't you?"

Once again, Cassie was confused. Richmond seemed genuinely concerned about her. He was also acting as if he wasn't the one who broke into her bedroom. Logically then, if he hadn't broken in, that meant that he probably wasn't a spy. That was very good indeed, because she hated the thought of Richmond being a turncoat. If Richmond wasn't a spy, then the spy was definitely Lord Pembrook. Of course, they both could be French spies working together to get the information from her, but that explanation didn't ring true to Cassie. Finally, Pandora did say that Richmond had connections with the French government, and did practically say he was a spy. In fact, she might have even called him a spy. Cassie couldn't quite remember. If he was a spy, pretending to be concerned about her after the burglary that he had staged was a good cover. *This is just too complicated*, Cassie finally decided, staring off at the scenery.

"Miss Wyndmoore?"

Cassie snapped out of her reverie. "Yes?"

"You will tell me, or my father, if anything unusual happens?" he intoned in a very serious voice.

"Oh, Lord Richmond," she said gaily, " 'tis Bath. Nothing unusual happens here." *All I need to do is to giggle, toss my curls and gently tap him with my fan to convince him I'm as addlepated as Daphne.*

Richmond raised an eyebrow. "Are you all right, Miss Wyndmoore?"

"All right?"

His eyes sparkled. "Yes, for a moment there you sounded rather like your sisters, and I thought that perhaps you might be having an apoplexy," he said in a very serious tone.

Cassie giggled. "Yes, well, hopefully that won't happen again."

The sun glistened off his jet-black hair, and, when they locked eyes, Cassie forgot that he was only after Lloyd's book. For a moment, she let herself believe in the illusion that he was genuinely interested in her.

"And he stayed out with the mouse for well over an hour," Pandora whined, making herself more comfortable on Daphne's bed.

Daphne stared at her oldest sister as if she'd never seen her before. It actually sounded like Pandora, a diamond of the first water who'd married very well, was jealous of Cassie. "I told you, Lord Richmond has taken a liking to Cassie. That's why their drive was so long," Daphne explained.

"But Richmond and Cassie! The idea is ridiculous! He should be spending his time paying court to me instead of dancing attendance on that mouse!"

Daphne frowned. Pandora had changed a lot since she'd married, and not all for the better. "But, Pandora, be reasonable. Richmond can't be dangling after you. You're married."

Pandora let loose a sparkling giggle and patted Daphne's hand. "Little Daphne, you know nothing about polite Society. Lyntwoode doesn't care about me.

It's expected that I take a lover. That's the way it's done," she said simply, wrapping a stray strand of her golden hair around her finger.

Daphne was shocked, to say the least. Mama never mentioned anything about married women taking lovers. It was scandalous. "But don't you love Lyntwoode?" she blurted out.

Pandora laughed again. "Love Lyntwoode? I never loved him, my dear. I love his money and his title."

Daphne looked out the window, completely confused. "I think I love Pembrook," she said in a small voice.

"Oh, really?"

"Yes. Will you help me catch him?"

"Of course, Daphne. On one condition."

Daphne looked up and stared into Pandora's cold blue eyes. "What condition?"

Pandora smiled slyly. "You have to help me keep Cassie and Richmond apart."

Daphne looked away and thought for a long while. *Cassie really likes Richmond,* she thought, *but I need to catch Pembrook. The way Mama has been acting, I'll never have my Season, and by that time, Pembrook will be married to someone else.* "I'll help you keep them apart," Daphne said, and as soon as the words came out of her mouth, she regretted them.

Chapter 12

"Cassie, will you please walk down to Madame Babette's with me? Please? I want to talk to her about a new gown," Daphne implored, her eyes large and pleading.

"Why don't you ask Pandora? You know how she loves shopping."

"I talked to Pandora before breakfast, and she said she was going to be busy all day writing some letters. Please, Cassie? I don't want to go alone with Mary. It's not any fun."

"Oh, all right. But I don't need you to lecture me on my clothes," Cassie warned, heading toward the stairs to go fetch her blue pelisse.

"I'm sorry I ever did that, Cassie. You look all the crack and you don't ever show too much of your bosom."

Cassie did look all the crack in her royal blue walking dress with the high neck and the ruffles at the sleeves and hem. It was one of the busier dresses that Madame Babette had suggested for her, but it was fashionable for walking about town, so Cassie didn't mind it much.

As the ladies strolled down Great Pulteney Street, it was apparent that Daphne had much on her mind. "We haven't seen Lord Pembrook in a long time," Daphne commented ever so casually.

"No, we haven't. But I think Aunt Honoria is ready to

let you start socializing again, so we might run across him," Cassie replied.

"I miss him terribly. He's the most handsome man I've ever met. Do you think he's taken a liking to me?"

"One never knows with gentlemen. They can be rather fickle," Cassie replied. *Gads, I hope she hasn't developed a* tendre *for him,* Cassie thought. *He's not quite respectable, and is much too sophisticated for her.*

"Oh," Daphne said and sighed again. Dramatically. "Do you think you'll ever get married?" she asked suddenly.

Once again, Cassie frowned. *What is Daphne thinking today?* she wondered, staring at her younger sister. "I'm quite on the shelf, Daphne, you know that, and I don't have any particular expectations. It would be nice to be married, but I don't think it will happen."

"Would you marry someone even if you didn't love them?" Daphne asked, flashing a smile at a handsome young buck standing in front of the jeweler's across the street.

"Well, I know it's not particularly fashionable to marry for love, but I don't think I could marry someone I didn't care about."

A radiant smile appeared on Daphne's face. "Then you don't think it's silly to marry for love?"

"Not at all. And I hope you love the man you marry," she replied, admiring the ornate carriages and excellent horseflesh that trotted down the street.

"I'm glad you said that. I think people who marry for a title are awfully selfish."

What was Daphne talking about? Was this about Pandora and Lyntwoode? "Daphne, people do it all the time, and many of them muck up their lives. I'm just glad that you're not hanging about for a title," Cassie replied, spotting Madame Babette's store across the street.

Daphne grinned impishly. "Oh, I'm not hanging about for a title, but I wouldn't mind having one. Lady Daphne Something or Another sounds grand, doesn't it?" she asked, giggling a bit.

Cassie grinned back at her as they stopped at the corner, waiting for the street to clear. She paid no heed to the boy behind her, and was just about to tell Daphne that Lady Cassandra had quite a nice ring to it as well, when she felt a hand at the base of her spine.

The next thing Cassie knew, she was tumbling into the street, trying to regain her balance as two huge black stallions pulling a phaeton bore down upon her. Daphne screamed, and Cassie caught the heel of her walking boots on the hem of her dress and fell to the ground. Her head hit the cobblestones with a dull thud, and she heard nothing.

Pandora sat at the escritoire, staring at the letter in front of her. It just wasn't right.

She knew for a fact that Derek had feelings for her, and that he was feigning interest in Cassie so he could see her. She was certain of that. It meant that he had put all of their former disagreements aside—and there had been many of them—and was ready to take his rightful place in her bedchamber. He just needed some encouragement from her, which she was more than glad to provide.

"You never know about head injuries," Cassie heard an unknown male voice proclaim. *Where am I?* she wondered, her eyes closed. She tried to open them, but she couldn't. She tried to move, but she couldn't seem to do that either. All she could really do was listen to the conversation around her.

"It might help to bleed her," the male voice added.

Bleed me? They'd best not bleed me, she thought in a panic.

"I don't think that will be necessary," she heard Aunt Honoria say.

Thank goodness, she thought, relief running through her immobile body.

"When will she wake up?" she heard Daphne ask in a tiny voice that made her sound like a young girl.

I'm all right, Cassie thought, willing herself to speak. The words just wouldn't come out of her mouth. As she struggled to wake up, she realized how much her head hurt, and how very, very tired she was. *Maybe if I try to sleep, I won't have a headache when I wake up,* she reasoned and let herself drift into the darkness.

Stanton was in the study, reading a copy of the *Bath Gazette* and drinking a glass of hock, when his son burst into the room.

"Father, you'll never believe what I just received," Derek said, sitting down on the morocco leather chair next to his father.

Stanton looked up and raised an eyebrow. "A letter from Castlereagh," he replied, only to see how Derek would react.

Richmond frowned. "No, not at all. Read this," he said, thrusting the scented paper at his father.

The romantic missive, which left little to the imagination, was signed, *your Greek goddess.* "So, should I ask the identity of your Greek goddess?" Stanton asked with a slight smile, handing the letter back to Richmond.

Richmond crumpled it up and threw it on the small table next to the chair. "It's Pandora, of course. Can you imagine her gall? Summoning me like I'm her lapdog?" Richmond stood up and headed over to the liquor.

"It's none of my concern, but are you going to meet with her?"

Richmond poured himself a glass of hock and sat back down. "I think not. Lady Lyntwoode has all but become a doxy. I can't imagine what I ever saw in her in the first place," he admitted, sipping his hock.

Stanton smiled. Maybe all wasn't lost. "Now her sister Cassandra is something else entirely," he said softly.

Richmond smiled over at him. "Yes, she certainly is. Rather like her Aunt Honoria."

Stanton smiled. Maybe his son wasn't as unaware as he'd imagined.

"Truly, Aunt Honoria, I'm fine," Cassie said reassuringly, sitting up on her bed, reaching for her teacup.

"My dear Cassandra, you've had a trying day. You have a prodigious bump on your head, and you slept most of the day. Are you sure you're feeling all right?"

"I'm right as rain, honestly, Aunt Honoria," Cassie said confidently. Although her head did still ache somewhat, and she did feel dizzy every now and again.

"If you feel well enough, come down for dinner. Pandora has been up in her room all day and has begged off dinner, so it might be less of a strain on you. But if you're not up to it, I'll send up a tray," Honoria added.

"After dinner, do you think Daphne would play the pianoforte for me? I'd really love to her hear play, and I think that it might help me get my mind off things," she said vaguely.

Cassie had many things on her mind, most prominently the fact that someone had pushed her into the street. *Who would want to hurt me?* She knew she couldn't tell Aunt Honoria again. She'd simply call the magistrate, and Cassie was certain that he wouldn't believe a word she said.

"I'll see you later this evening, then," Honoria said, heading toward the door. "You rest up until then," she added and closed the door behind her.

Cassie was certain her accident wasn't an accident. And the only thing that would cause anyone to try to hurt her were Mr. Lloyd's papers. Someone was trying to scare her.

She still didn't know who that someone was. It could be Pembrook or Richmond, or both of them, although she was certain that it was one of their minions who pushed her. On the other hand, it could be someone else. That was a possibility as well. Maybe there was someone else out there who was trying to find out what she knew . . .

Cassie shuddered and pulled the covers over her head. It was a long time before she drifted off to sleep.

"Miss Wyndmoore is recovering from an accident, and I don't know if she is at home to visitors," Laughton intoned in his most regal butler voice.

"An accident? Is Cassie, Miss Wyndmoore, all right?" Richmond blurted.

"Miss Wyndmoore doesn't seem to have sustained any permanent injuries," Laughton said stiffly.

Richmond let out a sigh of relief. "Would you be so kind as to inquire if Miss Wyndmoore would indeed see me?" he asked politely. Richmond had learned long ago that life was much easier when one was cordial to the servants.

Laughton smiled, took his card, and ushered him into the parlor to cool his heels.

Richmond stood alone in the parlor, staring out the window. It was another lovely late summer day, and he was planning to ask Cassie to go riding. He had found a neighbor who would lend him a sidesaddle, and he thought she might enjoy an afternoon in the sunshine.

In an instant though, everything had changed. Whatever happened to Cassie wasn't public knowledge, since his father would have heard about it at the Pump Room. What had happened to her? He could feel a strange tightness in his chest, and decided to ask to see Lady Raverston if Cassie wasn't seeing visitors

The large wooden door to the parlor opened, and he turned, fully expecting Cassie or at least Laughton.

Instead, Pandora stood in the doorway, her hand lingering on her milky white breasts, which were fringed by the finest Belgian lace. Her peach walking dress was much too low cut to be respectable, especially in Bath, and Richmond gaped at her indecency.

She closed the door behind her and sauntered over to him, a pout appearing on her face. "You ignored my letter, Derek," she said in the voice that, at one time, had driven him mad with desire. Now it just grated on his nerves.

She looks like a doxy, he thought, his eyes traveling over her lithe form. Her cheeks were painted, her lower lip jutted out like a spoiled child's, and he had seen Cyprians in Covent Garden who displayed less of their bosoms. "Lady Lyntwoode, you seem to have some sort of misconception about our relationship," he said calmly.

She stepped forward and began to finger his cravat provocatively. "Derek, I've missed you so. I've been so miserable without you," she purred seductively.

"Pandora, really, I . . ." he muttered, completely flustered. Her perfume engulfed his senses, and he didn't want to chat with her at all, but he couldn't quite figure out how to extricate himself from the situation.

He stepped back, she stepped forward, and, much to his utter surprise, she threw her arms around his neck and pressed her lips to his as if he were the last man on earth.

Richmond wasn't used to being accosted by gently bred ladies, but, since he was a government agent, he should have been able to push Pandora away and say something cutting to discourage her. He did want to do that. Except that he had forgotten how pleasant kissing Pandora was, and let himself enjoy it for a moment.

Somewhere in the background, he heard a door open, but it seemed far away. He knew he should push Pandora away, but for a moment or two more . . .

"Pandora, that is enough. You will go to your room, and I'll attend to you later," Honoria said in a clipped voice.

Richmond thrust Pandora away from him and said, "There is an explanation for this, Lady Raverston." He didn't even notice Cassie standing behind her.

"It was lovely seeing you again, Derek," Pandora cooed, giving him a telling look as she sashayed out of the room. "He's mine, mouse," she muttered as she passed Cassie.

"May I ask for your explanation, Lord Richmond?" Honoria said, taking a step into the doorway.

It was then that Richmond noticed Cassie. She had seen everything, he realized, and felt his heart sinking. He didn't know why, but he most certainly didn't want

Cassie to think he was interested in Pandora, and now she had seen this. *She'll really think I'm a blackguard now,* he realized with a jolt.

"Lady Raverston, I have no interest in Lady Lyntwoode, and it was she who initiated the scene you witnessed," he said formally.

"Really? I certainly hope your loud protests didn't disturb the rest of the household."

"Lady Raverston, you have my word as a gentleman that nothing like this will ever happen again," he said passionately.

Cassie swayed a little in the doorway and looked as if she was going to faint.

"Cassie, come sit down," Honoria said, leading her to the settee. Cassie followed her silently, not looking at Richmond.

He craned his neck to see her, but all that was visible was her right cheek, which was bright red and swollen.

"Miss Wyndmoore, what happened?" he said, his voice filled with concern.

"Cassie was involved in a carriage accident," Honoria explained.

"A carriage accident? When? How?"

When Aunt Honoria didn't reply, Cassie sighed. "Daphne and I were attempting to cross the street, and I somehow lost my balance and ended up on the cobblestones under a moving carriage."

Richmond stared at her, his heart in his throat. She could have been killed. What was going on? "You seem to have recovered nicely," he said blandly. What he really wanted to do was rush to her side and hold her in his arms, but he was certain that course of action wasn't advisable at the moment.

"Thank you," she replied, and then turned to Honoria.

"I think I need to rest a bit more, Aunt Honoria," she said as she stood up slowly.

"Yes, of course, my dear," Honoria replied, as Cassie slowly walked out of the room, completely ignoring Richmond.

"Is Cassie going to be all right?" he asked Honoria, his voice filled with concern.

"I find it rather amusing, Lord Richmond, that you appear to be courting two of my charges, one of whom is married," she observed.

He had the temerity to blush a bit, and couldn't meet her eyes. "It was a mistake, Lady Raverston," he said softly, feeling like an utter heel.

"Yes. Yes it was. And unfortunately because of that mistake, I will not be able to receive you here any longer," she said, sitting down on the settee.

Richmond stared at her in disbelief. "Pardon me? Are you barring me from your house, Lady Raverston?"

"I'm just notifying you that my nieces will not be home if you call," she said in a steady voice.

He stared at Honoria in disbelief. He was a member of the *ton* and was accepted in the best houses in London. The matchmaking mamas declared him one of the best catches in Town. Yet Lady Raverston, who, in the grand scheme of things, was simply a well-to-do matron in Bath, had the audacity to ban him from her house! He was about to give her a piece of his mind, then thought better of it. "As you wish, Lady Raverston," he said coldly, turning towards the door. "I would watch the situation with Miss Wyndmoore carefully. She could be in great danger here, and should leave Bath immediately," he added as he strolled out the door, certain that Honoria wouldn't listen to his advice.

So he would have to try to find a way to keep Cassie safe.

"What did Richmond mean, Cassandra? What kind of danger are you in?" Honoria asked, bringing the chair next to Cassie's bed in the attic.

Cassie didn't know what to say. It was so complicated and so . . . bizarre. She sighed deeply and decided to try to untangle the story for Aunt Honoria. "Do you remember Mr. Lloyd? The gentleman who died?"

"Yes . . ."

"Well, the book I found was his, and that was the book that was stolen," Cassie began. Her head was already starting to hurt.

"Yes, I recall. The book that you said Richmond and Pembrook wanted."

"They wanted the book because it was in code. Mr. Lloyd was a spy, and the book led me to some papers in the cemetery," Cassie said. *This sounds so very strange. I don't think Aunt Honoria will believe a word of this.*

"Papers in the cemetery? What are you talking about, Cassandra?"

"I know it sounds strange, Aunt Honoria. Well, the papers were in Greek and when I translated them, I realized they were troop movements."

"Troop movements?"

"Yes. French troop movements for the next few months," Cassie explained.

"My dear, this is quite the story," Honoria commented with a frown.

"I know it's hard to believe. That's why I didn't tell anyone," Cassie explained.

"So I'm to understand that you found sensitive

government documents hidden in a tree in the cemetery that were put there by Mr. Lloyd, who was a spy for our government?"

She doesn't believe me at all, Cassie thought in a panic. *She thinks I'm making the whole thing up.* "Yes."

"And Mr. Lloyd was a spy. For the English. Working in Bath. Not in Dover, not in some other coastal town, but in sleepy little Bath."

Cassie gulped. It sounded strange even to her eyes. "Yes."

"And you have his papers. Papers that show French troop movements."

"Yes. No, I mean, not now. I sent them to Papa and asked him to take them to Castlereagh," she explained.

Honoria raised her eyebrows. "You involved your father in this little drama?"

"I know it sounds strange, Aunt Honoria, but it's true. Lord Richmond and Lord Pembrook both wanted the book and now they want the papers."

"Cassandra, this is quite the yarn. It's like something out of a Minerva Press novel."

"I know," Cassie said with a sigh. "I didn't tell anyone, but I didn't stumble in the street. Someone pushed me. I felt their hand on my back," she murmured, her eyes brimming with tears.

"Someone tried to hurt you?

"I think so," Cassie said, trying to keep herself from crying.

"And what does Richmond have to do with this?"

Cassie stared at the floor. "Lord Richmond loves France, he has family there, and he has a dubious reputation. And he was curious about Mr. Lloyd's book and the papers, even though he hasn't asked me for either of them directly," Cassie explained.

"You think Richmond is a spy for the French?"

"Pandora all but accused him of that years ago, although she'll probably deny it now. That's why he's been hanging about pretending to be interested in me. It could be Lord Pembrook as well. He was asking the same questions as Lord Richmond. I don't know, it's all very confusing."

Honoria reached over and patted Cassie's hand gently. "Cassie, my dear, you're overwrought. You've had a horrible accident and a bad bump on the head. If these papers are what you say they are, your father will know what to do with them and everything will work out fine. As for Richmond, you don't have to worry about him. I've barred him from the house. And Pembrook isn't welcome here, you know that," she said calmly.

She doesn't believe me, Cassie thought wildly. *She thinks the bump on my head has caused me to have delusions.* She sighed again, and slumped into her pillows. "Did you talk to Pandora about Richmond?" she asked curiously.

A hint of a smile appeared on Honoria's face. "We had a little coze. I've sent for her husband, although she doesn't know that. The sooner he gets here, the better," she added.

Cassie smiled weakly. "I'm glad. It's rather trying to have Pandora underfoot."

"Yes, it most certainly is," Honoria said in complete agreement.

Pandora sat in Honoria's morning room, a frown etched on her face, pretending to work on her needlepoint. Things were not going well at all.

Richmond was not coming around to her way of thinking. He was all but ignoring her, and, if she didn't know better, she would almost swear that he had developed a *tendre* for her sister, the mouse. That certainly was a ridiculous idea!

Then there was Aunt Honoria. *She's even more tedious than my husband is,* Pandora mused, poking at her needlepoint. Just because Honoria had seen her kissing Richmond, she completely overreacted and barred Pandora from receiving visitors. *If Lyntwoode wasn't so stingy with his money, I'd set up my own residence in Bath,* Pandora decided. *Then I'd be able to do whatever I wanted, just like when I lived with Mama and Papa.*

A door closing down the hallway brought her out of her reverie, and she put down her needlepoint and decided to investigate. She opened the morning room door and saw Laughton in the hallway, carrying a huge bouquet of deep red roses.

"Flowers? Are they for me?" she exclaimed and dashed down the hallway.

Laughton raised an eyebrow. "I haven't read the card yet, Lady Lyntwoode," he exclaimed stiffly.

"I will, then," she proclaimed and grabbed the card out of Laughton's hands. *It's from Richmond, I know it is,* she thought and was correct. The missive read:

Cassie,
   I hope your injuries don't keep you out of Society for very long. I look forward to seeing you soon and giving you a proper apology for my actions.
                                        Your Servant,
                                        Richmond

Pandora turned red with rage. *He's writing Cassie! That . . . blackguard!* She was about to throw the card at Laughton and stomp off, then thought of a better course of action. She smiled prettily at the butler and said, "Thank you, Laughton, the flowers are for me. You can put them in the parlor," she ordered, heading toward her room, the card still in her hand.

Cassie would never find out the flowers were for her and would never know that Richmond had feelings for her. Ever.

Chapter 13

Cassie sat quietly in the Pump Room, silently cursing Aunt Honoria. She knew her aunt had the best of intentions. Aunt Honoria thought that it would be good for her to get out of the house and into the social whirl again.

That didn't help matters much. Cassie spent the afternoon explaining her bruised and red cheek as a riding accident to every single person who visited their table. Since Aunt Honoria had lived in Bath for ages, she knew everyone. In addition, this was the afternoon that everyone wanted to talk to Aunt Honoria.

Although it seemed as though Cassie explained her rather unpleasant facial contusion to everyone in Bath, as well as their relatives from London and the continent, the company in the Pump Room was actually dreadfully sparse. The most notable absences were Lord Richmond, his father, and Lord Pembrook.

Cassie sighed and gazed around the room. Daphne was a few feet away from their table, chatting with some young bucks who were vying for her attentions. It was the repeat of what happened at every social occasion in Warwick.

Cassie's eyes continued to scan the room until she spotted Pandora. Her sister was dressed in a tan walking dress that almost matched the shade of her skin, which, at first glance, made her look almost nude. Of course, Pandora was also showing off a grand expanse of her lovely bosom and as a result, she was surrounded by a set of bucks as well, just a slightly more mature version than Daphne's. While Daphne's admirers seemed to be pasty-faced youths, Pandora's admirers had an air of dissipation about them that made them seem much less appealing to Cassie.

"Is that your older sister?" Miss Chesterton, a connection of Lady So and So, who was currently chatting with Aunt Honoria, inquired.

Cassie looked over at Miss Chesterton, eated on her right. She appeared to be about twenty, had luminous skin, soft brown eyes, and long brown hair that was piled atop her head. She was a bit withdrawn, though, so Cassie tried to coax her into a conversation. "Yes, that's my sister Pandora, Lady Lyntwoode," Cassie explained.

"Is she in Bath with her husband?" Miss Chesterton asked, wringing her gloves in her hands.

"No, she came to visit our Aunt Honoria alone," Cassie replied, wondering what Miss Chesterton really wanted to say.

Miss Chesterton stared at her hands for the longest time, as if she were trying to find a polite way to say something unpleasant. "The gentlemen who are talking to your sister aren't the best *ton*. I don't think your aunt has noticed, or she would have called your sister back to the table."

Cassie shrugged. "I'm sure if it becomes a problem, Aunt Honoria will call her back here," she said calmly, hoping upon hope that Aunt Honoria didn't notice, so she didn't have to spend any more time with Pandora.

Miss Chesterton glanced over at the table where

Cassie's water was sitting. "Aren't you going to try your water?"

The glass of Bath's famous medicinal waters had been sitting on the small table in front of Cassie for a while. She hadn't even asked for it. The water had just appeared, as if by magic. It smelled bad and looked bad, and Cassie had no urge to try it at all.

"My aunt, Lady Paice, swears by the waters, and they've helped me when I've been feeling out of sorts," Miss Chesterton offered with a bland smile.

Cassie sighed again. *I might as well get it over with or Miss Chesterton will get offended that I didn't take her advice,* she thought and picked up the glass, gulping the murky liquid down. To her shock, it was surprisingly tasty. It didn't even smell that bad, and the smell of the waters at Bath was legendary. It smells like our cellar at home, Cassie thought, putting the glass on the table. "Have you been to the Assembly Rooms yet, Miss Chesterton?" she asked politely, trying to keep the conversation alive.

"Oh yes, it was the most wonderful experience!" Miss Chesterton said with a smile. "I loved the dancing, and everyone was so lovely to me," she began and started prattling on about her dancing partners.

As Miss Chesterton talked on and on, Cassie began to feel deuced odd. It suddenly became unbearably hot, and she didn't have a fan with her. And her stomach began to feel frightfully queer.

She got up slowly and walked over to Aunt Honoria, who was standing with Lady Paice. "Excuse me, Aunt Honoria?" she said weakly.

Honoria glanced at her and frowned. "What's the matter, Cassandra? You look dreadful."

"I think I'm going to disgrace myself," she said and

hoped upon hope that she didn't jerk the cat on Lady Paice or Aunt Honoria.

"Will she be all right, Aunt Honoria?" Daphne asked, worry filling her eyes.

"She'll be fine, Daphne," Honoria said in what she hoped was a calm voice. The sounds of Cassie's retching could be heard all the way down the hall, but the doctor had assured her this was perfectly normal. "She has to empty her stomach," she added.

The doctor, a youngish man with large hands and an aversion to fashion, walked into the upstairs sitting room and announced, "I'll be by tomorrow. She needs to sleep now."

"Why did she fall ill?" Honoria asked.

"Rat poison. Probably in her water. It happens now and again. It's nothing to be worried about," the doctor said, buttoning his ill-fitting brown jacket.

"Rat poison? In the water? Shouldn't we call the authorities?" Honoria asked, paling a bit.

The doctor shrugged and picked up his bag. "I don't believe so. I've never had a case like this from the Pump Room, but it isn't unheard of. Servants get careless in the kitchen and accidents happen. No harm done," he said, edging toward the door.

"Will my sister be all right?" Daphne blurted anxiously, her usually rosy cheeks rather pale and drawn.

A placid smile appeared on his face. "Yes, of course. She just needs her rest. I'll be by tomorrow to see her. If she gets hungry tonight, just give her tea," he finished as he hurried out of the room.

Honoria sat back down on one of the stiff-backed chairs and thought about Cassie. First the carriage accident and now this. Maybe the cock and bull story Cassie had told her about the papers she had found in the tree wasn't the product of an overactive imagination.

But they were in Bath. Not Dover or another coastal city. It made no sense at all that the city would be crawling with spies.

"And not only that, she's all but barred me from her home," Richmond raged, pacing the study.

Stanton sipped his claret. "Correct me if I'm wrong, Derek, but you did say that you were found embracing Lady Lyntwoode in her aunt's house. Don't you think she might take exception to that behavior?"

Richmond stalked over to the window and stared into the twilight. "Lady Lyntwoode accosted me like a common trollop." *Now I'm paying the price for her reckless behavior,* he thought, his blood boiling. *It's just not fair!*

"Nonetheless, you were caught in a compromising position with her. Why are you so incensed? It's not as if you're courting either of the available Wyndmoore ladies," Stanton commented.

"I'm just worried about Miss Wyndmoore. I have reason to believe that her accident was actually deliberate," he said softly, walking over to the chair next to his father and sitting down.

Deep frown lines furrowed Stanton's brows. "May I ask how you've come to this conclusion?"

Richmond was evasive. "I have my reasons. I've spoken to Lady Raverston, but she doesn't appear to take my warning seriously," Richmond said in a voice filled with defeat.

"Would you like me to speak with Lady Raverston tomorrow morning?" Stanton asked calmly.

The thought never occurred to Richmond. He rarely involved his father in his personal life, but this time, his friendship with Lady Raverston might help the situation. "Would you? I really don't want to see anything happen to Cassandra, and I can't be there to protect her," he said passionately.

Stanton smiled ever so slightly. "I'll check on her tomorrow. I'm sure she's fine," he said reassuringly.

"I sent Cassandra some flowers with an apology. Can you ask if she's received them?" he asked, his cheeks turning a slight shade of red.

"Of course," Stanton replied, draining his glass of claret.

Richmond's eyes fell back on the window. He knew Pembrook was after Cassie. Moreover, he was the only one who could stop him.

"Have you been entertaining much since you've been in Bath, Lord Stanton?" Pandora practically purred, her large blue eyes gazing seductively at Richmond's father.

Stanton stared at the intricate pattern on the dark maroon and golden carpet. Lady Lyntwoode, her womanly charms on view in a low cut, ruffled lavender walking dress, was incredibly tedious. No wonder his son was avoiding her like the plague. "No, we haven't been entertaining at all. We've taken a rather small house in town. It's not really suitable for a large rout," he explained blandly, straightening his cravat.

Pandora's rosebud lips curved into a smile. "I'd be more than happy to serve as hostess for any affair you're planning. These sort of things require a woman's touch, you know," she said in a sage voice.

"I think not," Honoria said in a firm voice from the parlor door.

Stanton looked up, and a wondrous smile appeared on his face. Honoria had saved him from the scheming doxy.

"But, Aunt Honoria, it's my Christian duty to help Lord Stanton," Pandora explained as Honoria settled herself in the Chippendale chair next to Stanton.

"My dear, it is your Christian duty to help the poor in Lyntwoode's parish. It's not your duty to help Lord Stanton plan a rout. It's just not done. Now why don't you go upstairs and help Daphne pick out a gown for Lady Hamilton's ball while I speak to Lord Stanton?" Honoria said in a tone that said her suggestion was an order.

"But, Aunt Honoria, I was just getting reacquainted with Lord Stanton!" Pandora whined.

Honoria raised an eyebrow. "Perhaps I didn't make myself clear, Pandora. We no longer require your company in the parlor. If you refuse to leave, you don't need to come down to dinner tonight," she said simply.

"You cannot treat me like you do Daphne!" Pandora exclaimed as she stomped out of the room in a full rage.

Stanton smiled. He had loved Honoria years ago, and he still loved her. Not just for her sparkling wit, her charm, or the way she smiled at him. He loved her for the way she handled her wayward nieces. She was magnificent. "Ah, Honoria, you rule your house with an iron fist," he said, certain that she would realize that he meant that as a compliment.

Honoria blushed slightly. "Yes, well, Daphne and Pandora are both spoiled beyond belief. They need someone to take them to task. Thank goodness Lyntwoode is on his way."

"Sending for the husband. I take it Pandora isn't aware?"

"Of course not."

"Of course not. Very good. Now to the matter of my son," Stanton said, ready to tackle Derek's brangle.

"Your son. The one who was embracing Lady Lyntwoode?"

Stanton sighed. "Yes, that one. Did Cassandra receive the flowers and the apology letter he sent over?" he asked, noticing the glow to Honoria's cheeks. *Gads, she's a handsome woman,* he thought.

"Flowers? He never sent Cassandra any flowers."

"Derek very definitely sent Cassandra flowers. He told me so himself," he said firmly.

Shaking her head, Honoria replied, "I'll look into it. Suffice it to say that Cassandra never received them."

"And has our brave girl recovered from her carriage accident?" he asked, sitting up in his chair.

Honoria frowned. "Then you haven't heard? Cassandra fell ill at the Pump Room yesterday. The physician says her glass of water contained traces of rat poison, but she seems to be doing well today."

"Rat poison? Have you alerted the authorities?"

"The doctor said these kinds of accidents are somewhat common, so we didn't call the authorities. As for Cassandra, she hasn't been herself since the carriage accident. She's been imagining all sorts of things. I'm thinking of sending her home in a sennight or so," she concluded.

Stanton had to think fast. Cassandra was obviously involved in something; Derek had all but confirmed that. Now there had been a second attempt on her life. There weren't any males, save their elderly butler, in the household to protect Cassie. "I'm sure it's nothing but a run of bad luck," Stanton said mildly, "but why don't I send over one of our footmen? If something goes awry, then it might be beneficial to have a strapping young man about."

A small smile appeared on Honoria's face. "I don't know if a strapping young footman is the answer with Pandora and Daphne underfoot," she said lightly.

Leaning back into the horribly uncomfortable chair, Stanton smiled. "I don't think it will be a problem. We have very reliable servants in our establishment, and if I send one of our footmen here to watch over Miss Wyndmoore, that's exactly what he'll do," he said with confidence.

"If you're willing to do without one of your staff, then I suppose there's no harm in giving the idea a try," Honoria conceded, then added, "but please send over one of your less attractive men!"

Richmond stared at the letter in his hand in utter astonishment. Alone in the study, the afternoon sun was warm on his back, and he felt as if he was in some sort of bizarre dream. The letter read:

> *Congratulations on a job well done! Sending Lloyd's papers to London through Wyndmoore from Warwick was a stroke of genius!*
> *We're now one step ahead of Boney and his men, thanks to you and Lloyd. Enjoy the rest of your holiday.*
>
> Castlereagh

She sent the papers to Castlereagh, he thought in a daze. Cassie had known enough to send the documents to Castlereagh, and did it covertly, without arousing any suspicion.

Richmond leaned back in his chair and stared at the letter. Miss Cassandra Wyndmoore had obviously been very busy. While Pembrook was robbing their house, and he was busy trying to gain her trust, she simply sent the papers to her father, who delivered them to Castlereagh without mentioning his daughter. Cassie handled the entire affair like a seasoned operative.

Cassandra Wyndmoore, bluestocking spinster who was fond of reading Greek tomes, had done his job for him. She accomplished his mission single-handedly and deserved the thanks of the government, as well as his own gratitude.

There was the problem. If he told her that the papers were safe in London, then he would be admitting that he did indeed work for Castlereagh, and that would put an end to his career as an operative. However, he would send her flowers again, dance with her all night at Lady Hamilton's ball, and beg for her forgiveness for the episode with Pandora.

Richmond sighed and leaned back in the chair. He missed his little bespectacled spy and cursed Honoria for banning him from the house.

However, she can't forbid me to see Cassie at the ball, he thought with a sly smile.

Dinner with his father turned out to be quite enlightening for Richmond.

"Yes, you missed quite an entertaining visit, Derek. You really should learn how to behave yourself so you can be received in the better houses," Stanton teased, attacking the sweetbreads in white sauce on his plate.

A slight smile appeared on Richmond's face. Once again, his clothes were wrinkled, his hair was a mess, and he needed a shave. However, he was a bit more relaxed, since his mission was accomplished. "Is Lady Lyntwoode still trying to inveigle her way into my bedroom?" he asked, scooping up a forkful of potatoes.

"Of course. What you ever wanted with that dull, cosseted *demi-rep* is beyond my understanding," Stanton muttered as he continued to eat.

"I must have had a brain fever," Richmond replied, and added, "Did you see Cassie?"

"No, Honoria said she hasn't been about much since the incident at the Pump Room."

Richmond leaned forward, his eyes riveted on his father. "Incident? What incident?"

"The doctor doesn't seem to think there's any reason for concern. It appears that a bit of rat poison found its way into Miss Wyndmoore's waters. She's fully recovered, and the doctor said it happens now and again, careless kitchen staff and all that," he concluded, finishing up his sweet breads.

Poisoned? Cassie had been accidentally poisoned? "I don't think it was an accident," Richmond said firmly, pushing his plate away from him. "She's got to leave Bath. She's in danger here," he announced dramatically.

Stanton continued eating. "I sent Robert, our footman, over. When I explained the situation, he seemed to understand what needed to be done."

Richmond's mind was whirling. They were trying to scare Cassie. If they scared her enough, they were sure that she would hand over Lloyd's papers. Only she didn't have them, a fact that they obviously didn't know. "Damn Pandora! If it wasn't for her antics, I could be there, helping Cassie! Is she going out in public soon?"

"Honoria says she'll be attending Lady Hamilton's ball later in the week. By the by, she never received the flowers you sent," Stanton added, finishing the last bit of greens on his plate.

The claret was tasteless in Richmond's mouth as he drained the glass. "What? Never received the flowers? I'll wager the charming Lady Lyntwoode had a hand in diverting them." Richmond was highly annoyed, and actually wanted to go to Honoria's and box Pandora's ears like a child.

"I'm sure she did. Lady Lyntwoode is very determined," Stanton observed.

"And I'm just as determined," Richmond replied. Even though he wasn't being received at Honoria's house, he would make sure that Cassie was safe. No matter what.

Cassie sat alone in the parlor, reading a rather ghastly gothic novel. Pandora, Daphne, and Aunt Honoria were out making morning calls, and were then headed out for some shopping, so Cassie had the house to herself. Aunt Honoria had suggested that she stay in until the rout, and Cassie didn't particularly mind being housebound.

Cassie was at sixes and sevens. Part of her was utterly convinced that someone was trying to hurt her because of Mr. Lloyd's documents. Yet there was a tiny part of her that thought everything was just a coincidence and that she was having a run of bad luck. In any case, she thought it was more prudent to stay home, so home she was, reading a novel. At least until Lady Hamilton's ball.

She stared at the page, wondering what was really going on in her life. All Daphne did was complain about Pembrook and his lack of attentions, and, if Cassie wasn't mistaken, she was convinced Daphne had formed an attachment to him. That wasn't a good thing.

Then there was Richmond. He wasn't allowed to call at Honoria's house, so she'd probably never see him again. This caused her heart to sink even lower, even though Cassie knew he was only using her for information about Mr. Lloyd. Except that she truly enjoyed his company, she always had. Now she had to cope with the fact that once she left Bath, she'd probably never see him again. That thought made Cassie even more blue deviled.

And there was the matter of Lord Stanton. He appeared to be developing some sort of *tendre* for Aunt Honoria, but she hadn't seen him around lately. And she certainly couldn't ask her aunt about her feelings for Lord Stanton. That wasn't done at all. Cassie was sure that Aunt Honoria did have feelings for him, but she had no idea how to help their budding relationship.

Then there was Robert, the new footman. He was the only man who was constantly around their house. In fact, he was constantly underfoot, and Cassie thought he might be helping Daphne forget Lord Pembrook. Robert was tall, muscular, and had wavy blond hair and striking blue eyes. Yes, he was handsome enough to be an actor on Drury Lane and appeared to be rather bright. So why was he suddenly part of their household, and why was he always on Cassie's heels, watching her every move?

She closed the book and stared at the landscape on the wall. *Maybe it would be best if I went home immediately,* she mused. *I'll be safe there and I won't have to worry about anything,* she decided with a sigh.

"Sir, you cannot just burst into the parlor! Miss Wyndmoore isn't at home," Laughton said, his voice traveling down the hallway. A moment later, the door to the parlor swung open and Lord Richmond stepped in.

"Of course Miss Wyndmoore is at home. She's in the parlor reading. I'll only keep her a moment, and, yes, keep the door open and send in her abigail if need be," Richmond said coolly, striding over to Cassie.

I look like a dowd, Cassie thought, turning a bright shade of red. Her hair was a fright, her glasses were perched prominently on her nose, and she wasn't even wearing any shoes! To complete the awful picture she presented, she was wearing her oldest morning gown, a drab brown thing that Aunt Honoria had tried to get her to throw out. She had rescued the offending frock from the trash. "Lord Richmond!" she exclaimed, sitting up on the brown leather chair and trying to hide her feet.

Richmond smiled and sat down on the chair next to her. "I'm dreadfully sorry to call on you uninvited, Miss Wyndmoore, but I wanted to make sure you were . . . all right. My father informed me of your recent illness, and I wanted to see for myself that you had indeed recovered," he said calmly.

Cassie frowned. What was going on? Richmond was Pandora's suitor. Why was he calling on her and inquiring after her health? It made no sense. "I'm fine, Lord Richmond," she said, blushing under his intense scrutiny.

A guarded smile appeared on Richmond's face, as if he wasn't completely sure she had recovered. "My father also informed me you didn't receive the roses I sent you," he said, leaning towards her.

"Were they red hothouse roses?" she asked, already knowing the answer.

"Yes, they were."

Cassie stared down at the book on her lap. Should she

tell him where the flowers had ended up? Pandora did swear her to secrecy. Finally she said, "Pandora told me in confidence that you sent them to her."

"I thought as much. Cassie, I didn't send any flowers to your sister. In fact, my life would be perfect if I never had to see her again."

Cassie looked into his eyes. He seemed so sincere. Yet it made no sense. Lord Richmond was a catch on the Marriage Mart. She was a spinster on the shelf. There was no world where he could ever care about her. She finally smiled a bit wryly and said, "Ah, you say that now, but once Pandora walks into the room, you'll fall under her spell. All men do," she concluded in a sage voice.

He leaned even closer to her, much to her surprise. "I realize you have no reason to believe me, Cassie, but I don't carry on with married women, no matter how willing they are. You're the only female in this household who holds any interest for me," he said, reaching over and grasping her hands in his.

Cassie tried to think of some suitable response. She couldn't think of anything but the fluttering of her heart, so she finally made a joke of it. "You'd best start spending your time with more eligible ladies, Lord Richmond, or Society will label you a bedlamite," she said lightly.

"I think not, Cassandra," he said, his eyes never leaving hers.

Cassie blushed, and waited for him to let go of her hands. He made no effort to do so. It was very inappropriate, but she liked the feel of his strong hands gripping hers.

"You will be careful?" he said worriedly, gazing into her golden green eyes.

"Aunt Honoria has suggested that I stay at home until Lady Hamilton's rout."

He looked so concerned. "You know, you've gotten yourself into quite the fix, and your aunt has barred me from the house, so I can't be here to look out for you."

Cassie was completely confused. If he was the spy, he was the one trying to scare her. Yet here he was, risking Aunt Honoria's wrath to come and reassure himself that she was all right. It made no sense. Unless he wasn't a spy, or at least was a spy for England. It was either that or he was very, very devious and trying to cover his tracks by pretending he wasn't behind her accidents. "Yes, well, I'll be fine," she replied awkwardly.

He stared at her for the longest time, without saying anything. His hand felt firm around hers, and she felt so . . . safe when he was around. This made no sense at all, since she thought he could be behind her run of bad luck. Nevertheless, when he sat close to her and gazed at her so intently, she was certain that he wouldn't try to hurt her.

Of course, if he was working for England, he should have gotten word that the papers were with Castlereagh, she reasoned. If they got to Castlereagh. They could have been intercepted. Cassie was utterly confused. "I expect to be leaving Bath soon," she said, breaking the long silence.

A million expressions crossed his face before he replied. "Leaving? When?"

"Sometime after Lady Hamilton's rout. I don't have any definite plans yet," she said, her heart tightening in her chest. She didn't want to leave Bath and face the fact that she'd never see him again.

He frowned. "Where will you be going?"

"I don't really know," Cassie said vaguely. She wanted

to tell him she was going home, but she wasn't sure if he could be trusted. Even if he was completely innocent and wasn't working for the French, it didn't matter, since he was only feigning affection for her.

He was silent for a long while. It was as if he wanted to say something, but kept deciding against it. Finally, he asked, "You said you'd be attending Lady Hamilton's rout?

"Yes."

"I'll see you there then," he said and gently kissed her hand. "Now I really must be going. I'd rather not meet up with your aunt. And be careful," he said rather abruptly.

Utterly confused, Cassie turned bright red as he stood up and headed toward the door.

"And, Cassandra?" he said in a soft, seductive voice.

"Yes?"

"You have lovely feet. You don't need to keep them hidden under your clothes," he said with an impish smile and swept out of the parlor.

Chapter 14

"Cassie, why isn't Lord Pembrook calling on me?" Daphne asked innocently, sitting on the edge of Cassie's bed.

Sunlight streamed through the window, and Cassie wondered what time it was. Daphne rarely woke up before noon, and was rarely up before Cassie. Yet here she was, looking definitely agitated, sitting on Cassie's bed. It was two days until Lady Hamilton's rout, and Daphne was paralyzed with anxiety. This wasn't a natural state for Daphne at all. Cassie propped her overfilled goose down pillow against the headboard and leaned back, studying her sister.

Daphne was always a vision of loveliness. Always. Even when she was ill, the beads of perspiration on her brow made her look dewy and radiant. However, she certainly wasn't radiant today. Daphne looked wan, her usual rosy blush was definitely absent, her hair looked absolutely lackluster, and there were even faint dark circles under her eyes.

"Gentleman aren't always the most predictable, Daphne, especially those who have been around Town for a while," Cassie said gently. *She's fixed her interest on him,* Cassie mused. *Now he's thrown her over for some unknown reason.*

Daphne frowned and began to finger the white Belgian lace on her morning dress. "I did something wrong, didn't I? That's why Lord Pembrook has made himself scarce lately."

"Daphne, I'm certain that you didn't do anything wrong at all. It's just that being in Society can be difficult, and you're accustomed to the lads back home. Lord Pembrook is a stranger, and they don't always act as we expect," Cassie explained.

"It's not Lord Pembrook. Pandora said I'm not beautiful enough, that's why I can't hold on to someone like him," Daphne admitted in a soft voice.

Cassie reached over and took Daphne's hand in hers. "Daphne, why in the world would you listen to Pandora? You know she's only interested in herself."

Daphne sniffled. "I know. She even wanted me to keep you away from Richmond, and I told her I'd help her, but I changed my mind," she admitted.

"Why would Pandora want to keep me away from Richmond?"

"Silly goose! Because he's taken a fancy to you and Pandora doesn't like it," Daphne explained.

"I don't know, Daphne," Cassie said nonchalantly.

"There's something else as well. Something I didn't tell you about, and I know that's why Lord Pembrook isn't interested in me any longer."

Cassie's mind was in a whirl. Did Pembrook attempt to take liberties with her sister? Did he try to comprise her virtue? *What in the world is Daphne talking about?* she wondered, a frown appearing on her brow. "Why, Daphne?" Cassie asked, trying to conceal her curiosity.

Daphne stared at the floor. "Remember when Lord Pembrook called and you and Aunt Honoria were out?"

"Yes."

"Well, when we were alone, he asked me about the book you found," Daphne said cautiously.

Cassie's heart skipped a beat. Pembrook. A spy who was looking for information. Of course. It wasn't surprising, since he had been on her trail for quite a while. "And?"

"And, well, he asked me to show it to him. I went to look for it, but I couldn't find it," Daphne murmured.

"Why did he want to see it, Daphne?" Cassie asked cautiously.

"Well, he said he was working for the government and that the book belonged to Mr. Lloyd. It was all very secret. And that's when he told me that Lord Richmond was a spy."

Cassie mulled over the information. Things were getting more complicated by the moment. Pembrook and Richmond both wanted the book. Why would a spy admit to anyone that he was a spy? That would seem to be against the spying code, whatever that was. Since Pembrook was the one fingering Richmond, it appeared that Pembrook was more likely to be the spy. Unless Pembrook was, well, stupid, and didn't realize that he shouldn't admit to anyone that he was a spy. It was all very suspect to Cassie. "Well, none of that matters now since the book was stolen," Cassie observed wryly.

"I suppose you're right," Daphne replied with a sigh.

"You know, Daphne, when a gentleman genuinely takes a liking to you, he doesn't ask you particular favors, and he certainly wouldn't do anything that would hurt your reputation," Cassie observed.

"Oh."

"And you know you're just as lovely as Pandora, and more importantly, you have a bigger heart," Cassie said, squeezing Daphne's hand.

"Do you really think so?" Daphne said softly.

Cassie smiled. "Yes. Yes, I do. Lord Pembrook isn't the most handsome man in England, you know, and choosing a partner on looks isn't always the best idea, either," she added for good measure.

Daphne looked up and smiled slightly. "I know. Have you seen Robert, the new footman? He's very handsome."

"Yes, I've noticed him," Cassie replied.

Daphne winked at her. "I think he has formed an attachment for you, Cassie. Haven't you noticed he's always hanging about your heels?"

"Yes, well, it's probably just a coincidence," Cassie replied. She had noticed that Robert was always underfoot, and thought it was just a coincidence. Moreover, why did Aunt Honoria even hire a new footman? Her house was filled with old retainers, so why did she need to hire someone else?

Of course, there could be another reason. Robert, the new footman, could be an accomplice to whoever was looking for Lloyd's papers, she mused. If he wasn't an accomplice, perhaps he was the person who was behind all of her accidents. Perhaps he was the French spy and Pembrook and Richmond were innocent. That made no sense at all though, considering their curiosity about the book.

"You know, Pandora was much nicer to me when I was younger," Daphne said suddenly.

Cassie sighed. *Pandora is ruining our entire trip to Bath,* she thought angrily. "People sometimes change as they grow older," she finally replied.

"You haven't changed, Cassie. I've always been able to talk to you."

Cassie grinned. "And you always will, since I'm

dreadfully old and set in my ways. Before you came along, Daphne, Pandora was always the beautiful Wyndmoore. Now she has to share the spotlight with you, and I don't think she likes the idea."

"But you're beautiful too, Cassie. Most of your beauty is inside, that's all."

Cassie leaned over and wrapped her arms around Daphne in a short hug. "That's very sweet of you to say, Daphne."

Daphne smiled. "It's true. And I know Lord Richmond likes you. That's why Pandora's been so mean to you lately."

Looking everywhere but at Daphne, Cassie replied, "Lord Richmond is just being polite to me. I'm quite on the shelf, you know."

"You're wrong, Cassie. You'll see. I bet he spends all his time with you at Lady Hamilton's ball," Daphne predicted.

"I hardly think that's possible," Cassie commented. "He's an earl and I'm just the mousy Miss Wyndmoore."

Daphne smiled again. "You'll see."

Cassie sighed. *If only Daphne is right, and Richmond really is interested in me. But it's only Lloyd's papers that are keeping him here, not my charms,* she thought, becoming more blue deviled by the moment.

The rest of the day was quiet, until Laughton called Cassie to the front door.

"What's amiss, Laughton?" Cassie asked, standing at the bottom of the stairs. A charming young urchin in tattered clothes was standing at the front door with Laughton, holding an impressive bouquet of flowers.

"This young person," Laughton began haughtily,

"insists that she must deliver the flowers with a message to you personally."

Cassie studied the young girl. Her clothes were a bit on the dirty side, she had a streak of what looked to be soot across her face, and her long hair looked utterly tangled. Overall, she looked like every other harmless street urchin. "That's quite all right, Laughton. I'll speak with the young lady," Cassie said, effectively dismissing him.

"I'll be down the hall if you need my assistance," Laughton intoned and walked away stiffly, his disapproval very apparent.

She walked down to the door and smiled at the girl, who appeared to be around ten. "How can I help you, young lady?" Cassie said with a smile.

"You're Miss Cassandra Wyndmoore?" the girl said, playing with a long, rather matted strand of hair.

"Yes, I am."

The girl gave her a broad smile, revealing a set of very yellow teeth. "Then these flowers are for you, miss," she said calmly and handed the flowers to Cassie.

"Thank you," Cassie said, opening the door.

The girl stepped outside and was ready to leave, then turned to Cassie, as if she had forgotten something. "I have something for you to read," she said quickly, digging in her pockets for a folded piece of paper. She handed it to Cassie and waited. Cassie put the flowers down on a small table and unfolded the piece of paper slowly. It read:

> *Bring Lloyd's papers to the Hamilton rout. At midnight, take them to the Bath Abbey and leave them on the altar. Go alone, or you will be killed. Tell anyone, and your next accident will be fatal. We are watching you right now.*

Cassie stared at the note in her hand, the hairs on the back of her neck standing on end. She was still staring at it when the girl grabbed the note from her hand and ran quickly down the street, disappearing.

Cassie looked around. The street seemed quiet. Her heart was beating wildly in her chest when she closed the door. *What am I going to do?* she thought in a panic. *I don't have the papers, and the little girl took the note. No one will believe me when I tell them about the threat. And the Hamilton ball is tomorrow evening. What am I going to do?*

As Cassie stood near the door, she saw a figure watching her out of the corner of her eye. It was Robert, the footman.

Cassie retreated to her bedroom, weighing her options. *I can't run away. They're watching me. So if I leave Bath, they'll simply follow me,* she reasoned.

I can tell Aunt Honoria. Will Aunt Honoria believe me? Will the magistrate believe me? I don't even have a copy of the letter. They'll just think I'm having some sort of strange episode because of my fall, she thought, staring out the window yet seeing nothing.

Even if they do believe me, what can they do? I'm being watched, they said so. Maybe even by someone in this very house. I don't have Lloyd's book, and what do my notes prove? They'll just say I fabricated everything, and I can't prove otherwise, she thought.

Cassie stared out the window. It was a beautiful day, the birds were singing, and sky was as blue as Daphne's favorite walking dress. *Why didn't I just give back Mr. Lloyd's book?* she thought, her face frozen in a scowl. *Why did I have to be so bloody curious? I should have just turned his book over to the magistrate, or his heir, and just forgotten about it. Now I have to put up with the consequences of my horrid curiosity.*

Running away wasn't an option. Telling someone wasn't an option. *Papa always says I have to handle my own problems, and this is something I'll handle myself,* she thought, trying in vain to figure out a reasonable solution.

The French spy, whoever he was, knew about the papers in the tree. He thought she still had them. What he didn't know was the information they contained.

I'll just forge a fake set of papers, Cassie suddenly decided. *I'll write them in Greek and make them similar to the ones from the tree, but not exactly the same. By the time they figure out what happened, I'll be out of Bath. Even if they come after me, I'll be safe in Warwick; our servants will make sure of that. It's the perfect solution,* she decided.

Cassie went over to one of her trunks in search of a quill pen and some paper. She rustled through her belongings until she found them, sat down at the small escritoire and began writing. She was certain her plan was the best course of action.

"This won't do. I look like a prize cow in it," Pandora shrilled, throwing a red satin gown at Suzette, her abigail.

Suzette was obviously accustomed to Pandora's antics and easily dodged the flying garment. "Yes, m'lady," she said very subserviently and picked up the offending garment.

"Didn't you bring any suitable gowns at all? I cannot believe that Honoria's modiste doesn't have time to make me a new gown. Doesn't she realize that I'm Lady

Lyntwoode?" she raved, not really expecting any sort of answer.

Suzette didn't give her one, and instead began rifling through Pandora's wardrobe in search of a suitable gown. "How about this one, m'lady?" she suggested, holding up a low cut cerise creation.

Pandora stared at her as if she had lost her mind. "That's all wrong," she stormed and walked over to the gowns that were on the bed. "I'll find something myself, since you obviously have no idea what I need," she said in a withering voice.

Suzette sighed imperceptibly and stepped aside.

Pandora sorted through the gowns with a vengeance, flinging the unacceptable creations onto the floor in disgust. Finally, after the floor was covered with Pandora's clothes, she held one out to Suzette. "This one will have to do for the Hamilton ball," Pandora hissed, thrusting a crimson gown at her abigail.

Suzette stared at the gown in horror. For it was a horrid gown, more suitable for a Cyprian than a lady. The sheer crimson confection, which was worn with dampened petticoats, was full of flounces, which Pandora enjoyed. It was also cut in a most daring fashion, which Pandora also enjoyed. In fact, it was cut so low that there were times Pandora displayed her nipples, which caused Lyntwoode to actually comment on her daring. *However, Lyntwoode won't be at the rout, and Richmond will,* Pandora thought with a slight smile.

"And make sure my rubies are in perfect condition. I expect I'll be wearing them with the gown," she ordered, frowning at Suzette.

Suzette wasn't really vexing Pandora. It was Richmond. And Cassie. *Why is he spending time with my mouse of a sister?* she wondered, walking over to the window and gazing out into the garden. *He can't be interested in her, he just can't be!*

As she gazed at the lush greenery, everything suddenly became clear to her. *He's still angry that I married Lyntwoode,* she realized. *That's why he's courting the mouse—to get even with me! It all makes perfect sense now,* she decided, winding a strand of hair around her finger.

If he's trying to get even with me, then he still cares. He still loves me, she thought, a satisfied smile slowly appearing on her face. *And if he still loves me, I'm sure to be in his bed before long,* she mused.

"Miss Cassandra, aren't you up yet?" Sara questioned, opening Cassie's door slightly.

There was no answer.

Sara tried again. She knocked on the door a bit more forcefully and said, "Miss Cassandra, are you up yet?" in a much louder voice.

Cassie groaned. *What time is it?* she wondered, burying herself under the covers. "Yes, Sara?" she finally said, trying to rouse herself.

It had been dawn when she finally finished the falsified documents. She tried to remember the format of Mr. Lloyd's papers and tried to make her version similar. The papers appeared to detail French troop movements for the next four months; unfortunately, Cassie hadn't studied the papers as closely as she would have liked, so creating the new documents in Greek had been time consuming.

Sara entered the room and immediately frowned at Cassie. "Miss Cassandra, Lady Raverston sent me up to help you get ready for Lady Hamilton's ball tonight," Sara announced.

"What time is it, Sara?" Cassie muttered, still groggy.

"It's almost five, Miss Cassandra. Lady Raverston sent me up earlier today to see if you wanted tea, but I couldn't wake you. Lady Lyntwoode and Miss Daphne have already had their hair done and are waiting for their gowns to be pressed," Sara explained.

Cassie groaned. Not only had it been dawn before she fell asleep, but she spent the night engulfed in surreal nightmares of Mr. Lloyd, Richmond, and Pandora. "I'll be up soon, Sara. I'm just very tired, I didn't sleep well last night," she explained, hoping upon hope that she could get another hour of sleep.

"Are you sure you don't want me to post your letter?" Sara asked calmly.

Cassie frowned. *My letter?* "What letter?"

"The letter you were working on last night. I brought you two candles at midnight, and Robert said you were up until dawn. Do you want me to post it?" she asked with a frown.

Cassie could feel her chest tightening. Robert. The footman who was spying on her. *Damnation, I hope he doesn't know what I'm working on,* she thought in a panic. "No, I'm not done with it yet," Cassie replied, making a mental note to send some sort of letter in the next day to cover her tracks.

"So you don't need Lady Raverston to frank it?"

"No, I'm not quite done with it yet."

"Oh," Sara said, looking somewhat confused.

"Why don't you come back in about an hour, Sara? It won't take me any time to get ready, and I'm sure I'll feel more the thing then."

"Yes, Miss Cassandra," Sara replied and disappeared out of the door.

Cassie nestled back into the covers and expected to drift to sleep immediately.

All she could think of were the papers and Richmond, and she couldn't fall asleep.

"Yes, Robert, you have some information for me?" Stanton said, wondering what had brought his footman back from the Raverston household so soon.

"Yes, Lord Stanton. You wanted me to tell you if anything strange was happening at the household, especially if it involved Miss Cassandra," Robert replied.

"Yes," Stanton said with a frown. What could be amiss now?

"Miss Cassandra was up all night, working on some papers."

"What kind of papers?" Stanton asked, studying his footman.

"I'm not certain, m'lord. At first, I thought it might be a letter, but it seems deuced odd that she would spend all night writing a letter and then not see to it that it's posted first thing in the morning. In addition, if I may be so bold, Miss Cassandra seems to know her mind. I can't see that it would take her all night to write a letter," Robert said boldly.

"That's a good observation."

"And Lady Hamilton's ball is tonight. All of the ladies in the house were in bed early, except Miss Cassandra. Ladies always turn in early the night before a rout. But Miss Cassandra was writing until dawn. Sara said she thinks the papers were in a foreign language," Robert added.

Stanton frowned. Cassie had been up all night before the biggest rout in Bath working on papers in a foreign language. That was dashed odd. Dashed odd indeed.

"But, Miss Cassandra, your reticule doesn't match your gown," Sara practically whined. Cassie was wearing a lovely golden shot silk gown, paired with an exotic golden and rose-colored Indian shawl. The offending reticule was blue. Not light blue, not blue and gold, not blue and rose, just blue. Midnight blue to be exact.

Cassie pulled at the gown, trying to cover her bosom. "Doesn't this gown seem rather . . . revealing to you, Sara?" she asked, gaping at what appeared to be a vast expanse of her own flesh. Much more flesh than she was accustomed to exposing in public. Or in private, for that matter.

Sara studied her critically. "The gown looks fine, Miss Cassandra, and, from what I hear, isn't nearly as . . . daring as the gown that Lady Lyntwoode is wearing," she said.

"Is Pandora wearing something indecent?"

Sara looked everywhere but at Cassie. "Yes, well, it isn't my place to say, Miss Cassandra. You look very nice, and I don't think your gown is indecent or too revealing," Sara replied tactfully.

"Oh" Cassie said, still staring at the mirror. She hadn't slept most of the night and had expected to look rather pale. However, the gown brought out her coloring and almost made her cheeks glow. Sara, who had finished helping Aunt Honoria dress quite a while ago, curled her hair a bit, so she did have some charming little ringlets framing her face. No one would ever be able to tell that she was up all night falsifying papers.

"Are you sure you want to take the blue reticule?" Sara asked again.

Cassie needed a reticule big enough to hold the papers. She had initially considered hiding them on her person, perhaps somewhere in her underclothes, but there was a problem. The gown. The lovely golden gown hugged her body and revealed every curve. It would also reveal a mass of papers, so that idea was out of the question. Therefore, she needed a large reticule, and the only large reticule she had was blue. Yes, it looked hideous. Cassie knew it looked hideous, but there wasn't any other option. "If you can find another reticule this size in the house that matches, I'll be happy to use it," Cassie replied, draping the shawl around her. *At least the shawl is large*, she mused. *If I'm lucky I'll be able to spend the night in a corner and not worry about having some bosky old lord looking down my cleavage.*

"I'll go look, Miss Cassandra," Sara said obediently and swept out of the room on her mission.

Cassie stared after her and sat on the side of the bed, enveloped by a feeling of dread. Everything was such a mess.

She knew Richmond was probably a spy. He was still hanging about her, while Pembrook had practically vanished. But her heart didn't want to believe that Richmond would hurt her. The way he smiled at her seemed so genuine, and he actually seemed interested in her. In addition, he seemed to be concerned about her safety. He had risked Aunt Honoria's wrath to come and see her after he was barred from the house. But then again, he was kissing Pandora. Again.

Cassie sighed. It was so much easier to see Richmond as a heartless womanizer than a spy. As for Pembrook, he was handsome, he was charming, and he had friends everywhere. He was the least likely person in Bath to be a spy. Yet there was something about him that just didn't ring true.

She stared at the door, waiting patiently for Sara to return with a new reticule. The papers were hidden in her escritoire, just waiting to be delivered to the Abbey. *If I give them the papers, maybe they'll be fooled, and this will all end,* she thought, sighing again.

Cassie didn't want to think about the fact that her life could be in danger.

"Pandora, your dress is so . . . so . . . colorful," Daphne managed to gulp, staring at her oldest sister in abject horror.

Pandora looked like a bird of paradise. Her crimson gown, accented with large black ribbons at the bosom, sleeves, and hem, was one of the most hideous creations Daphne had ever seen. True, her experience in polite Society was limited, but she was certain that crimson wasn't a color that was worn in Bath, at least not at this time of the year. If the color wasn't scandalous enough, there was the fact that the gown barely covered her womanly charms, and Daphne expected her sister to literally pop out of her gown when she moved.

Daphne, clad in a high waisted white satin gown adorned with pink embroidery at the bosom and the hem, frowned at Pandora. *She looks like a Cyprian,* Daphne thought, waiting anxiously for Cassie to appear so they could finally leave.

Pandora gave her a satisfied smile. "Yes, well, you know I am the *only* beauty of the family," she said haughtily.

For once in her life, Daphne found she had nothing to

say. She was going to the largest fête in Bath with her sister looking like a doxy. *At least we're not in London,* Daphne mused, sagging against the wall.

Pandora gave her a satisfied smile. "You shouldn't be so blue deviled, Daphne. It's not your fault that you're not a diamond," she said, gazing at Daphne as if she were an antidote.

Daphne didn't bother answering.

Pandora strolled over to the window and gazed out with interest. "Is that Richmond's carriage?" she asked curiously.

Daphne cringed. *Pandora has a husband. She should be thinking about him, not about Lord Richmond,* she decided. "It's Lord Stanton's carriage. He's escorting us tonight."

"I see." She turned to Daphne and gave her a wicked little smile. "Do you know why Richmond isn't escorting the mouse?"

Daphne frowned. *I hate it when she calls Cassie that, she's not a mouse at all,* she thought rebelliously. "You mean Cassie?"

"Yes, the mouse. He's barred from the house. I made sure Aunt Honoria and Cassie caught me kissing him, and they blamed him and said he couldn't see Cassie anymore," she proclaimed proudly.

"What? Why didn't anyone tell me?" Daphne said in shock.

"And why should they? It didn't involve you, and now I've made sure that dear Derek will stay away from the mouse. Wasn't it a brilliant plan?" Pandora asked.

Before Daphne could reply, Aunt Honoria bustled into the morning room. She looked lovely in a tasteful sage green gown, the famous Raverston emeralds around her neck.

"Lord Stanton is here. Where's Cassie?" she asked, looking around the room expectantly.

"She hasn't come down yet, Aunt Honoria," Daphne said, glancing from Honoria to Pandora, waiting for her to comment on Pandora's awful gown.

Instead, Honoria smiled at Daphne calmly. "Daphne dear, would you go upstairs and see what's keeping her? I hate to keep Lord Stanton waiting."

Daphne sighed. No one ever stood up to Pandora. Ever.

Cassie wrapped the colorful Indian shawl around her shoulders tightly and tried to be brave. Except that she wanted to lose her lunch. Once she did that, she wanted to go home. Immediately.

But she couldn't do that. She had to deliver the papers, and perhaps that would put an end to the awful intrigue that was taking over her life.

"Cassie, are you ready to leave yet?" Daphne asked, standing in the doorway.

Cassie grabbed her blue reticule, and nervously pushed her spectacles up her nose. "I suppose," she replied, standing up.

"Why didn't you come downstairs? You're ready, aren't you?" Daphne asked curiously.

Cassie grinned. "I didn't want to listen to Pandora," she said as they headed down the stairs. "I thought someone would eventually come and get me."

Daphne smiled. "That was a good idea."

Cassie studied her sister. "You look lovely tonight, Daphne. I'm sure all of the gentlemen at Lady Hamilton's rout are going to be spellbound by your charm."

"I hope so. I certainly didn't charm Lord Pembrook, did I?" Daphne asked.

"Lord Pembrook isn't the only man in Bath, or in London," Cassie noted, hiding the blue reticule in the folds of her shawl.

"Pandora's being dreadful and looks like a Cyprian," Daphne commented.

Cassie smiled at her. "Remember, Daphne, she's not a Wyndmoore any longer. If you just ignore her, she won't have any fun taunting you," she said in a level voice.

As they reached the bottom of the stairs, Daphne turned toward Cassie. "Pandora told me about what happened with Lord Richmond."

"Daphne, it's not like I haven't seen him kiss Pandora before," she said in a calm voice. At least she tried to be calm.

"Cassie, he didn't kiss her, she kissed him. So that he wouldn't be able to see you anymore," Daphne proclaimed, just seconds before Aunt Honoria and Pandora stepped out of the morning room.

Before Cassie had a chance to reply, Aunt Honoria started hustling them into the carriages to go to Lady Hamilton's rout.

Chapter 15

"Oh, Cassie, this is the most wonderful ball ever," Daphne exclaimed, sitting down next to Cassie, her pink cheeks flushed with excitement.

Cassie surveyed the crowded ballroom and had to agree. Lady Hamilton had spared no expense to create the social event of the summer.

Pink, yellow, orange, and blue hothouse flowers filled every corner, engulfing the room in a rich, heady fragrance. The gentlemen were dressed to the nines, and Cassie even heard some mutterings that the legendary Beau Brummel was in attendance, although no one had actually talked with him personally. The ladies present wore the loveliest French silk gowns, although a few of them were adorned with the most dreadful turbans, which were, of course, the style. It reminded Cassie of her very short time in London during her Season.

"I'm quite overwhelmed myself," Cassie said, clutching her reticule to her chest, her eyes searching the room for Richmond. *Of course he won't be here,* she chided herself. *He's lingering at the Abbey, waiting for me to arrive,* she thought.

"Why aren't you dancing?" Daphne asked innocently.

"You know I don't dance, Daphne. And I am on the shelf, so I'm perfectly content to sit here with the dowagers and the more literary types," Cassie lied. Usually, sitting with the dowagers didn't bother her, but tonight it was getting on her nerves. She was tired of not having any fun and of people treating her as if she was in her dotage.

"I haven't seen Lord Pembrook here tonight," Daphne said casually.

"Perhaps he's left Bath," Cassie suggested.

"Oh no, I was talking to Miss Shropshire, and she said that she saw him driving yesterday afternoon."

"Daphne, Lord Pembrook is just the first of many handsome men you'll meet," Cassie said philosophically.

"I suppose you're right. You know, Cassie, you look much prettier without your spectacles," she said mischievously.

"I know. Aunt Honoria asked me to remove them for the rout."

"Well?"

"I can't watch the crowd very well without them," Cassie replied.

"But you look so much prettier. Won't you take them off just for a while, for me?" Daphne pleaded.

Cassie smiled slightly, then capitulated. "Oh, all right," she said, slipping the spectacles into her reticule.

Richmond stared at Cassie from across the room and frowned. *Why is she covered up with a shawl as if it's the middle of winter,* he wondered. He found the room quite stuffy, so he reasoned that she had to be near heatstroke.

Then there was the fact that she was with the dowagers. Even though she was hiding her dress under a shawl, she was still one of the most beautiful women in the room. *Why isn't she wearing her spectacles?* he wondered. With them, she was very, very pretty. Without them, she was stunning, and he realized with a start that he didn't want anyone else in the room to notice her. She was his, and he most definitely didn't want the other bucks at the rout taking any interest at all in her.

He smiled as he made his way toward her. When she turned her head a certain way, she looked just like the charming young woman he had met at the Pig and Crow Inn. She was everything he wanted: smart, charming, and resourceful. He didn't know many men who would have made sure Lloyd's documents got to Castlereagh, but she had. In fact, she had potential to be an operative for the government. That wasn't something he'd ever mention to Castlereagh.

Cassie looked into the crowd, searching for Richmond. She was certain that he wasn't at the rout. Because if he was at the rout, he could hardly be waiting at the Bath Abbey for her—unless he left early to meet her.

There was a man that could have been Richmond on the far side of the room talking with a group of young bucks. He was about the same height and the same weight, and he had dark hair. Cassie squinted. *It could be him, but I can't tell without my glasses,* she thought with a frown. She almost put them on and then remembered that she had told Daphne she wouldn't wear them for the evening.

She was still staring at the man who might be Lord Richmond when she heard someone talking to the dowager a few seats away. Cassie ignored the voice and continued squinting. Then the male voice got louder.

"Excuse me, Miss Wyndmoore. Would you care to dance?" the voice said, and Cassie realized that it was Lord Richmond. Talking to her.

She looked up and saw him gazing down at her expectantly. His hair was combed into a Brutus, as much of a Brutus as he could muster. The blue-black mane practically glistened tonight, and his eyes were sparkling with mirth. "Lord Richmond, I'm so sorry, I wasn't attending," she admitted, blushing. *He must think I'm a complete idiot,* Cassie thought, noticing the perfect fit of his black waistcoat and the shine of his Hessians. Once again, he looked like a gypsy masquerading as a gentleman.

He smiled again, a dazzling smile. Almost like the smiles he used to give Pandora. "I asked if you'd care to dance."

At that very moment, the band struck up a waltz, and before she could refuse, he took her hand in his and gazed at her entreatingly. The shawl slipped from her shoulders and her reticule sat on the chair with it, forgotten, as she followed Richmond to the dance floor.

As the music flowed sweetly through the fragrant summer night, Cassie let him hold her closer than what was respectable, and she didn't care. She was certain that everyone was taking note of the spinster who was dancing with the eligible Lord Richmond, but it didn't matter. *Tonight might be my last night in Bath,* she realized. *It might be the last time I see Lord Richmond before I go home.*

"You look enchanting tonight," he said softly into her ear, drawing her a bit closer.

Cassie sighed. Richmond was so romantic, but she knew that. Pandora told her time after time. It was too bad that he was probably a spy. And not interested in her at all. She sighed and didn't reply.

"You seem preoccupied this evening," he commented, as they continued to whirl across the floor.

"I've just been thinking about everything that's happened since I came to Bath," she said softly, still clinging to his tall, muscular form. *What an inane comment to make,* she thought, chiding herself. *I sound like Daphne.*

He smiled down at her. "You don't have anything to worry about, Cassandra. You've handled everything that's happened to you perfectly," he said in a reassuring voice.

Cassie frowned. *What is he talking about?*

The music stopped and as he led her back to her seat, she casually remarked, "I believe my sister Pandora is in the garden."

To her utter amazement, he smiled and took the seat next to her. "Then I most assuredly won't be there."

She moved closer to him and enjoyed the feel of his strong, muscular form against her.

"You will save another waltz for me, won't you?" he said into her ear.

Cassie smiled up at him and forgot about propriety. "Of course."

It certainly felt as if she was being courted, and for the moment, Cassie wanted to forget about her suspicions and believe that Richmond was interested in her.

"Derek, may I ask what you're thinking?" Stanton asked as they stood in the hall, studying the Hamilton family portraits.

"What am I thinking? I suppose I'm thinking that Lady Jane Hamilton wasn't the most attractive member of the family," Richmond replied, gesturing to the portrait.

Stanton frowned. "That's not what I mean. I'm talking

about Cassandra Wyndmoore. You're paying marked attention to her."

"Yes, I suppose I am," Richmond replied calmly.

"The tabbies are speculating that you'll take Miss Wyndmoore under your protection," Stanton said sharply, hoping to scare some sense into his son.

"I'd hardly take Miss Wyndmoore under my protection. She's quite respectable," he replied warily.

"Quite respectable?"

"Yes. And anyone who knew of her character would know that she doesn't behave in that manner," Richmond added, obviously offended.

Stanton smiled. *So Derek has become attached to the chit, just as I suspected.* "But you have to be aware of her reputation. By singling her out, you're subjecting her to all sorts of gossip."

"I'm not singling her out. We're just spending some time together. And I thought the tabbies would be busy trying to find out the name of the Cyprian who sold Lady Lyntwoode her gown," Richmond said calmly.

Stanton smiled. Lady Lyntwoode's gown was one of the major topics of conversation that night. "That's not the point, Derek. You are singling her out, you know. She's the only chit you've danced with all night, and you've spent the rest of the time hanging on her coattails."

Richmond smiled. "I enjoy her company."

"Just be careful. She is a respectable young lady," Stanton added for good measure.

The pair stared at the portraits for a while longer, until Richmond suddenly commented, "Cassandra seems to be preoccupied tonight."

Stanton sipped the glass of hock in his hand. "I hear she was up all night writing," he said calmly. He wasn't sure why he was telling his son this tidbit of information, but if Cassandra had involved herself in something unsavory, then Derek was the one man who could help her.

"Writing? All night?" Richmond questioned, a look of concern on his face.

"Yes, she was up until dawn, from what I hear. I sent Robert, our footman, over to Honoria, Lady Raverston's, to watch over her. He told me today. It's all very mysterious."

Stanton glanced over at his son. He was frowning. That was a good sign. He was obviously worried about Cassie.

"Perhaps I should keep an eye on her tonight," Richmond said, glancing toward the ballroom.

"Do you think there'll be any . . . unpleasantness?" Stanton asked, frowning to himself.

"I don't know, Father. I don't know," Richmond said warily.

Cassie sat alone in the study, curled up like a cat in a large, luxurious leather chair next to the fire. She glanced down at her father's pocket watch. She had nearly an hour before she had to leave.

The small fire was burning steadily, and since the window was open, the room was quite comfortable. Cassie closed her eyes and went over every detail.

When Papa's pocket watch reads a quarter to the hour, I'll go outside and get a hackney, she thought. *It's still early, so that shouldn't be a problem.*

Once we get to the Abbey, I'll make him wait for me, she decided. *I'll give him some extra blunt to come inside if he hears any strange noises. Or if I'm gone for more than a few minutes.* The extra money she'd brought from home was coming in handy.

The rest of the plan was simple: walk up the aisle, drop the papers on the altar, and walk back to the hackney. It all seemed very simple and straightforward.

Then, when she got home, she'd tell Aunt Honoria everything and ask to go home. That way, if anything went wrong, she'd be safe at home. It was a logical plan and nothing could really go wrong—that is, unless the traitors realized that she'd forged all of the documents. If that happened, and things started happening in Warwick, she'd simply go to Castlereagh.

Cassie sighed and disappeared into the chair. She still had time.

Richmond followed Pandora into the study, completely annoyed. He wasn't in the mood to chat with her, but Pandora had said it was about Cassie, so he gritted his teeth and followed her.

Pandora closed the door behind them. They were alone in the study; there was a roaring fire, the window was open, and a large leather chair that looked very welcoming was facing in the other direction.

"So what do you need to tell me about Cassandra?" Richmond asked irritably, staring at the door. *I shouldn't have let her close it,* he thought, glaring at Pandora.

Pandora smiled at him and closed the distance between them, standing closer than what was appropriate or necessary. "I wanted to tell you that my little sister is practically engaged," she murmured, stroking her neck sensually.

"My felicitations. It seems unusual that her family in Bath is unaware of that fact, though," he replied, taking a step back from Pandora. *What was I thinking walking into a room alone with her?* he wondered, glancing at the door.

Pandora stepped forward and placed her hand on his lapel. "Yes, well, she's being married off to the pock-faced son of the curate. It's not something that the family talks about."

The heavy, unnatural scent of Pandora's perfume wafted up to Richmond, and he began to feel a bit light-headed. *Gads, she smells worse than a brothel,* he decided and coughed.

What happened next was a blur to him. As he coughed, Pandora leaned forward, wrapped her arms around his neck, and kissed him as if he was the last man in the world. Once again, Pandora's audacity stunned him, and he didn't even react for a moment or two, he was so shocked.

He was even more stunned when the door to the study was flung open and the usually meek Earl of Lyntwoode appeared.

"Unhand my wife and name your seconds, Richmond," Lyntwoode said passionately.

Richmond thrust Pandora away from him in disgust. "Lyntwoode, I'm not going to duel you. Take your . . . wife and keep her away from me. She's been a thorn in my side ever since she's come to Bath," he said, glaring at Pandora.

Pandora looked at Richmond, and then at her husband. Then she broke down and started to cry. "Oh, Giles, it was horrible, he . . . he . . . he tried to force himself on me," she sobbed, flinging herself into her husband's arms.

Stroking her golden hair, Lyntwoode murmured something to Pandora before looking over at Richmond.

"I'll not stand for this. You will meet me on the field of honor," he said hotly.

Unfortunately, Richmond was a crack shot. He knew this. Everyone in London knew it. However, obviously Lyntwoode was unaware of the fact. "I refuse. I came into the study to discuss Lady Lyntwoode's sister Cassandra. Then she thrust herself into my arms, much the same way she just did to you," he replied.

Pandora muttered something to Lyntwoode, and he cooed something in her ear.

"Excuse me," Cassie said from the other side of the room.

Richmond, Pandora, and Lyntwoode all stared at her in disbelief.

"I'm sorry to say, Giles, that Lord Richmond is telling the truth," she said simply.

Pandora turned a rather unattractive shade of purple. "How dare you lie to my husband?" she began, tearing herself out of Lyntwoode's arms and walking over to Cassie. "You've been nothing but a trial to me all of my life. Do you know what it's like to be cursed with a pasty-faced, mousy bluestocking for a sister? Now, because you're still in love with Richmond after all these years, you're lying for him. He'll never ever love you, because he's in love with me!" Pandora shrieked, losing all of her self-control.

Cassie turned bright red, but didn't back down. "Giles, please believe me. Lord Richmond wasn't in here to seduce Pandora," she said in a level voice.

Richmond was reeling. Cassie loved him? Was that possible? He wasn't even sure she liked him. She was always so suspicious and distant, especially after he had kissed her. He was in shock.

Lyntwoode looked at Cassie, shifted his gaze to

Richmond, and then settled his eyes on his wife, who was rigged out like doxy. Then he took a deep breath. "I think it's best if this episode is forgotten," he announced, much to everyone's surprise.

Pandora's beautiful blue eyes bulged out of their sockets, presenting a less than perfect picture of the diamond of the first water. "How dare you believe them and not me! You're a half-wit disguised as an earl," she hissed.

Lyntwoode grabbed her wrist and held it firmly. "You will be quiet, or I'll give you the beating you so richly deserve," he said, as the entire room gaped at him.

That was when Cassie slipped out of the room.

She was halfway down the hall when she heard him behind her.

"Cassie, wait a moment, I need to talk to you," Richmond said, calling after her.

Cassie sighed. *He's the last person I want to talk to right now,* she thought, looking for an escape route. There was none. She was in the middle of a straight hallway that eventually led back to the ballroom. He knew she heard him, so she couldn't just duck behind a closed door. Knowing Richmond, he'd more than likely follow her, and she didn't particularly want to be alone with him.

He caught up with her a moment later. "Thank you for telling Lyntwoode the truth," he said softly, looking down at her.

Cassie didn't want to look at him. She was horrified that Pandora had told everyone in the room she had a *tendre* for Richmond, and she just wanted to be alone. She stared at the dark red Aubusson carpet. "He deserves to know how Pandora's behaving," she replied, her eyes still on the carpet.

He put his thumb under her chin and ever so gently

made her meet his eyes. "And there's no son of a curate waiting for you back home?" he said seductively, leaning closer to her.

I can't look at him, she thought, gazing at the wall behind him, refusing to meet his eyes. "I haven't heard from Papa lately, so I can't say for certain," she replied.

He smiled, a slow, seductive smile that transformed his rather angular features. "Ah, but, Cassandra, you forget. I've met your father, and he would never marry off his favorite daughter without consulting her first," he reasoned.

She didn't have a reply for him. *Damnation, why does he have to be so smart?* she wondered, frowning. *Yes, I did tell him I was Papa's favorite, but I didn't think he was paying attention,* she mused.

Before Cassie could think up a suitable reply, or even escape their conversation, he leaned over and lightly kissed her.

All she wanted to do was lean into him and wrap her arms around his tall, muscular frame. She wanted to forget the fact that he had been kissing her sister less than a quarter of an hour ago. She wanted to forget that he was probably a spy for the French. Most of all, she wanted to forget that he really wasn't interested in her.

But she couldn't. He kissed her gently, and seemed to be genuinely surprised when she didn't respond quite as ardently as she had in the carriage. "Cassie?" he asked softly, his hands wrapped around her waist.

Cassie took a step back, and he released her, frowning. "What's wrong?" he asked.

Once again, she couldn't meet his eyes. "Aunt Honoria will be looking for me," she said and darted down the hall toward the ballroom, never looking back.

* * *

Richmond watched Cassie from the corner of his eyes as he went through the paces of a country dance with Lady Hamilton's young, eligible daughter Elizabeth, who smiled prettily at him at every possible opportunity. She was a taking little thing who rather reminded him of Daphne Wyndmoore, except that the young Lady Elizabeth had already been presented at Court and had one very successful Season behind her. At least according to her doting Mama. In addition, since it was Lady Hamilton's ball, courtesy dictated that he dance at least once with the decorative Lady Elizabeth, who was, like Daphne, incapable of any sensible conversation.

Cassie was on the other side of the room, and, when they came around at a certain angle, he could see her. She was sitting next to a huge potted palm near a door. He glanced around the dance floor and saw Daphne dancing with a young buck. Lady Raverston was dancing with his father. Cassie was alone, for the moment, and appeared to be checking a pocket watch every now and again. *That's strange,* he mused. *Why in the world would she care about the time?*

The country dance, which seemed to last an interminable amount of time, finally ended and Richmond led Lady Elizabeth back to her mama. She was prattling on about something or another when Richmond noticed Cassie stand up and head for the door, her shawl and reticule in hand.

Lady Elizabeth stared at him, waiting for an answer. He had no idea what she had asked and instead smiled and said, "Excuse me," and strode quickly out of the room, trailing behind Cassie, much to the shock of Lady Hamilton and her daughter.

* * *

Richmond entered the Abbey through the south doors, making sure they closed silently behind him. He had no idea why Cassie would leave Lady Hamilton's rout for no apparent reason and head to the Abbey in a hackney, but he wasn't about to let her out of his sight.

As he lingered in the shadows, he saw her move slowly through the nave, shrouded in darkness. The Abbey was filled with shadows, and he couldn't see much, but his senses were sharp. He knew he wasn't alone there with Cassie.

Richmond studied the room. There was a pillar near the altar. Someone was there, he was sure of it. He heard a rustling that he knew didn't come from Cassie. She was still near the center of the main aisle; the sounds were coming from the pillar. So there was at least one other person with them.

He watched Cassie make her way down the main aisle purposely. This wasn't a spur of the moment journey to get away from the rout. No, she was there for a reason, he could tell by her very erect, almost defiant stance.

Then he heard someone else. Near the north transept. A footstep that was very light, a footstep from someone who didn't want to be heard. Two men were waiting for Cassie in the dark in the Abbey at midnight. Something was amiss, and he instinctively reached for the revolver in his coat. As silently as a cat, he moved through the darkness toward the altar.

Cassie's hands were shaking as she walked slowly up the aisle. All she wanted to do was run to the altar, drop the papers, and run out of the Abbey as fast as she could. But she decided against that course of action. *If*

*they think I'm afraid, they'll come after me in Warwick.
I have to be brave,* she thought, forcing herself to walk
casually toward the altar.

To make matters worse, the Abby was shrouded in
darkness, which didn't help her frazzled nerves. The
eerie glow of the full moon illuminated the Abbey just
enough for her to see the altar, and to keep her from
bumping into things. However, she really couldn't see
much of anything, and the moonlight made the vaulted
ceiling look vaguely sinister.

She began to count her steps. *Two, three, four, five.
Only about ten more steps to go,* she thought, terror
sweeping through her body. *Eight, nine, ten, almost
there.* Once in a while, she heard a strange noise, and
she came to realize that she wasn't alone. She was sure
her heart was going to burst out of her chest, it was beating so hard.

Her count was at thirteen when she reached the altar.
She had to believe that it was Richmond waiting for her
in the darkness, since she was sure he wouldn't hurt her.

She didn't want to think about what might happen if
she was wrong and there was someone else lurking in
the shadows.

Richmond could see someone on the other side of the
Abbey in the transept. The man in question was wearing dark clothing and hiding in the darkness. *Pembrook
perhaps?* he wondered, trying to focus on the figure.
*No, he's not tall enough to be Pembrook. Maybe it's one
of his allies,* Richmond reasoned. The figure ducked
around a corner, out of range of Richmond's weapon.

A chill ran up his spine as Cassie walked up to the
altar and delicately put down a thick parcel of papers.

He saw the figure near the altar move slightly; he was obviously waiting for Cassie. She then turned and began to walk toward the huge Abbey doors.

Then, from the corner of his eye, Richmond saw glint of metal across the room. It was a gun, pointed straight at Cassie.

Chapter 16

"No," a man screamed and lunged toward Cassie as she turned away from the altar.

Cassie couldn't move. Her terror kept her rooted in place, like a statue. *It's as if I'm in a play,* she thought, unable to move away from the figure rushing toward her. As he collided with her, a gunshot rang through the Abbey. It sounded like a cannon.

Cassie felt the man's body against her and could smell his cologne. It seemed familiar yet wasn't. She couldn't see his face in the moonlight, but he struck her with such force that it took the breath out of her. She hit the ground with a thud, and then everything went black.

When Pembrook screamed, it took every bit of Richmond's self-control not to go after Cassie. He knew Pembrook and knew that he didn't have a stomach for violence.

His heart lurched in his chest when the gun went off. Every instinct told him to go to Cassie, to see if she was hit. He didn't move. Instead, he focused every sense on the shadow that was now against the wall. He silently leveled his gun at the man in the north transept, waiting for the right opportunity. He wasn't going to waste a shot. He would shoot to kill.

Cassie and Pembrook were both on the floor, and both were silent. It was possible they were both dead. He didn't care about Pembrook; Cassie was his only concern. Every fiber of his body told him to go to her. He stood waiting. If he were any other man, he would have rushed to the side of his beloved.

He wasn't just any man. He was an agent for the Crown, and he knew what had to be done. He silently moved through the shadows, waiting for the gunman to make a mistake.

Richmond didn't have to wait long. The gunman in the north transept moved ever so slightly to his left, into the light from the great east window. Richmond aimed the pistol at the gunman's heart and pulled the trigger. He could think of nothing but Cassie's prone figure on the floor a few feet away.

The shot resounded through the Abbey, and the gunman fell to the floor as if he were a child's doll. Richmond wasn't the richest, the most handsome, or the most charming peer in London, but he was a crack shot. His opponent had no chance.

Pembrook was moaning softly when Richmond reached his side. "Why did you save her?"

"She wasn't supposed to die. I couldn't let her," Pembrook gasped, as he clutched his side.

Richmond took off his coat and pressed it against Pembrook's wound. "We'll get a doctor. You'll be fine," he said in his most reassuring voice.

I have no idea if he'll be fine, he thought, moving toward Cassie's crumpled form. He knelt down next to her and cradled her in his arms, lightly kissing her temples.

"Cassie, my darling, wake up, wake up," he crooned, hoping upon hope she hadn't suffered another head injury.

Cassie's eyes fluttered open in the darkness of the Abbey, and she was incredibly confused. *What happened?* she wondered, gradually becoming aware of her surroundings.

"Everything's over, Cassandra. You're going to be all right," Richmond crooned, stroking her hair gently.

What's going on? she wondered. Why is Richmond comforting me? Shouldn't he be gone with the papers? "Derek," she said softly, using his Christian name for the first time. "What happened?" she asked, the words resounding in her aching head.

Richmond took her hand in his and gently kissed it. "Pembrook pushed you out of the way. It would appear that he was here to retrieve the papers you were carrying. They're fake, aren't they?" he asked softly.

"Yes. How did you know?" she asked.

"It appears that my father took measures into his own hands and sent our footman to Lady Raverston's to watch over you. He noticed you were working on the papers and told my father, who then told me."

"I noticed he was hanging about. I thought he was a spy as well. Why did Pembrook try to save me?"

"Pembrook didn't want you to die for the papers. He took the bullet that was meant for you."

Cassie tried to sit up, and suddenly, it was as if someone had turned her upside down and she almost jerked the cat. She fell back into her previous position, and simply let Richmond cradle her in his arms. "Pembrook? He's the spy?" she gasped softly.

"Yes, my love. It was Pembrook, not me," he said softly, still gently stroking her hair.

"I was up all night writing. I thought I could fool them," she said in a barely audible whisper. *My head hurts so much,* she thought. *Even worse than when I had the accident in the street.*

"I know. Robert told my father, who told me. The papers are safe. You did everything right, and the Crown owes you a great debt," he said seriously.

He's not the spy. The words ran through her head, over and over again. *Richmond's not the spy.*

Somewhere, far away, she heard another voice.

" 'Ere now, what's happened?" her hackney driver said to no one in particular.

Richmond picked Cassie up as if she weighed nothing and addressed the hackney driver. "She lives with Lady Raverston; take her there immediately and return with the magistrate and a doctor. If you forget that the young lady was here, I'll reward you handsomely," Richmond said seriously.

"The young lady, is she all right?" the hackney driver asked, his voice filled with concern.

"I'm fine," Cassie replied, enjoying the feeling of being held in Richmond's arms, and once again was carried away by a wave of nausea.

"I'll take care of it, governor," the hackney driver said, as they followed him out to the hackney.

"One of your men?" Richmond said, smiling down at Cassie.

She tried to smile. "My hackney driver. I told him I'd give him a guinea if he waited for me, and another to come in if he heard any strange noises," she explained. Richmond's body was warm and strong, and she quite enjoyed being nestled against him.

Moonlight illuminated the night sky, and the hackney was strangely warm and inviting. Richmond placed her in carefully and turned to the driver. "Can I count on your discretion?"

"Yes, guv," he said casually.

"Then go, and be careful," Richmond ordered. He then turned to Cassie, who was beginning to feel a bit queasy. "Don't talk to anyone until I see you. If Lady Raverston asks, tell her you were ill and needed to go home," he said and leaned forward and gently kissed her.

"All right," Cassie said weakly. It would have been wonderful to have Richmond lavishing all this attention on her if she was feeling well, but her head was feeling not at all the thing. *At least Pembrook didn't bleed on my dress,* she thought as Richmond closed the door and the hackney lurched forward.

Honoria was getting worried. She had been looking for Cassie for the past half hour, and she seemed to have disappeared. She even went so far as to search the rest of the house, which was a trifle embarrassing, since she walked in on more than one couple having private . . . encounters.

Still, she had no clue to Cassie's whereabouts. Daphne was dancing with some spotty young lord, and Pandora had left with Lyntwoode. Stanton was dancing with some young chit—it looked like she was Lady Hamilton's daughter, which was the proper thing for him to do.

When the dance ended, Stanton reappeared at Honoria's side. "Something wrong, Honoria?" he asked curiously.

"Yes. Cassandra. I can't seem to locate her."

Stanton frowned. "Cassie? Did you check the library?

And the study? Maybe she got tired of the dancing and fell asleep somewhere," he suggested.

Honoria kept checking the crush of people. Cassie wasn't there. "Yes, I checked everywhere, and she's not here. It's quite vexing," she said, her eyes never leaving the crowd.

"Perhaps Derek's seen Cassie," Stanton offered, looking for his son.

"When I couldn't locate her immediately, I looked for him. He's disappeared as well," Honoria said dramatically.

Stanton frowned. "You don't suppose . . ."

Honoria shook her head. "No. Not Cassie. She wouldn't elope. Now if it was Daphne or Pandora, that would be something else entirely. But not Cassandra."

"Could she have gone home? In a hackney?"

Honoria was quite put out. Cassie wasn't one to act irregularly, and she was worried. "That's the only explanation that makes any sense. But why would she leave without telling me?" she asked, gazing at Stanton, her eyes filled with concern.

"I can stay here and keep an eye on Daphne, while you check the house for Cassie," he said calmly.

Honoria gazed around the room, until her eyes settled on a clock. "Well, the rout just started, so I don't think it will be a problem getting the carriage. And I am worried about Cassie," she admitted.

Stanton smiled. "Take the carriage and have my driver wait for you. If Cassie is at home, send word with him. If she's not, tell him that as well, but stay there. If there's been some foul play, they may try to contact you at home. If she's home, I'll return Daphne later this evening; if she's not, I'll collect Daphne and return immediately."

He's so commanding, Honoria thought. She liked men of action, and Stanton certainly knew how to handle a crisis. "That sounds like a good plan, Hugh. You don't think there's been foul play, do you?"

"Of course not. She probably just didn't feel well, couldn't locate you, and just went home. You'll see," he said, patting her arm reassuringly.

I hope he's right, Honoria thought as they made their way to the front door.

"What do you mean I can't see Cassandra?" Richmond said, his temper flaring. "I have to see her. Tonight."

Laughton sighed. "Lord Richmond, Lady Raverston barred you from the house," he said dramatically.

"I know that. But I must to talk to Cassandra. Just for a moment," he entreated.

"Lord Richmond, it's almost three in the morning. Miss Cassandra is in bed, sleeping."

"Laughton, I have to talk to her. I know it's not done, but I need to see her. Tonight," he said, desperation in his voice.

"I'm very sorry, Lord Richmond," Laughton replied, then added, "Miss Cassandra is usually an early riser; she's always up by nine. The day after a large rout, Lady Raverston usually doesn't receive callers until the afternoon," he explained.

Richmond sighed. He needed to see Cassie tonight, but he could see the determination in the elderly butler's eyes. "Perhaps I'll stop by tomorrow morning then," he said calmly.

Laughton smiled. "Yes, Lord Richmond, that might be a good idea," he said as he closed the door.

* * *

"Miss Cassandra, wake up," Mary said, nudging Cassie gently.

Cassie was confused. *What time is it? Where am I? And why does my head hurt so dreadfully?* "Yes, Mary, what is it?" she muttered.

"You have to get dressed, Miss Cassandra, you have a caller," Mary announced.

"What time is it?" Cassie said, sitting up in bed. She still felt a bit out of sorts but better than last night.

"It's just after nine."

"Who would be calling this early? It's just not done."

Mary grinned. "It's Lord Richmond. Laughton said he came by late last night, but Laughton wouldn't let him see you, and told him to come by this morning. He looks ever so handsome, Miss Cassandra, and I think he's here to offer for you!" she concluded.

Cassie frowned and stood up. "He's not here to offer for me, Mary. Help me find a dress and I'll go talk to him, though," she said calmly, even though she didn't feel very calm.

Richmond paced the parlor, trying to avoid knocking into any of Honoria's strange statuary. The room was an eclectic mix of numerous design styles, and he thought it was a bit much.

He was utterly exhausted. He hadn't gotten to sleep, and spent the night tidying up the loose ends at the Abbey. Thankfully, he was able to remove Cassie from the scene and conceal her involvement. If any word leaked out that a respectable young lady had been involved in a shooting at the Abbey, it would be the death of her social life. *Not that she cares much about her so-*

cial life, he mused, walking over to the window. *But no wife of mine is going to be embroiled in an intrigue.*

The door opened, and Cassie appeared, clad in a bright peach walking dress. The color made her skin all but glow, and she looked like she spent the night dancing at Lady Hamilton's instead of being a witness to a shooting. "Good morning, Lord Richmond," she said with a small smile.

"Good morning, Cassandra. And you must stop calling me Lord Richmond. My name is Derek," he corrected with a smile.

"All right," she said and sat down on one of the Chippendale chairs.

Richmond pulled the nearest chair closer to her and sat down himself. "What did you tell them last night?"

"I said I felt sick and that I couldn't find anyone at the rout, so I went home in a hackney," she replied simply.

He studied her carefully. When the light hit her a certain way, he could see a small bump on her head above her right ear. "Did they notice your new injury?"

"Not yet. Aunt Honoria has ordered me to stay in my room and rest for the whole of the day," Cassie reported.

"Good. When your aunt receives callers this afternoon, this is what she's going to hear. There was an altercation last night at the Abbey. Lord Pembrook was attempting to sell classified government information to a French informant. There was a scuffle, and the Frenchman was killed accidentally. The magistrate has taken Pembrook to London, and he'll be investigated," Richmond said, his eyes never leaving Cassie. *She was so brave last night. She never got hysterical, and did exactly what I told her,* he marveled inwardly.

"Will Lord Pembrook be hanged?" she asked worriedly.

"Probably not. He did save your life, and, if he

cooperates with the Crown, they may even let him go into exile," Richmond said.

Cassie looked down at her hands. "I'm sorry about everything," she finally said.

"What do you mean you're sorry?" he said with a frown.

"I'm sorry I didn't trust you. Pandora more than hinted to me that you were a spy for the French a long time ago, and Pembrook told Daphne the same thing. You were behaving so suspiciously, I was sure you were the turncoat. Then I thought you were working in tandem with Pembrook. I didn't know who to believe," Cassie confessed. "I tried to do the right thing," she added in a small voice.

He leaned over and took her small hands in his. "You did do the right thing, Cassandra. I don't know why Lloyd chose you, but he did. And it was a wise choice. Lloyd was aware he was being watched, and he knew that his covert status was compromised, so he couldn't just post the information. Lloyd was much sicker than he realized and wasn't thinking properly. I know that now."

"Did Pembrook murder him?" she asked in soft voice.

"No. He died of natural causes. He knew he was ill, he needed an accomplice, and you did exactly what he wanted you to do. You found the papers and got them to Castlereagh."

"I've been wondering about them for ages. I thought that it would cause a ruckus if I posted something to Castlereagh, but no one would take notice if I sent a parcel to my Papa," Cassie explained.

He smiled. She was very, very clever. "And you were exactly right. I'm just sorry I couldn't have been there for you all along. But I couldn't compromise my mission," he admitted.

"Of course," she said, then added, "spies in Bath. It doesn't even sound possible."

"We are at war, Cassandra," he said in a very serious voice.

"I know."

They sat in silence for a long time until he said, "I'm sorry about the episode in the library with Pandora." He never wanted to talk about Pandora again, but he knew he had to clear the air.

"Aunt Honoria is sending her away today with Lyntwoode."

"I'm glad. You know I don't have any interest in her, don't you?"

Cassie didn't answer.

"I don't," he said gently.

"Does anyone know I was involved in the . . . intrigue?" she asked, looking up at him, her eyes wide.

"No. I managed to keep your name out, as well as mine. If you were linked to something like that, it would have had horrific consequences."

"I would have been compromised," she said simply.

"Yes. And it might have done damage to your reputation, even though you are a hero," Richmond replied, squeezing her hands lightly.

"I'm not a hero," she said, looking away from him again.

"Yes, you are," he said, as he leaned over and kissed her lightly on the lips. She kissed him back ever so slightly, and her lips were soft and warm.

There was a cough at the door, and Richmond looked up. It was Laughton.

"Excuse me, Lord Richmond, but you've been in the parlor with Miss Cassandra for a dreadfully long time, and someone else in the family might take note if you don't leave soon," he said in a very serious voice.

Richmond got up and smiled at Laughton. "Yes, well, you're right. Perhaps it is time to leave before I call attention to the situation," he said, moving toward the door.

"I'll see you soon, Cassandra," he said as he left the parlor.

"I hear that Laughton had a lapse of judgment, and not only let Richmond into the house but that you were in the parlor alone with him. Can you explain yourself, Cassandra?" Honoria demanded.

Cassie was still in bed, and Aunt Honoria was sitting on the chair at her escritoire. "Lord Richmond came by to apologize," she said simply.

"Apologize for what?" Honoria asked suspiciously.

Cassie had known that although Laughton was discreet, someone else was bound to notice that Richmond had called on her. Therefore, she spent the morning fabricating an excuse. "There was an . . . episode at Lady Hamilton's involving Pandora," she said simply.

"Yes?"

"I was alone in the study; I wasn't feeling quite the thing. Pandora lured Lord Richmond in, and then she threw herself at him. Lord Lyntwoode came in and challenged Lord Richmond to a duel, but then decided against it," she explained.

"And where were you during this attempted seduction?"

"I was sitting in one of the rather large chairs Lord Hamilton has near the fire. The chair was facing the other way, so no one noticed me," she added.

Honoria frowned. "And Richmond came by today to apologize?"

"Yes, he didn't want me to think that he was the type of person who dallied with married ladies," Cassie said simply.

"That's fine. Pandora and Lyntwoode left a while ago," Honoria reported.

"Is he still barred from the house?" Cassie asked.

"I suppose not, now that Pandora has left with Lyntwoode."

"I'm glad Pandora's gone. Can I go home soon?" Cassie said softly.

"You need some time to rest, Cassandra. Maybe in a week or so. Would that suit you?"

Cassie wanted to leave immediately. Not because of the episode at the Abbey and not because she was frightened. But she had a strange feeling that Richmond felt obligated, and was going to offer for her. She certainly didn't want anyone to offer for her out of an obligation.

Richmond was at sixes and sevens. He had no reason to stay in Bath, but if he left, he'd never see Cassie again.

Oh, he might see her once every few years, if she decided to come to London. From what his father had said, there was more than one man who had taken notice of the lovely Miss Wyndmoore last night, so she was a social success, at least in Bath. So she might decide to partake in London Society.

However, he didn't think he'd see her in London unless Lady Raverston dragged her there to try to find a suitable husband.

Therein lay the problem. He was a suitable husband. She would be a wonderful wife. Unfortunately, he had no idea how she felt about him. Of course, Pandora had said Cassie had loved him from afar for years. Pandora could have been lying to humiliate Cassie, which was always possible. But he'd seen the look on Cassie's face when Pandora made her declaration, and she was devastated. That led him to believe that perhaps it was true. Perhaps she wasn't immune to his charms.

Cassie came down to dinner, and they all tried to pretend that everything was fine.

Except things weren't fine. Daphne was so blue deviled that she wasn't talking, while Aunt Honoria seemed to be overly preoccupied with something she wasn't sharing with the girls. The dinner conversation was sparse to nonexistent.

"Did you enjoy the ball last night, Daphne?" Cassie asked curiously. She hadn't spent any time at all with her younger sister, and had no idea how she handled herself.

Daphne sighed. Loudly and dramatically. "It was lovely," she said in a passionless voice. "There are flowers in the parlor. Some are for you," Daphne added, picking at her creamed asparagus.

"Really?" Cassie hadn't expected any flowers at all.

"Oh, yes. The loveliest are from Richmond. He sent you two dozen red roses," Honoria added, trying to sound interested.

"I didn't see them. I thought all the flowers were for Daphne," Cassie replied.

Daphne managed a wan smile. "Everyone was asking about you last night, even the younger gentlemen who danced with me. You looked so pretty last night, and I was proud to be your sister," she said in all sincerity.

Cassie smiled back at her. "Why, thank you, Daphne."

Honoria looked at both girls and got up from her chair. "I've got a bit of a headache. I'm going to retire for the night," she said, and slowly walked out of the room.

"Good night, Aunt Honoria," Daphne called after her.

"I hope you feel better," Cassie said loudly, as the door closed.

Daphne looked over at Cassie. "You heard about Lord Pembrook?"

Cassie frowned. *How much does Daphne know?* "Not really."

"He's a spy! A spy for the French," Daphne wailed.

"Daphne, he was much too old for you, and his affections were never constant," Cassie said mildly.

"But he was so handsome. How could he be a traitor?"

"Daphne, people aren't always what they seem. Pandora is very beautiful, but she's not always so nice to us, is she?" Cassie remarked.

"No, she's not."

"Just because Lord Pembrook was handsome and caught your fancy doesn't mean that he was a good person. He was good at pretending, that's all."

Daphne frowned, and seemed to consider Cassie's words. "So I'm not the only one Lord Pembrook deceived?"

"Not at all. He deceived all of Bath."

Daphne pondered her words for a moment. "You're right, Cassie. I don't feel so bad now," Daphne admitted.

Cassie smiled indulgently at her. "And now do you know why Mama wants you to wait for your Season? She doesn't want a man in London trying to deceive you."

Once again, Daphne seemed to consider Cassie's words. "So Mama is just trying to make things easier?"

"Yes. She wants you to make a good choice, Daphne, not like Pandora."

Daphne folded her napkin and placed it on the table. "I know Mama will be happy with *your* choice," she said.

Cassie was confused. *What is she going on about,* she wondered. "My choice, Daphne?"

Daphne grinned and stood up. "Oh, Cassie, everyone knows that Lord Richmond is in your pocket," she said as she scampered out of the room, a smile on her face.

Cassie stared after her. Richmond? In her pocket? It seemed unbelievable. Daphne had to be wrong.

Richmond was slowly going mad. He was sure of it. All he thought about was Cassie. All day and all night.

He wanted to marry her. He was sure of it. He tugged at his cravat, which, once again, seemed much too tight.

Cassie was another matter. He wasn't sure that she wanted to marry anyone. She seemed happy. At least, it seemed like she was accustomed to her life as a spinster.

But who wants to live as a spinster, he wondered, pacing the study. *Who wouldn't want their own family?*

He needed a plan. He had made sure Cassie wasn't compromised at the Abbey so she wasn't forced into marrying him for propriety, even though he wanted to marry her with all of his heart. However, he wanted her to want him as well.

Richmond paced the room, thinking. He was certain that his father approved of Cassie; he was always trying to force the two of them together. He thought that Lady Raverston favored the match. If his father and Lady Raverston both approved, they could talk to Mr. Wyndmoore if needed.

He walked over to the side table and poured himself a glass of port. *Why am I so anxious?* he wondered, sipping the dark liquid. *I should just ask her outright and get it over with,* he decided.

Then he thought again, and smiled. He knew two things about Cassandra Wyndmoore. She was curious. And she had no idea that he loved her.

He was an experienced agent of the Crown. He knew that if he put his mind to it, he could figure out a way to win Cassie's heart.

Chapter 17

It was a long day, and Cassie was tired. She still didn't feel quite the thing, and spent most of the day reading in the parlor. Dinner was quiet, and Aunt Honoria wanted her to start accompanying her on morning calls, but she wasn't interested.

Cassie wasn't interested in much of anything. She tried to read, but she couldn't concentrate. She played cards with Daphne, and lost worse than usual. After their card game, Cassie found herself in the parlor, staring out the window, thinking of Richmond.

Then she would force herself to stop swooning over him and try to get interested in anything. It didn't work. After she spent an entire day of wondering if she'd ever see him again, she retired early, in defeat. He probably wasn't even in Bath.

When she opened the door to the attic, there was a box with a pretty red bow sitting on her bed. Cassie looked around. Mary wasn't about, and neither was Sara. Yet there was a box on her bed. *Why would someone leave a box on my bed?* she wondered as she sat down and opened it.

The box wasn't large, and Cassie's heart was beating rapidly as she opened the lid. Nestled inside were two small wooden toys: a pig and a bird. Specifically, a blackbird.

Cassie stared at the toys. There was no logical reason why anyone would send her children's toys. She put the toys back in the box and decided to find out who had sent them.

She bounded down the stairs and located Laughton. He appeared to be completely unaware of the package. Her next suspect was Mary. Cassie found her in Daphne's room, getting the hot bricks ready. Mary wasn't helpful, either.

Then she tried Sara, Aunt Honoria's abigail. She found Sara in Aunt Honoria's room.

"Excuse me, Sara?" Cassie said softly.

"Yes, Miss Cassandra?" Sara said pertly, looking up from the nightgown she was folding.

"There was a package left on my bed. Do you know anything about it?" she asked, waiting for another refusal.

"Yes, Miss Cassandra," Sara said, looking back down at the gown and continuing her work.

"There wasn't a card. Who is it from?" Cassie asked, relieved to have found someone who knew something about the mysterious gift.

"I'm not at liberty to say, Miss Cassandra," Sara said simply, walked over to the dresser and placed the nightgown inside.

"Pardon me?" Cassie said, her mouth dropping open. Sara occasionally tended to be a bit cheeky, but this was beyond the pale. "If you know who the box is from, I want you to tell me."

Sara smiled. "I'm sorry, Miss Cassandra. I'm not at liberty to tell you."

"Must I go to Aunt Honoria?" she asked, hating herself for the tone she was using with Sara.

Sara shrugged. "I suppose you can. But I can't help you," she added simply.

Cassie sighed. After all she went through with Mr. Lloyd, she had to be sure the box wasn't some sort of ruse. "The box isn't a trick, is it, Sara?" she asked suspiciously.

"Oh no. It's a gift," she said with a smile and sauntered out of the room before Cassie could ask her another question.

Her next stop was the parlor, where Aunt Honoria was reading. Cassie bounded into the room, determined to find out who had sent her the package.

"Excuse me, Aunt Honoria?"

Honoria looked up from her book. "Yes, Cassandra?"

"There was a box on my bed, a gift. Do you know who it's from?"

"Isn't there a card?" Honoria asked innocently.

Cassie studied her aunt. She was certain that Aunt Honoria knew who sent the box, as did Sara and probably everyone else in the household. So she tried a different line of questioning. "Is it from Richmond?"

"I don't know, dear."

Cassie sank into the chair opposite Aunt Honoria. "Is it a prank?"

"Not that I'm aware."

Cassie thought about the gift. Two children's toys. Who would send her two children's toys?

The next afternoon, it happened again. Cassie decided to work on her needlework and headed toward the parlor. Sitting on the small black lacquer table was a package with a bright yellow ribbon on it. Once again, the room was empty. Aunt Honoria and Daphne were still out making morning calls, and she was alone in the house, except for the staff. Cassie was sure there weren't any callers that morning, so it couldn't have come from a visitor, since there were no visitors.

She walked over to the package and stared at it. This time, there was a small card attached. It read simply 'Cassandra.' It was another present.

Cassie tore open the wrapping paper, which revealed a book. Not just any book. A rich, leather-bound edition titled *A Dictionary of Phrases and Words from the Greek*. Once again, Cassie frowned. The book looked new, and most definitely didn't come from the Bath lending library, since all of their books in Greek were ancient. She sat down and thumbed through the book, which was actually quite a good reference document that served as an expanded English/Greek dictionary. *If only I'd had this when I was working on Mr. Lloyd's papers, I would have been done much sooner,* she thought. *Why would anyone give me a book of Greek phrases?*

If Pandora or Daphne were getting the gifts, she knew they would both be in alt, since both ladies relished the ideas of having admirers, especially secret admirers. Cassie never had a secret admirer in her life, except for the curate's son, and everyone knew he was overly fond of Cassie. She was not overly fond of him, and used every possible opportunity to discourage him, until he finally fixed his attentions on another unmarried lady of a certain age in town.

It all seemed so bizarre to Cassie. First, she got involved in a ring of spies in Bath. In *Bath*! That was completely unbelievable. Then she started getting gifts from what would appear to be a secret admirer. She was certain that she hadn't made that much of an impression on any man in Bath. In fact, she didn't know anyone in Bath that well, except for Lord Richmond, Lord Stanton, and Lord Pembrook, and Pembrook was in London. As for Lord Stanton, Cassie was certain that if he were behind the presents, they'd be addressed to her Aunt Honoria. That left Richmond, and the idea that he was sending her these mysterious gifts seemed so impractical and romantic that it was out of the question.

Cassie thumbed through the book and smiled. *It must be either the magistrate or the doctor,* she decided. *Those are the only other men I've spent any time with in Bath.*

"You've been getting gifts from a secret admirer and you didn't tell me?" Daphne questioned, as they sat and played piquet. As usual, Daphne was winning.

Cassie glanced over at Aunt Honoria. "I think Aunt Honoria knows who they're from. So does Sara. But they won't tell me."

Daphne's eyes sparkled. "This is so exciting, Cassie! What has he sent you?"

"Well, the first gift was two children's toys, a black-bird and a pig, and earlier today, I got a book of Greek phrases," she said.

"A blackbird and a pig? How strange. I can certainly see someone giving you a book, but children's toys? Why would they give you that?" Daphne questioned, playing her card.

"I don't know," Cassie replied, realizing that Daphne was going to win the hand again.

"Hmm . . . a blackbird and a pig. Wasn't that the name of the inn where we had the carriage repaired or something similar to that?"

"That was the Pig and Crow," Cassie said, suddenly suspicious of her sister.

"Could your blackbird be a crow?"

Cassie put down her cards. "Daphne Wyndmoore, what do you know about this?" she demanded.

"I don't know anything, Cassie, honestly. But we did stay at the Pig and Crow. Maybe it has something to do with that," she said innocently.

Cassie didn't know if she should believe Daphne or not. However, she did know what had happened at the Pig and Crow. That was where she had been reunited with Richmond.

"I doubt it," Cassie replied. Richmond wasn't the type to send anonymous gifts, she was sure of that. He'd certainly never sent anonymous gifts to Pandora, much to her sister's chagrin.

"Oh. I thought the gifts might be from Lord Richmond, but Aunt Honoria said he left Bath yesterday, so I suppose you're right," Daphne replied, putting down a card and winning the hand.

Cassie was flummoxed. If Richmond wasn't in town, who could it be? She was loath to admit it, but the gifts did connect to her experiences with Richmond, and she had spent time with him.

So who was sending her gifts? And why?

The next gift appeared the next day after dinner. When the ladies retired to the parlor, there was a rather large box with a purple ribbon on one of the tables.

"Cassie, is that your package?" Honoria asked curiously, gesturing toward the table.

Cassie frowned. *I know Aunt Honoria is in on this, I know it.* "I don't know," Cassie replied, and walked over to the table. There was another card on it, and it read 'Cassandra.' "It says Cassandra, so I assume it's mine," she replied, staring at the rectangular wooden box. *What is this about? Who's going to all this bother?* she wondered.

"Well, open it!" Daphne demanded, coming up beside her.

"All right," Cassie said, trying to hide her eagerness. She was vastly curious about the contents of the wooden box, but tried to remain nonchalant. She opened the lid, and inside was a bottle of wine. From France.

"It's wine. From France. Is that . . . legal?" Cassie said, frowning again. Why would someone send her wine from France?

"Well, not exactly, but those who are well connected can get it. As long as you're not smuggling vast quantities into the country, there's not a problem," Honoria explained.

"Why would someone send me French wine?"

"I can't say, Cassandra. Maybe someone wants you to think of France in a positive light. Their wines are delightful, even though they are ruled by that Corsican devil," Aunt Honoria said mildly.

The gifts were making Cassie crazy. One simply didn't start sending gifts for no reason. Toys, then a book, then wine. They all connected back to Richmond.

Yes, she was well aware he was out of town. However, he was resourceful and could simply have ordered one of his staff to bring them over to the house.

He was the only person who she could logically connect to all of the gifts. The first time she had become reaquainted with Lord Richmond was on the way to

Bath, at the inn, the Pig and Crow. Hence, the gift of the children's toys.

The next time she saw him was in the library, when she was in the Greek section. She was holding the Aesop book when she found him talking to Daphne. She was sure he knew that Lloyd's papers were written in Greek.

When they went on their picnic, he talked about France, convincing her that he was a spy. The wine was something from France that was positive, like his family, rather than negative, like Pembrook and his cronies.

Cassie had only one question: why was he doing this?

She didn't have an answer.

"So, how is the courtship going?" Honoria asked, sipping her tea. It was high time that Richmond came up to snuff, and she expected Stanton to have good news.

Stanton smiled at her. "I don't really know. He's in London now, but when he left, he seemed to be pleased with his plan, whatever that may be," he said simply.

Honoria smiled knowingly. "It's gifts. He's been sending her gifts that relate to the time they've spent together," she explained.

"Really? Why?" he said, furrowing his brow. "Wouldn't it just be easier to simply ask the gel? She is . . . she will accept him, won't she?" he asked, somewhat worried.

Honoria took another sip from her white and blue teacup. "Yes, well, I suppose only Cassandra knows that."

Stanton loosened his cravat a bit. It was tied in a waterfall, and looked quite impressive, until he started fussing with it. Now it looked rather wrinkled. "You mean there's actually a chance she might refuse him? He's my heir, for goodness sake. He's quite the catch on the Marriage Mart, I've been told that for years," he said, a slight edge to his usually velvety voice.

"Yes, well, Hugh, perhaps your Derek is a bit full of himself and a bit too sure. That's why I banned him from the house when Pandora was here, to take him down a notch. Cassandra isn't Daphne, or even Pandora. She is quite valuable in her own sake, and seems to be quite accepting of her single state," she said mildly.

"My Derek? A bit full of himself? Do you really think so?"

Honoria put down the teacup gently. "Yes, well, you also have to remember that Cassandra knows every detail of his romance with her sister. That has to be off-putting as well."

Stanton sank into the chair. "So he doesn't have a chance?"

"I wouldn't say that. He seems to have aroused her curiosity with the gifts, which is a good sign," Honoria replied calmly.

Stanton studied her for a very long while before replying, "How long are the girls going to stay, Honoria?"

"I'd say for another week or two. Why?" she asked curiously.

"Because, my dear, it's difficult for me to do my courting when we're both so tied up with my son's and your niece's . . . situation," Stanton said simply.

Honoria blushed ever so slightly. "You're courting me, Hugh? I didn't know."

He smiled at her. "Well, now you do."

Daphne and Cassie were playing piquet, and Daphne was winning once again, much to Cassie's dismay.

"Did you get another gift today?" Daphne asked with a smile.

"No, nothing today. The last gift was the bottle of wine," Cassie explained.

"It's so exciting, being courted, isn't it?" Daphne said.

"Being courted? Just because someone is giving you gifts doesn't mean you're being courted," Cassie said mildly.

"Cassie, you are such a slow top! Of course you're being courted! Everyone is expecting Lord Richmond to offer for you. I even heard one of Aunt Honoria's friends mention it, " Daphne added in a soft voice.

"Oh, I don't know, Daphne. Lord Richmond has certainly been kind to me, but I don't know if I'd say he was courting me," she replied, as she pondered the idea. *Is Richmond really courting me? I suppose that if one looked at the situation in a certain light, one might think that he's interested. But I'm much too old and he likes his female companions to be beautiful, like Pandora and Daphne.*

"Well, I'll bet you a guinea that he proposes," Daphne said confidently.

"Oh, we're betting on it now? I think not," Cassie said, smiling at her sister.

"You'll see, Cassie. Lord Richmond is going to offer for you. Didn't you see the way he looked at you at Lady Hamilton's ball? Everyone knows he's smitten with you. Everyone."

Cassie thought back to Lady Hamilton's ball. The night she was almost shot. The night that she once again saw Richmond embracing her sister. "I don't think so, Daphne."

Daphne played her last card and once again won the hand. "Fine, don't believe me. You'll see. I'm sure your gifts are from Lord Richmond, and a man doesn't give out gifts unless there's a real reason. Moreover, they're such strange gifts. He has to have something in mind. Think about it, Cassie. He's not going to ask you to be his bird of paradise, is he? I doubt if he's trying to get in your good graces because he wants to offer you some sort of employment. So what else is there?" Daphne reasoned.

Cassie's mind was in a flurry. *Is he really going to offer for me? And if he does, what will I say?*

A day passed without a gift. Then another. Then a third.

Cassie was convinced that the gifts were from Richmond. In her mind, he was probably leading up to something, perhaps even an offer.

Outside of her father, Cassie was the most practical one in the family. Oh, Pandora had her moments and knew that it would behoove her to marry well, which she did. In some way, Cassie also expected Daphne to realize that her life would be easier if she married a man of means. Papa wasn't a pauper, but he wasn't a lord, either. Consequently, Pandora and Daphne knew what they needed to do to ensure their comfort.

Cassie never thought about her future. Oh, in a way, she did. She knew that eventually her parents would fall ill, and she would end up running the household and taking care of their needs. It wasn't the future she had expected, but she wasn't going to be forced into being a governess or a companion either. Her future wouldn't be glittering and exciting like Pandora's or Daphne's, but it would be . . . adequate. She had no expectations. Oh, she could probably find a curate or a spotty younger son to marry, but she didn't want to marry without affection, and her parents never pressed her.

Her future was planned out. She would simply spend her life in Warwick until she got old. Then she'd more than likely move in with Daphne and her husband and be a doting aunt. It was a lovely, quiet life, and she'd be happy with it.

Cassie knew there was a possibility that Richmond might propose to her. She was also well aware that he was a lord, his family's holdings were quite vast, and, in Society, he was very important. He was a man who should marry a diamond of the first water, not an aging spinster.

Even if Richmond proposed, Cassie decided to turn him down. He couldn't ever love her; he was just caught up in the drama of what happened in the Abbey and was confused. From what she could tell, most men who were involved with her sisters were in a near constant state of confusion. Richmond, although he didn't seem to be easily swayed, was just . . . unsettled by the events at the Abbey and would recover and find himself a pretty, young, and amiable bride in due time. He just needed some time to think.

Yes. He was confused. Cassie was sure of it.

She wasn't confused. Cassie knew that she was in love with him—oh, not in the same way that she had been in love with him when he was courting Pandora, but in love nonetheless. Cassie loved him enough to give him up so he could have the future that he deserved.

Two more days passed. Richmond wasn't in Bath, the gifts had stopped, and she was even more blue deviled than Daphne.

In the end, Cassie decided to forget about Richmond and the gifts and go home.

* * *

"You want to go home?" Honoria said, frowning at Cassie. "Why?"

Cassie didn't know what to say. She knew she couldn't be honest and admit that she was confused about Richmond and wanted time think. If she said that, Aunt Honoria would say she could think in Bath. She tried a different tactic instead. "I haven't been feeling quite the thing, and I think I'd do better at home," Cassie explained.

Honoria furrowed her brows. "I suppose I can make the arrangements, but it will take some time."

"Why?" Cassie was confused. How hard could it be to get from Bath to Warwick? They had their own transportation and their own coachman.

"Well, we've got to get you packed. I did promise your Papa I would get you properly rigged out, and you really don't have enough dresses to go back to Warwick, so you really shouldn't leave until you get a few more frocks from Madame Babette's. Daphne is finally coming along, I was thinking about taking her to the Assembly Rooms in a few days, so really, it will be at least a sennight before you can go," Honoria explained.

"A sennight? Can't John Coachman just take me home?" Cassie protested.

"No, now's just not the time, Cassandra," Honoria concluded, and the tone of her voice convinced Cassie that the subject was closed.

"Is he ever coming back to Bath?" Honoria asked impatiently, frowning at Lord Stanton. "Cassie wants to go home, and I had to fabricate some sort of cock and bull story to keep her here."

Stanton put down his teacup. "Yes, well, I believe he's due back in a day or two. Business, you see."

"Business? What kind of business?"

"Government business, very hush-hush. He doesn't think I know about it, but I do. Plus I believe he was at our country home as well."

"Your country home? Why on earth would he be there? If he's going to propose to Cassie, he'd better do it now instead of haring around the countryside."

"Honoria, my dearest, be patient. The reason he had to go to our country home is to retrieve something for your Cassandra. Trust me, he wants to get this settled as much as we do," Stanton assured her.

Honoria sipped her tea. "You're not just bamming me, are you, Hugh?"

"I would never lead you on, my dear. You're so much smarter than I am, you'd see right though me," he replied with a smile.

"Ha!"

Once again, Honoria had the last word.

It was a beautiful sunny day, and once again, Cassie was alone, in the parlor, reading. She read every afternoon, since she wasn't really in the mood for socializing. Aunt Honoria and Daphne had taken a stroll to the milliner's to look for a hat for Daphne, and she expected them back at any time. Then they'd have dinner and perhaps play cards. Or Daphne would play piano. Every night was the same, and Cassie couldn't wait until she got home.

"Miss Cassie, may I interrupt you?" Sara said, standing in the parlor door.

"Yes, Sara?"

"I'm sorry to bother you, Miss Cassie, but Lady Raverston told me that you were planning to leave soon, and I noticed you have still some old dresses in your portmanteau. Do you want me to pack them, or do you think you'll be wearing them?"

Cassie frowned. Why was Sara bothering with her wardrobe now? "Sara, this can wait, can't it? I'm not due to leave for a week or two."

"But, Miss Cassie, Lady Raverston asked me to get your wardrobe together, and I really need to know what dresses you want packed and which you prefer to wear. Lady Raverston did mention that you're going back to Madame Babette's, and we do need to know your favorite new dresses as well," Sara explained.

"Must we do this now, Sara?"

"I'm sorry, Miss Cassie, but Lady Raverston and Miss Daphne are gone, so it's the perfect time to work on your wardrobe," the maid said brightly.

"Oh, all right," Cassie said and followed Sara out of the room and up the stairs.

From Cassie's viewpoint, it took forever to look through her clothes. Sara had question after question about packing and traveling and then she even started asking questions about Daphne's wardrobe. This was even more confusing, since Cassie thought she heard Daphne and Aunt Honoria downstairs, so Sara could have asked Daphne. Instead, she asked Cassie, and Daphne never did appear. They were up in the bedroom forever, until Laughton finally appeared and whisked Sara off on another errand.

At that point, Cassie was going to take a nap. That is, until Laughton came over to her door and reminded her that she had left an open book in the parlor, and if she wanted to make sure she didn't lose her page, he suggested that she retrieve the book.

Cassie didn't particularly want to go down to the parlor, and could have simply requested that Laughton fetch the book for her. However, Cassie didn't enjoy making servants do those kinds of things, and he was correct, she had left her book out. If she left it out for any period of time, there was the chance that one of the maids would put it away, and she'd lose her place.

So she got off the bed, tried to smooth the folds out of her dress, and trudged down to the parlor from the attic. The house was still, which was odd, since she was certain she had heard her aunt and her sister return from shopping. In fact, she thought she'd heard Lord Stanton's voice as well.

Cassie opened the parlor door, fully expecting Aunt Honoria, Daphne, and Lord Stanton to be there, drinking tea and having biscuits. The room was empty.

Except there was something in the middle of the room. Something huge. Something wrapped in brown paper with a beautiful pink bow on top of it. Cassie walked over to it curiously. Was it another gift for her?

Next to the ribbon was a small card. It read 'Cassandra.' A smile appeared on Cassie's face. She wouldn't admit it to anyone, but she enjoyed the gifts. They made her feel special. At least for a little while.

Cassie carefully took the bow off the gift, and tore the paper away. It revealed something magical.

A dollhouse. A huge dollhouse that was fashioned like

Aunt Honoria's home in Bath. In fact, it was a good replica, from the parlor to the kitchen to the bedrooms. There even appeared to be an attic, but she would have had to lift the roof to reveal it. There was tiny furniture in the dollhouse, and in the parlor stood a small man and a small woman.

Cassie was delighted. It was a wonderful gift, even though it didn't make any sense. She peered into the house and looked at every little detail, from the furniture to the color of the walls and the tiny, tiny drapes. The dollhouse was an incredible work of art.

She was so intrigued by the gift that she never heard Richmond enter the room.

"Do you like the dollhouse?" he asked in a husky voice.

Cassie looked up, startled. He looked so handsome in his buckskin breeches and his black Hessians. His hair was tousled, as if he had been running his fingers through it nervously.

"Lord Richmond!" she exclaimed and found herself suddenly tongue-tied.

"I thought we were on a first-name basis, Cassandra," he said.

She blushed. "Yes, we are," Cassie conceded.

He didn't seem to notice. He walked over to her and looked at the dollhouse. "I thought you'd like it. I had someone in London create it especially for you. That's why it took so long," he explained.

Cassie was flustered. He was going to propose, she was sure of it. She didn't know if she wanted to stop him. "Lord Richmond, Derek, you've been very kind, but I can't accept your gifts," she said quickly, before she changed her mind. She loved his gifts and did want to keep them, but it wouldn't be proper.

He smiled. "I thought you might say that. But I commissioned the dollhouse especially for you, so it can't be returned," he countered.

"Oh. It is lovely, thank you," she managed to say.

"There's something else in it," he said with a smile.

"Something else?"

"Yes. You just have to find it."

Cassie frowned at him, then looked back at the dollhouse. The furniture was small, so there couldn't be anything in the tiny furniture, or even under it. The chimney looked sealed, so that left the attic. She gently lifted the roof to reveal the attic, and there sat a small jewelers' box. A ring box. "I can't accept anything from you, Derek," she said in a hopeless voice. More than anything else, she wanted to accept him, but she knew that she couldn't.

"You can at least look at what you're refusing, can't you? It wouldn't be polite to refuse a gift out of hand, would it?"

Cassie was torn. On one hand, she knew she should simply put the roof of the dollhouse down and explain to Lord Richmond that he wasn't behaving properly at all. On the other hand, she was curious about what was in the box.

In the end, curiosity won out, and she mentally conceded that it would be impolite not to see what he was trying to give her. She took the small box in her hand and opened it.

Inside was a very, very old wedding ring. There was a large diamond, offset by two rubies. Cassie stared at it, mute.

"When we met at that horrid inn, I thought you were the most charming woman I had ever met, everything a man could want in a companion," Richmond began softly. "Then when I arrived in Bath, I found out you were Pandora's sister and I made certain assumptions that were wrong, and I'm very, very sorry about that," he said, wrapping his hands around hers.

Cassie's heart was pounding in her chest. This was it. He was going to propose. Cassie knew a wedding ring when she saw one, and this was it. She had to say something to stop him before he did actually offer for her and she had to say no. She knew she had to say no. Unfortunately, she couldn't think of anything and simply gazed up into his eyes, transfixed by his words.

"I've known from the beginning that you were mixed up in Lloyd's business, but I certainly wasn't at liberty to divulge that I was working for Castlereagh. While I was trying to coax you into giving me Lloyd's information, I began to enjoy your company. In fact, I almost completely forgot about my mission once I knew Castlereagh had the papers. I just wanted to spend time with you," he said softly.

She looked away. *Why is he being so dashed difficult?* she wondered. *Why is he telling me all of this? He can't want to marry me.* "I'm sure we can always be friends, Lord Richmond," she said in a choked voice, close to tears. She didn't want to be friends with him. She loved him.

"Cassandra, I don't want to be your friend. I followed you into the Abbey because I was worried that something was wrong. When I thought the Frenchman shot you, it was worse than being shot myself. That's why I killed him. I couldn't bear to see anything happen to you," he admitted in a voice thick with emotion.

Cassie stared at the box in her hands. She didn't want to look at him. If she did, she would throw her arms around him and declare her everlasting love.

"I've only killed two other people in my life, Cassandra, and it's not a thing I take lightly. If you would have been hurt, I would have died," he said softly.

When she didn't answer, he took his hand and placed it under her chin, forcing her to meet his eyes. "This is my great-grandmother's ring. She was quite an accomplished woman, and even saved my grandfather's life when he was shot in a hunting accident and the doctor couldn't be found. She was quite a remarkable woman, just like you are," he concluded.

Cassie couldn't speak. She couldn't tell him all of the reasons why she shouldn't be his wife.

"Please marry me, Cassandra. I love you with all of my heart and I want to have a brave, intelligent, and beautiful woman as my countess, the same kind of woman that my grandfather had," he finished.

"I wouldn't be a very good wife," she said softly, her hands trembling. *He said he loves me,* she thought in amazement. *That has to mean something.*

Richmond smiled gently at her. "I've thought about proposing to you for a long time, my dear Cassandra. I knew you would be set against it because of my dealings with your sister, and I don't blame you. That's why I got you the gifts. The toys represented the first time I saw you again. That's when I fell in love with you. The book reminded me of when I found you in the library here in Bath. I was so happy to see you again, but so unhappy that you were related to Pandora. The wine was for the time we went on the picnic, and you asked me about France. I was so at ease with you that I forgot about Lloyd and the papers and wanted to share my memories of France with you. I ended up convincing you that I was a spy, which wasn't my intention at all," he explained.

"And the dollhouse?"

"Ah, the dollhouse. That was the most difficult of all. I once asked you what you wanted in life, and you didn't have a good answer. I refuse to believe that you'd settle for being a maiden aunt to your sister's children. But I do remember you said you'd like a house like Lady Raverston's, and that's what made me think of getting you a dollhouse," he finished.

"It really is quite lovely," she admitted.

"The dollhouse or the ring?"

"Both," she said in a whisper.

"Well, Cassandra, will you have me?"

"Are you sure?" she said softly.

"Of course I'm sure. I've loved you for ages, you know."

"I'm dreadfully old and not very pretty," she said, looking at the floor.

He smiled at her gently. "Well, you're younger than Pandora, who is nearer to my age. And no, you're not pretty. You're beautiful. You've always been beautiful to me," he murmured.

Cassie looked at the floor and said nothing.

"Would I be more convincing if I got down on bended knee and begged for your hand? I'm fully prepared to do that, you know," he added.

Cassie finally looked up at him and smiled. "You most certainly can't do that. You're the influential Lord Richmond and I'm just Miss Wyndmoore. That sort of thing just isn't done."

He smiled down at her. "Yes, but you're the brave and wonderful Miss Wyndmoore, and I would be honored if you accepted a proposal from a lackwit who works for Castlereagh. Pardon me, who worked for Castlereagh."

"You've stopped your work for the government?"

"A married man can't be haring around the countryside putting himself and his family in danger," he replied.

"You'd give up your work for me?"

"Of course, Cassandra. I love you and want to marry you. Must I bring in Lady Raverston's staff and announce my intentions? Must I post a notice in the newspaper to convince you?" he added lightly.

Cassie finally smiled a radiant smile. "Yes, Derek, I'll marry you. If you're certain it's what you want," she said, trying desperately to be sensible. She wanted to marry him more than anything and she had to be sure he wanted to be with her just as much as she wanted to be with him.

"Yes, Cassandra, it's definitely what I want," he said, leaning over and kissing her soundly.

"So did she finally say yes?" Stanton asked Honoria as she leaned against the parlor door, listening to the pair inside.

"Finally. Gads, I thought they'd never get around to it," she muttered, turning to face him.

Stanton smiled easily at Honoria. After all of these years, she was still his best friend, the first woman that he had wanted to marry. Now all he had to do was figure out a way to ask her to marry him. "Well, asking a lady to marry you isn't the easiest task, Honoria," he began, as he took her arm and led her down the hallway.

Her eyes twinkled merrily. "Oh, really?"

"Yes, it's quite taxing. What do you think the family would say if there was another marriage in offing?" he asked casually, wondering if she realized what he was hinting at.

Honoria smiled. "Do you have someone in mind for Daphne? How wonderful."

They reached the end of the hall and walked into the unoccupied parlor. Stanton closed the door and boldly took Honoria in his arms. She didn't protest, and instead, smiled at him merrily. "No, Lady Raverston, Daphne isn't the female I had in mind," he said, and for the first time in five and twenty years, he kissed Honoria soundly.

BOOK YOUR PLACE ON OUR WEBSITE AND MAKE THE READING CONNECTION!

We've created a customized website just for our very special readers, where you can get the inside scoop on everything that's going on with Zebra, Pinnacle and Kensington books.

When you come online, you'll have the exciting opportunity to:

- View covers of upcoming books
- Read sample chapters
- Learn about our future publishing schedule (listed by publication month *and author*)
- Find out when your favorite authors will be visiting a city near you
- Search for and order backlist books from our online catalog
- Check out author bios and background information
- Send e-mail to your favorite authors
- Meet the Kensington staff online
- Join us in weekly chats with authors, readers and other guests
- Get writing guidelines
- AND MUCH MORE!

**Visit our website at
http://www.kensingtonbooks.com**

More Regency Romance
From Zebra

Embrace the Romance of
Shannon Drake